ARTEMIS FOWL
THE ETERNITY CODE

THE GRAPHIC NOVEL

Adapted by
EOIN COLFER
&
ANDREW DONKIN

Art by GIOVANNI RIGANO

Color by PAOLO LAMANNA
Color Separation by STUDIO BLINQ

Lettering by CHRIS DICKEY

DISNEP · HYPERION BOOKS
New York

Adapted from the novel *Artemis Fowl: The Eternity Code*

Text copyright © 2013 by Eoin Colfer
Illustrations copyright © 2013 by Giovanni Rigano

Printed in the United States of America
First Edition
10 9 8 7 6 5 4 3 2 1
V381-8386-5-13105
Library of Congress Cataloging-in-Publication Data
Colfer, Eoin.

  Artemis Fowl. The eternity code / adapted by Eoin Colfer and Andrew Donkin ; illustrations by
Giovanni Rigano.—First edition.

    pages cm

  Summary: After Artemis uses stolen fairy technology to create a powerful microcomputer and it is
snatched by a dangerous American businessman, Artemis, Juliet, Mulch, and the fairies join forces to try
to retrieve it.

  ISBN 978-1-4231-4527-1 (hardcover)—ISBN 978-1-4231-4577-6 (pbk.)

1.   Graphic novels. [1. Graphic novels. 2. Adventure and adventurers—Fiction. 3. Fairies—Fiction. 4.
Magic—Fiction. 5. Computers—Fiction. 6. England—Fiction.] I. Donkin, Andrew. II. Rigano, Giovanni,
illustrator. III. Title. IV. Title: Eternity code.

  PZ7.7.C645Arw 2013

  741.5'9415—dc23   2013001136

Visit www.disneyhyperionbooks.com and www.artemisfowl.com

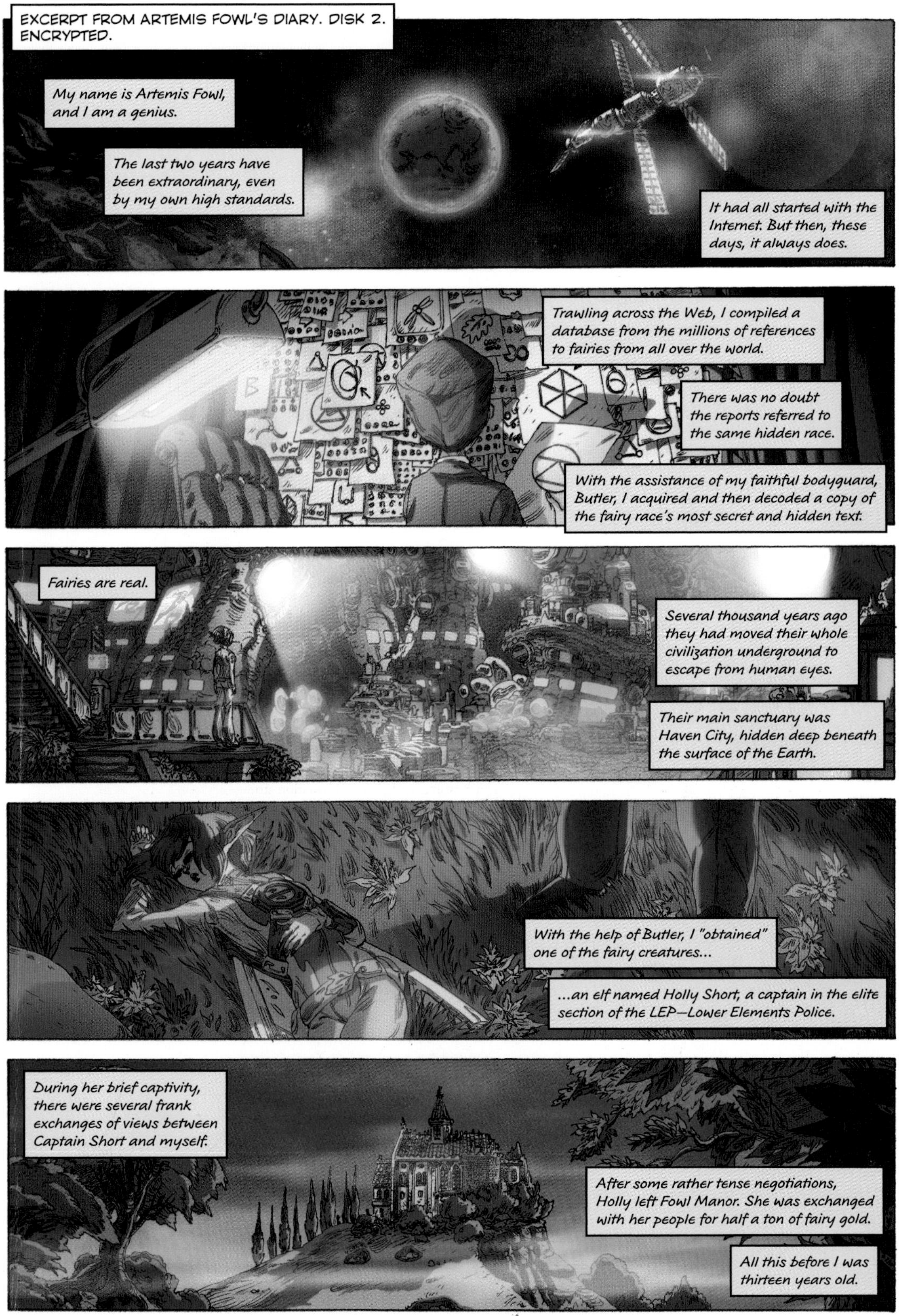
EXCERPT FROM ARTEMIS FOWL'S DIARY. DISK 2. ENCRYPTED.
My name is Artemis Fowl, and I am a genius.
The last two years have been extraordinary, even by my own high standards.
It had all started with the Internet. But then, these days, it always does.
Trawling across the Web, I compiled a database from the millions of references to fairies from all over the world.
There was no doubt the reports referred to the same hidden race.
With the assistance of my faithful bodyguard, Butler, I acquired and then decoded a copy of the fairy race's most secret and hidden text.
Fairies are real.
Several thousand years ago they had moved their whole civilization underground to escape from human eyes.
Their main sanctuary was Haven City, hidden deep beneath the surface of the Earth.
With the help of Butler, I "obtained" one of the fairy creatures...
...an elf named Holly Short, a captain in the elite section of the LEP—Lower Elements Police.
During her brief captivity, there were several frank exchanges of views between Captain Short and myself.
After some rather tense negotiations, Holly left Fowl Manor. She was exchanged with her people for half a ton of fairy gold.
All this before I was thirteen years old.

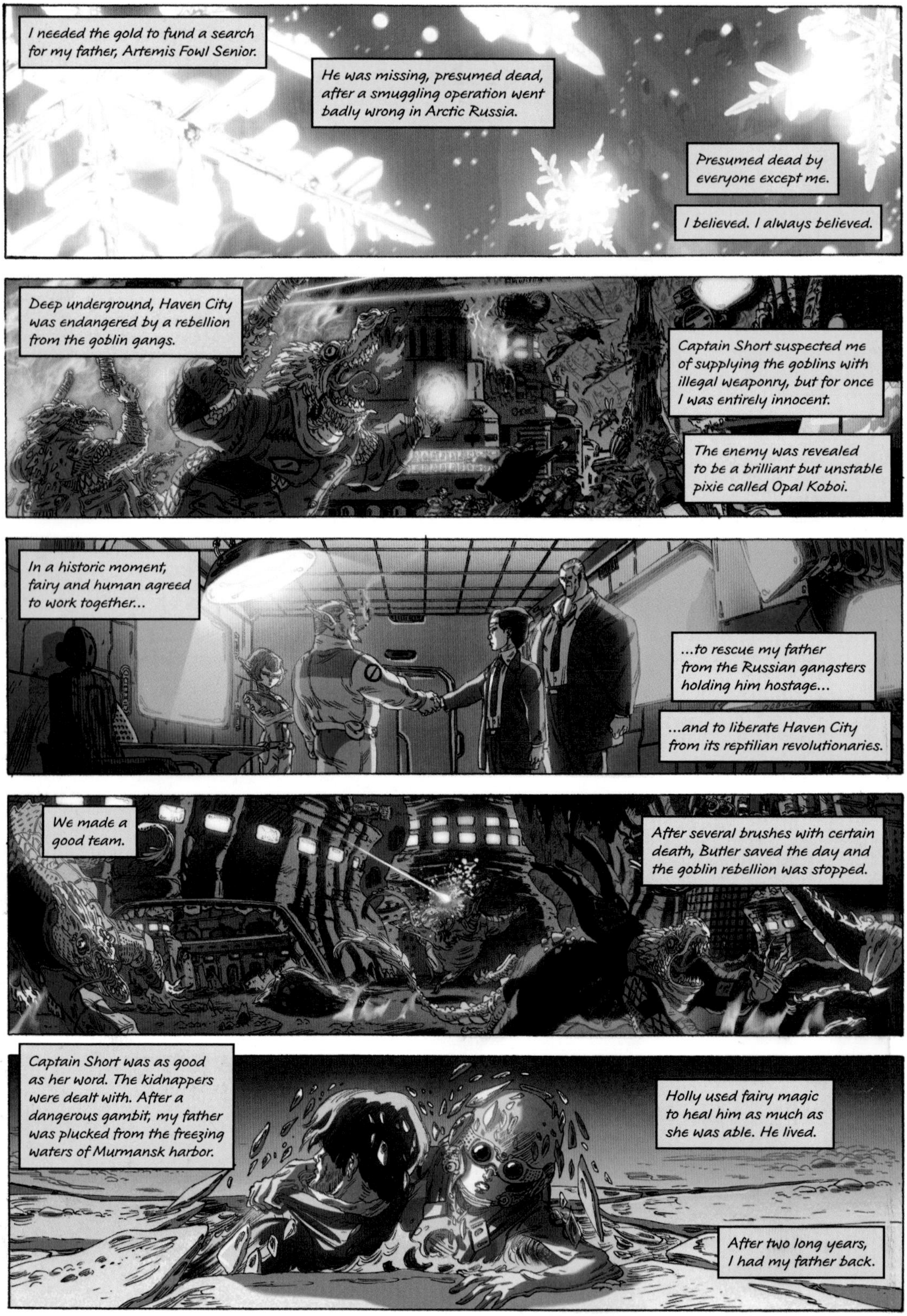
I needed the gold to fund a search for my father, Artemis Fowl Senior.
He was missing, presumed dead, after a smuggling operation went badly wrong in Arctic Russia.
Presumed dead by everyone except me.
I believed. I always believed.
Deep underground, Haven City was endangered by a rebellion from the goblin gangs.
Captain Short suspected me of supplying the goblins with illegal weaponry, but for once I was entirely innocent.
The enemy was revealed to be a brilliant but unstable pixie called Opal Koboi.
In a historic moment, fairy and human agreed to work together...
...to rescue my father from the Russian gangsters holding him hostage...
...and to liberate Haven City from its reptilian revolutionaries.
We made a good team.
After several brushes with certain death, Butler saved the day and the goblin rebellion was stopped.
Captain Short was as good as her word. The kidnappers were dealt with. After a dangerous gambit, my father was plucked from the freezing waters of Murmansk harbor.
Holly used fairy magic to heal him as much as she was able. He lived.
After two long years, I had my father back.

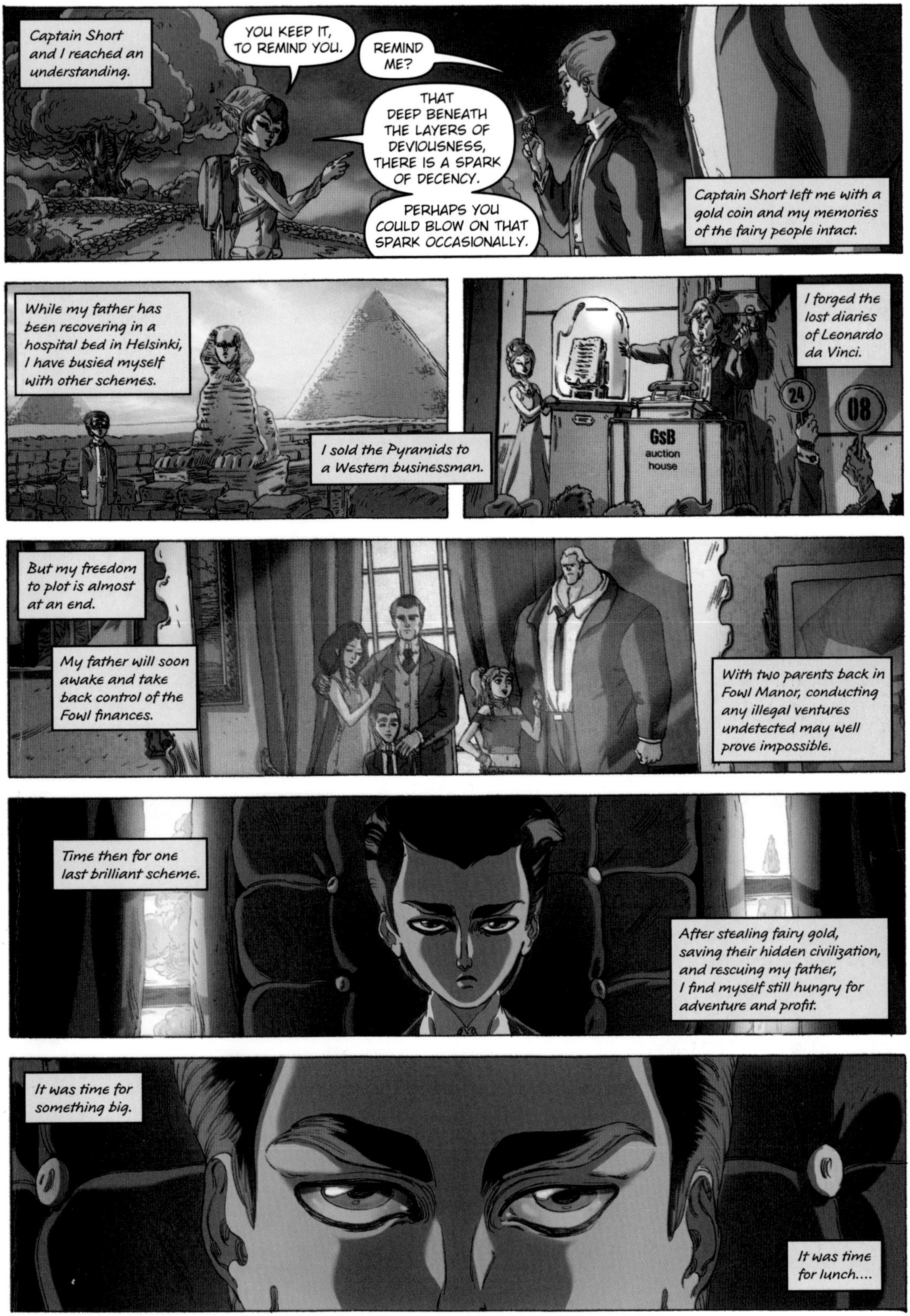
Captain Short and I reached an understanding.
YOU KEEP IT, TO REMIND YOU.
REMIND ME?
THAT DEEP BENEATH THE LAYERS OF DEVIOUSNESS, THERE IS A SPARK OF DECENCY.
PERHAPS YOU COULD BLOW ON THAT SPARK OCCASIONALLY.
Captain Short left me with a gold coin and my memories of the fairy people intact.
While my father has been recovering in a hospital bed in Helsinki, I have busied myself with other schemes.
I sold the Pyramids to a Western businessman.
I forged the lost diaries of Leonardo da Vinci.
GsB
auction house
24
08
But my freedom to plot is almost at an end.
My father will soon awake and take back control of the Fowl finances.
With two parents back in Fowl Manor, conducting any illegal ventures undetected may well prove impossible.
Time then for one last brilliant scheme.
After stealing fairy gold, saving their hidden civilization, and rescuing my father, I find myself still hungry for adventure and profit.
It was time for something big.
It was time for lunch....

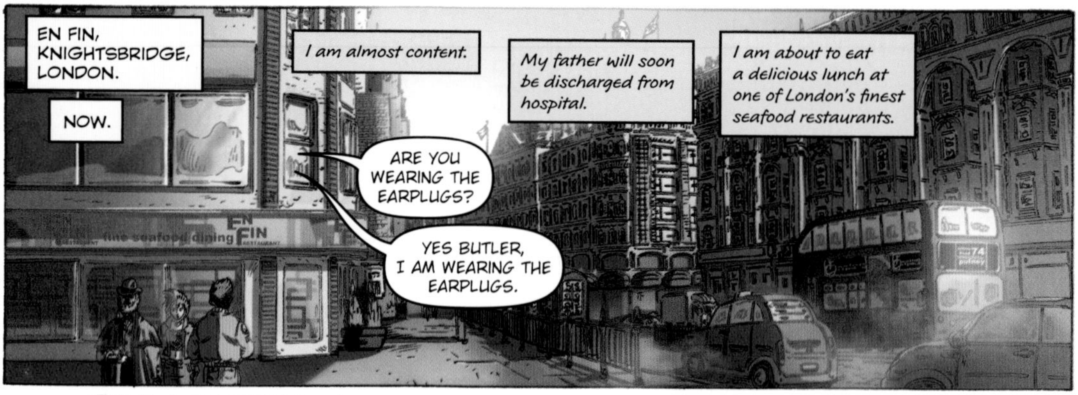
EN FIN, KNIGHTSBRIDGE, LONDON.
NOW.
I am almost content.
My father will soon be discharged from hospital.
I am about to eat a delicious lunch at one of London's finest seafood restaurants.
ARE YOU WEARING THE EARPLUGS?
YES BUTLER, I AM WEARING THE EARPLUGS.

CHAPTER 1: THE CUBE

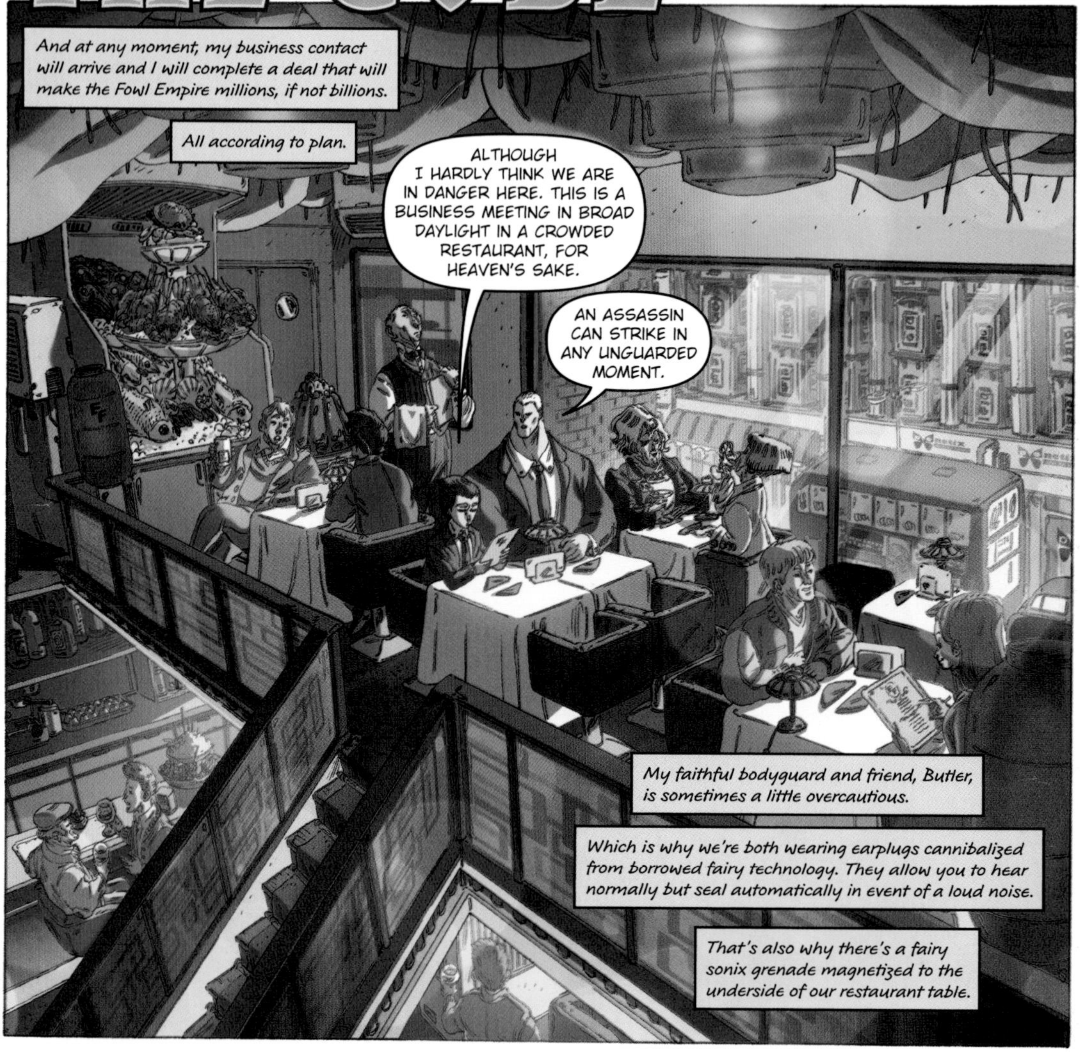
And at any moment, my business contact will arrive and I will complete a deal that will make the Fowl Empire millions, if not billions.
All according to plan.
ALTHOUGH I HARDLY THINK WE ARE IN DANGER HERE. THIS IS A BUSINESS MEETING IN BROAD DAYLIGHT IN A CROWDED RESTAURANT, FOR HEAVEN'S SAKE.
AN ASSASSIN CAN STRIKE IN ANY UNGUARDED MOMENT.
My faithful bodyguard and friend, Butler, is sometimes a little overcautious.
Which is why we're both wearing earplugs cannibalized from borrowed fairy technology. They allow you to hear normally but seal automatically in event of a loud noise.
That's also why there's a fairy sonix grenade magnetized to the underside of our restaurant table.

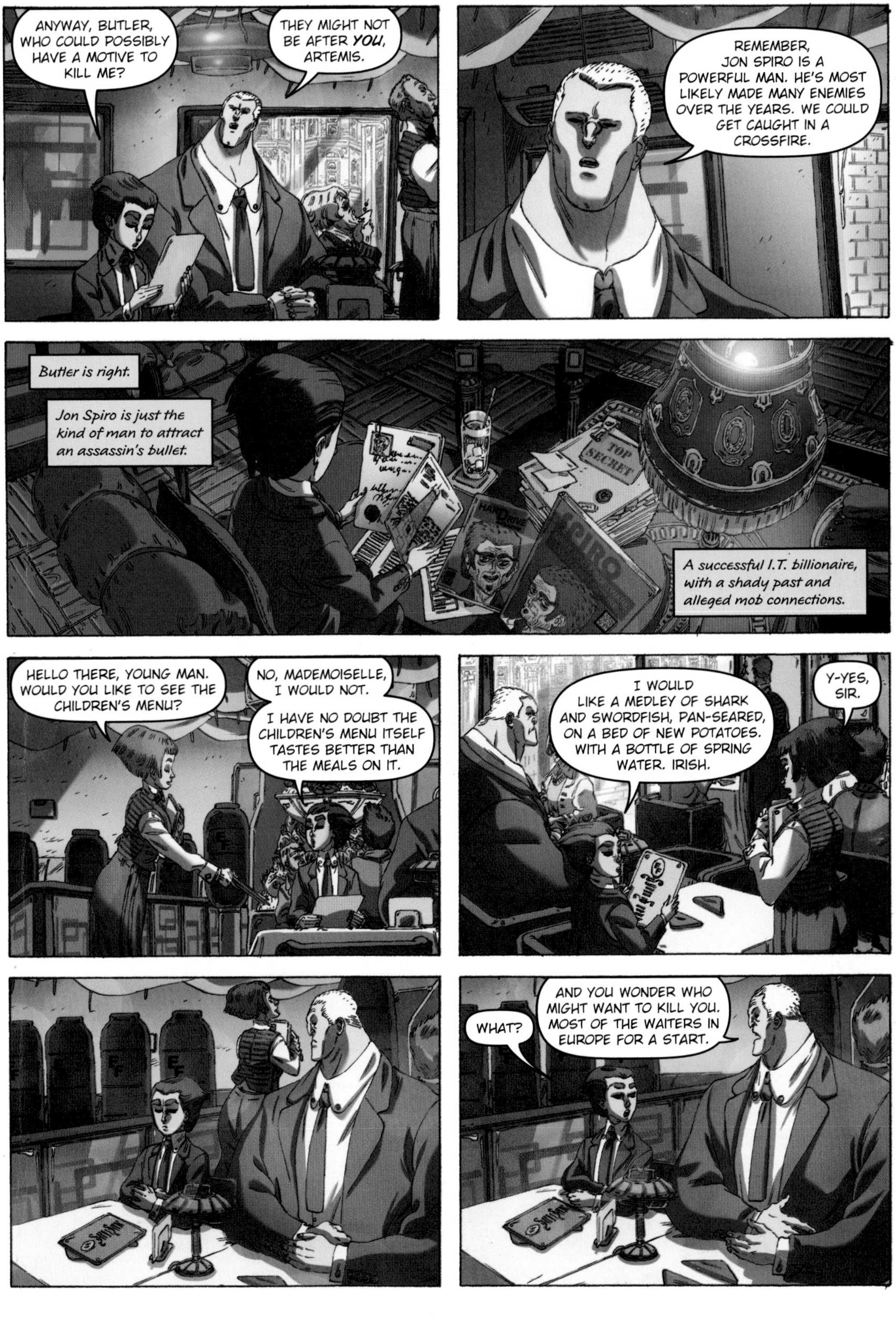
ANYWAY, BUTLER, WHO COULD POSSIBLY HAVE A MOTIVE TO KILL ME?
THEY MIGHT NOT BE AFTER YOU, ARTEMIS.
REMEMBER, JON SPIRO IS A POWERFUL MAN. HE'S MOST LIKELY MADE MANY ENEMIES OVER THE YEARS. WE COULD GET CAUGHT IN A CROSSFIRE.
Butler is right.
Jon Spiro is just the kind of man to attract an assassin's bullet.
TOP SECRET
A successful I.T. billionaire, with a shady past and alleged mob connections.
HELLO THERE, YOUNG MAN. WOULD YOU LIKE TO SEE THE CHILDREN'S MENU?
NO, MADEMOISELLE, I WOULD NOT.
I HAVE NO DOUBT THE CHILDREN'S MENU ITSELF TASTES BETTER THAN THE MEALS ON IT.
I WOULD LIKE A MEDLEY OF SHARK AND SWORDFISH, PAN-SEARED, ON A BED OF NEW POTATOES. WITH A BOTTLE OF SPRING WATER. IRISH.
Y-YES, SIR.
WHAT?
AND YOU WONDER WHO MIGHT WANT TO KILL YOU. MOST OF THE WAITERS IN EUROPE FOR A START.

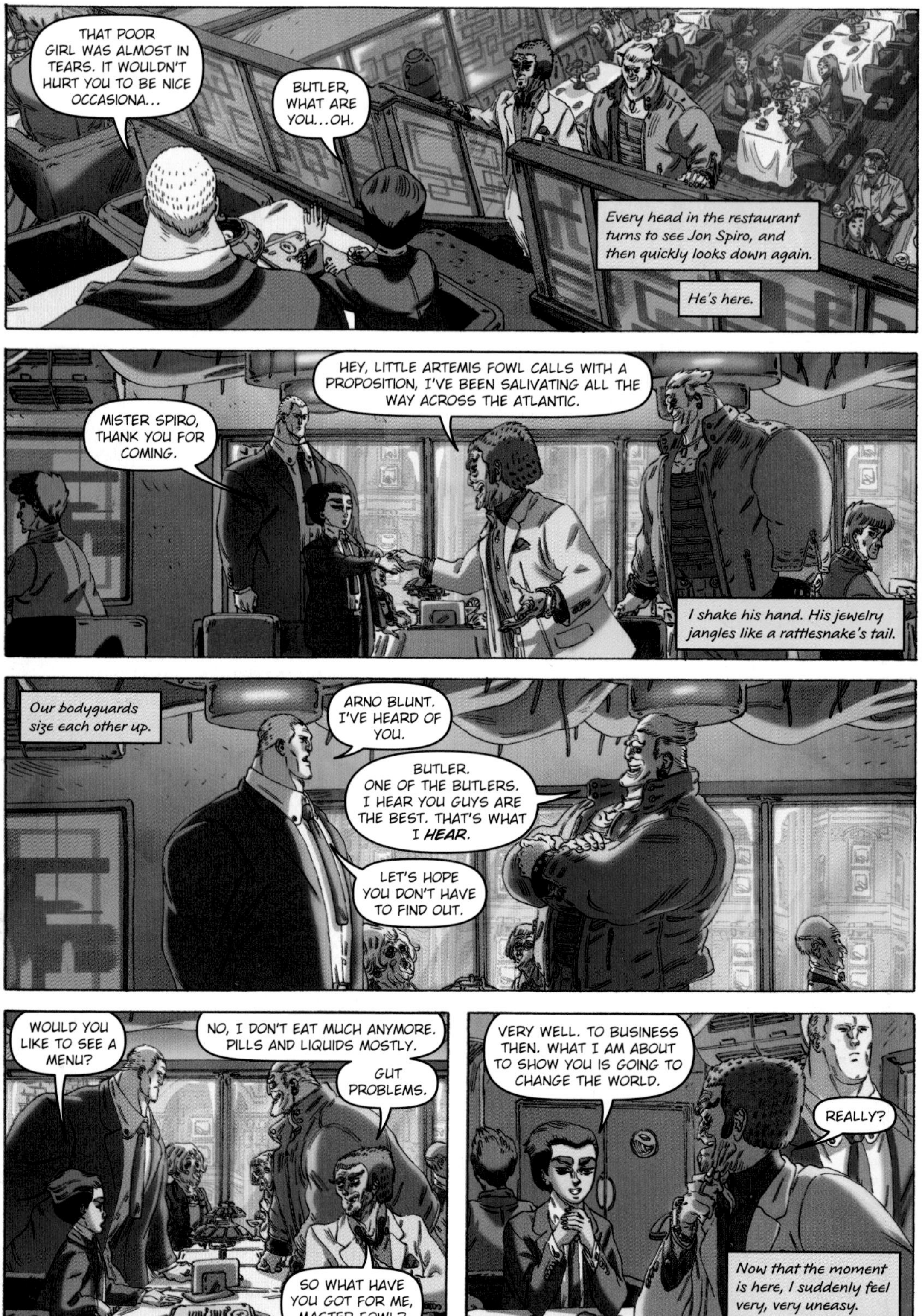
THAT POOR GIRL WAS ALMOST IN TEARS. IT WOULDN'T HURT YOU TO BE NICE OCCASIONA...
BUTLER, WHAT ARE YOU...OH.
Every head in the restaurant turns to see Jon Spiro, and then quickly looks down again.
He's here.
MISTER SPIRO, THANK YOU FOR COMING.
HEY, LITTLE ARTEMIS FOWL CALLS WITH A PROPOSITION, I'VE BEEN SALIVATING ALL THE WAY ACROSS THE ATLANTIC.
I shake his hand. His jewelry jangles like a rattlesnake's tail.
Our bodyguards size each other up.
ARNO BLUNT. I'VE HEARD OF YOU.
BUTLER. ONE OF THE BUTLERS. I HEAR YOU GUYS ARE THE BEST. THAT'S WHAT I HEAR.
LET'S HOPE YOU DON'T HAVE TO FIND OUT.
WOULD YOU LIKE TO SEE A MENU?
NO, I DON'T EAT MUCH ANYMORE. PILLS AND LIQUIDS MOSTLY.
GUT PROBLEMS.
SO WHAT HAVE YOU GOT FOR ME, MASTER FOWL?
VERY WELL. TO BUSINESS THEN. WHAT I AM ABOUT TO SHOW YOU IS GOING TO CHANGE THE WORLD.
REALLY?
Now that the moment is here, I suddenly feel very, very uneasy.

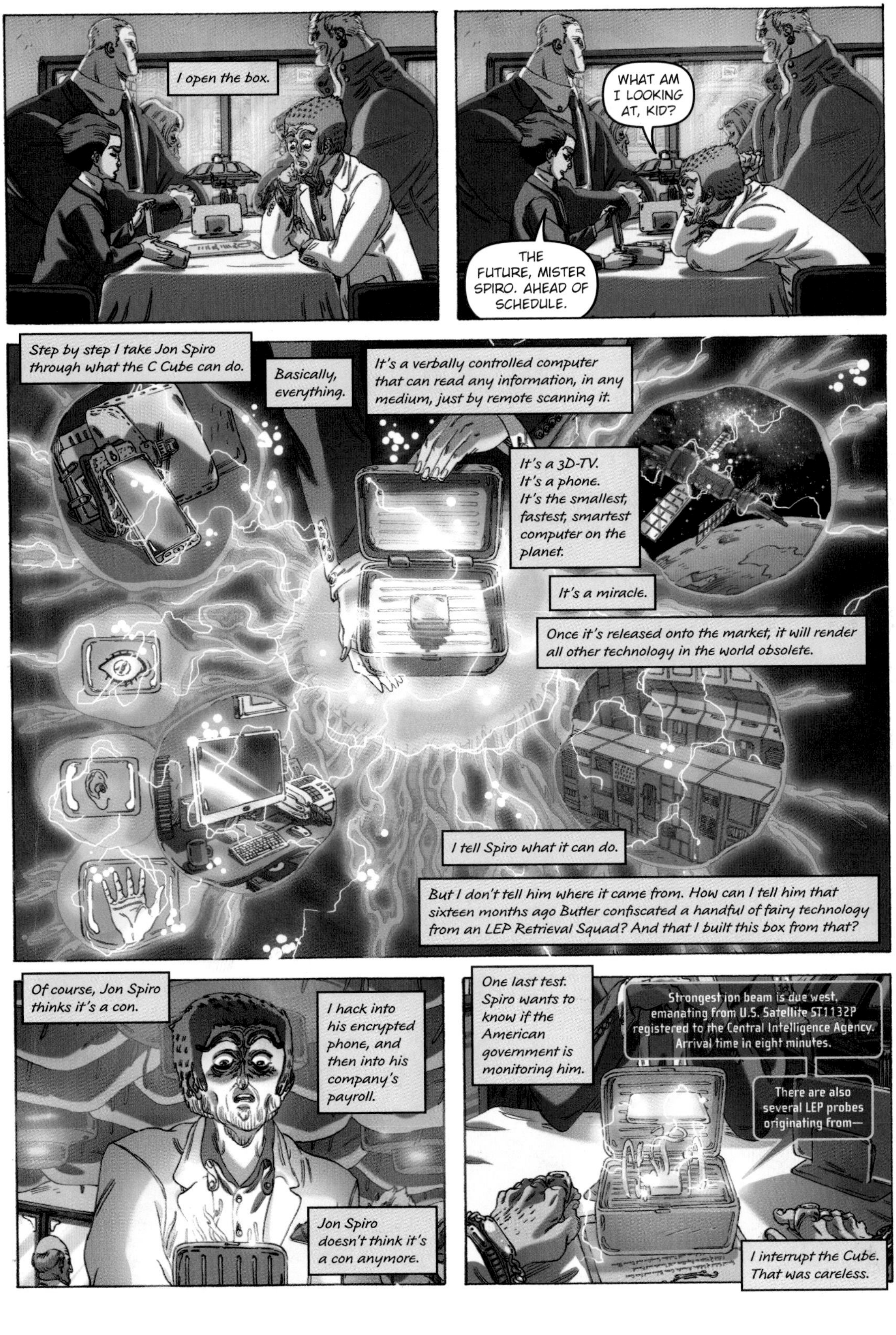
I open the box.
WHAT AM I LOOKING AT, KID?
THE FUTURE, MISTER SPIRO. AHEAD OF SCHEDULE.
Step by step I take Jon Spiro through what the C Cube can do.
Basically, everything.
It's a verbally controlled computer that can read any information, in any medium, just by remote scanning it.
It's a 3D-TV.
It's a phone.
It's the smallest, fastest, smartest computer on the planet.
It's a miracle.
Once it's released onto the market, it will render all other technology in the world obsolete.
I tell Spiro what it can do.
But I don't tell him where it came from. How can I tell him that sixteen months ago Butler confiscated a handful of fairy technology from an LEP Retrieval Squad? And that I built this box from that?
Of course, Jon Spiro thinks it's a con.
I hack into his encrypted phone, and then into his company's payroll.
Jon Spiro doesn't think it's a con anymore.
One last test. Spiro wants to know if the American government is monitoring him.
Strongest ion beam is due west, emanating from U.S. Satellite ST1132P registered to the Central Intelligence Agency. Arrival time in eight minutes.
There are also several LEP probes originating from—
I interrupt the Cube. That was careless.

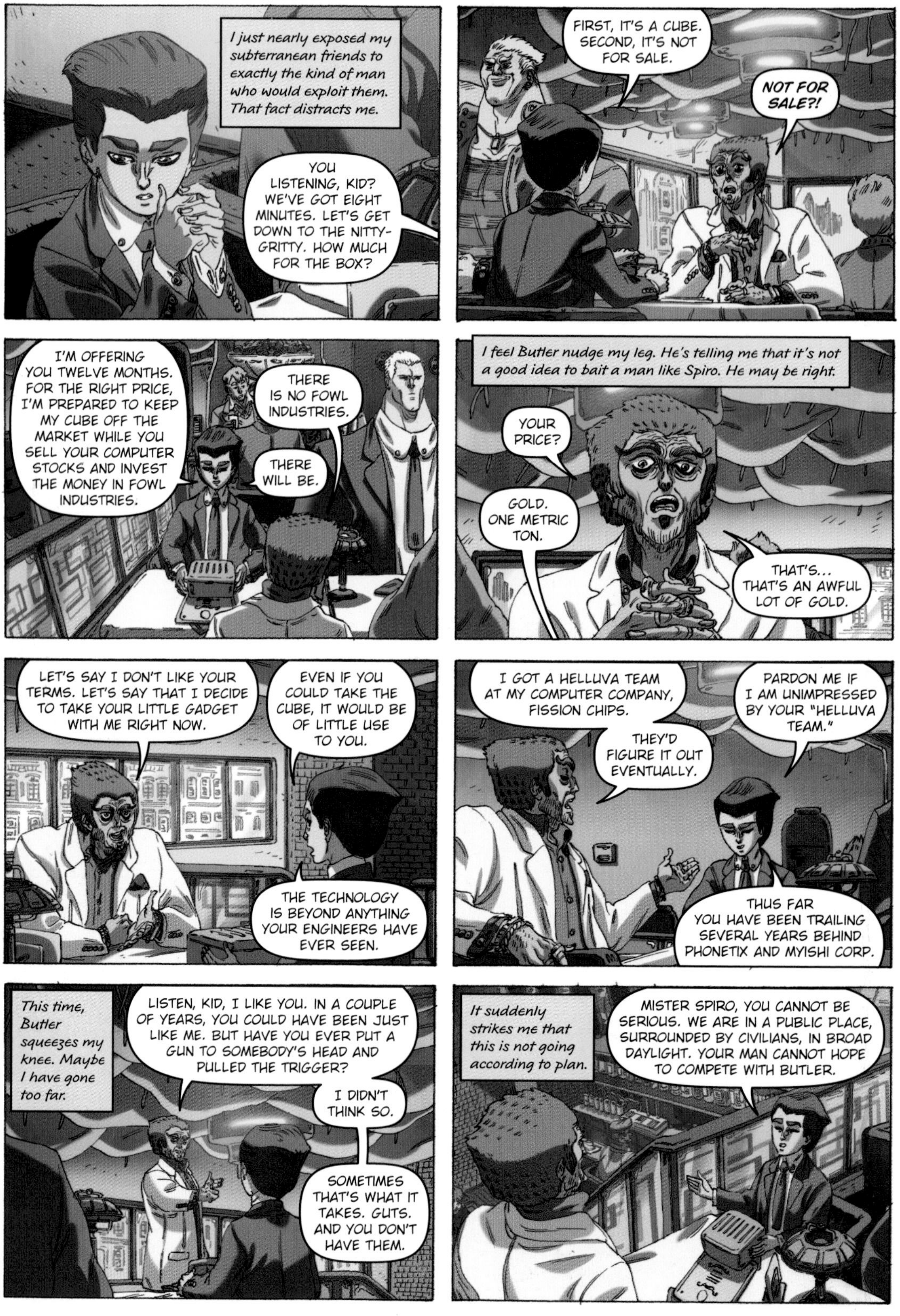
I just nearly exposed my subterranean friends to exactly the kind of man who would exploit them. That fact distracts me.
YOU LISTENING, KID? WE'VE GOT EIGHT MINUTES. LET'S GET DOWN TO THE NITTY-GRITTY. HOW MUCH FOR THE BOX?
FIRST, IT'S A CUBE. SECOND, IT'S NOT FOR SALE.
NOT FOR SALE?!
I'M OFFERING YOU TWELVE MONTHS. FOR THE RIGHT PRICE, I'M PREPARED TO KEEP MY CUBE OFF THE MARKET WHILE YOU SELL YOUR COMPUTER STOCKS AND INVEST THE MONEY IN FOWL INDUSTRIES.
THERE IS NO FOWL INDUSTRIES.
THERE WILL BE.
I feel Butler nudge my leg. He's telling me that it's not a good idea to bait a man like Spiro. He may be right.
YOUR PRICE?
GOLD. ONE METRIC TON.
THAT'S... THAT'S AN AWFUL LOT OF GOLD.
LET'S SAY I DON'T LIKE YOUR TERMS. LET'S SAY THAT I DECIDE TO TAKE YOUR LITTLE GADGET WITH ME RIGHT NOW.
EVEN IF YOU COULD TAKE THE CUBE, IT WOULD BE OF LITTLE USE TO YOU.
THE TECHNOLOGY IS BEYOND ANYTHING YOUR ENGINEERS HAVE EVER SEEN.
I GOT A HELLUVA TEAM AT MY COMPUTER COMPANY, FISSION CHIPS.
THEY'D FIGURE IT OUT EVENTUALLY.
PARDON ME IF I AM UNIMPRESSED BY YOUR "HELLUVA TEAM."
THUS FAR YOU HAVE BEEN TRAILING SEVERAL YEARS BEHIND PHONETIX AND MYISHI CORP.
This time, Butler squeezes my knee. Maybe I have gone too far.
LISTEN, KID, I LIKE YOU. IN A COUPLE OF YEARS, YOU COULD HAVE BEEN JUST LIKE ME. BUT HAVE YOU EVER PUT A GUN TO SOMEBODY'S HEAD AND PULLED THE TRIGGER?
I DIDN'T THINK SO.
SOMETIMES THAT'S WHAT IT TAKES. GUTS. AND YOU DON'T HAVE THEM.
It suddenly strikes me that this is not going according to plan.
MISTER SPIRO, YOU CANNOT BE SERIOUS. WE ARE IN A PUBLIC PLACE, SURROUNDED BY CIVILIANS, IN BROAD DAYLIGHT. YOUR MAN CANNOT HOPE TO COMPETE WITH BUTLER.

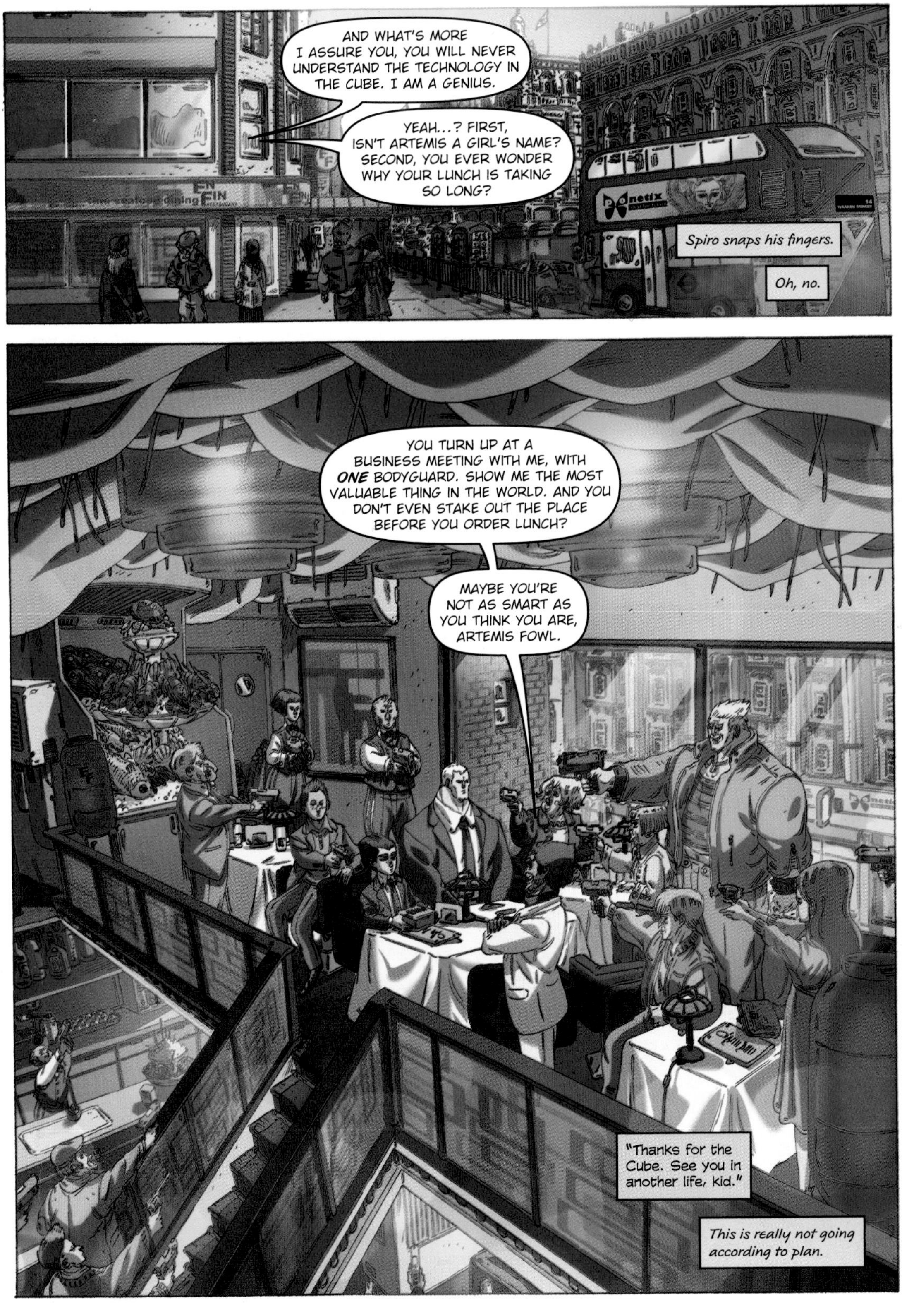
AND WHAT'S MORE I ASSURE YOU, YOU WILL NEVER UNDERSTAND THE TECHNOLOGY IN THE CUBE. I AM A GENIUS.
YEAH...? FIRST, ISN'T ARTEMIS A GIRL'S NAME? SECOND, YOU EVER WONDER WHY YOUR LUNCH IS TAKING SO LONG?
EN FIN
fine seafood dining
Spiro snaps his fingers.
Oh, no.
YOU TURN UP AT A BUSINESS MEETING WITH ME, WITH ONE BODYGUARD. SHOW ME THE MOST VALUABLE THING IN THE WORLD. AND YOU DON'T EVEN STAKE OUT THE PLACE BEFORE YOU ORDER LUNCH?
MAYBE YOU'RE NOT AS SMART AS YOU THINK YOU ARE, ARTEMIS FOWL.
"Thanks for the Cube. See you in another life, kid."
This is really not going according to plan.

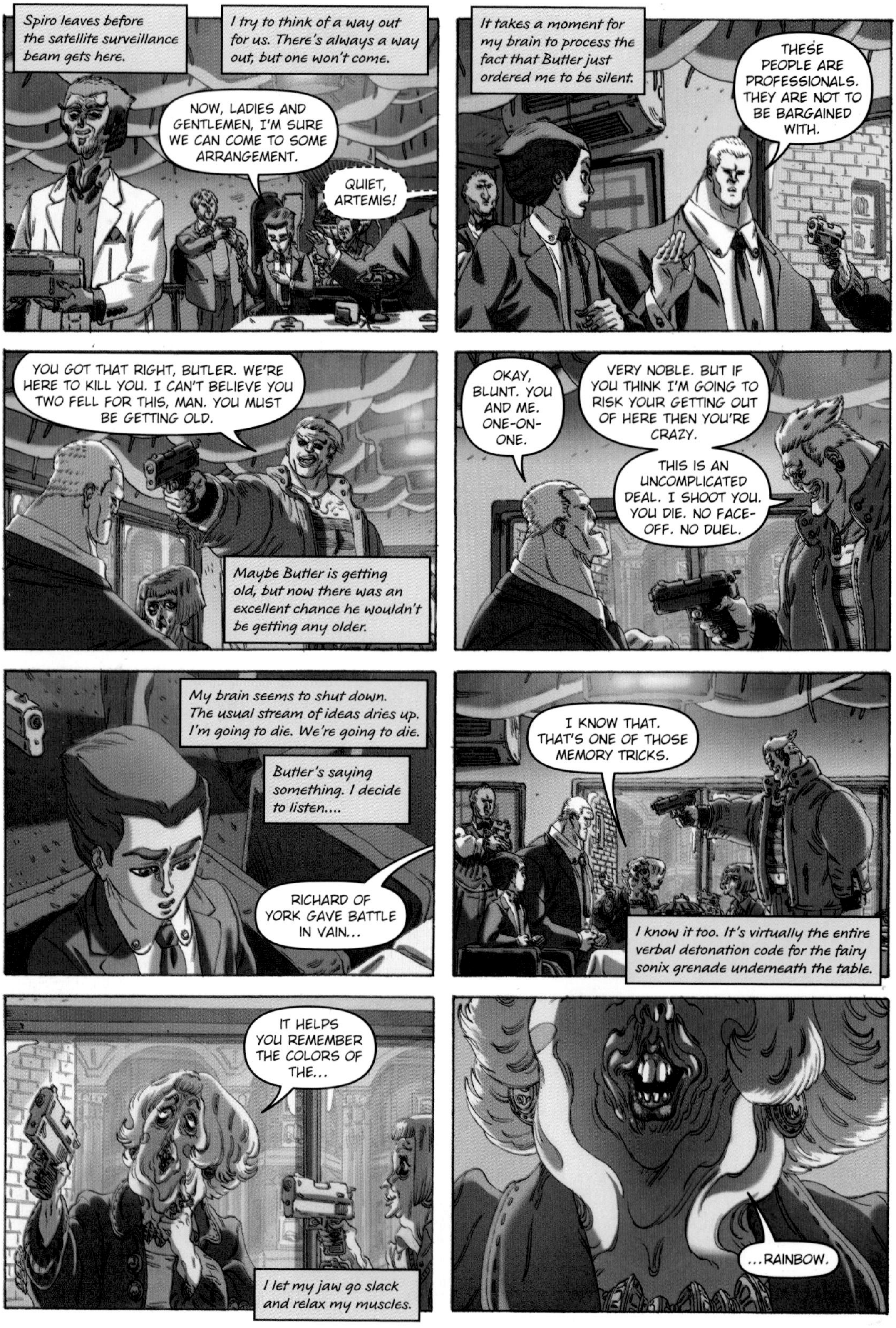
Spiro leaves before the satellite surveillance beam gets here.
I try to think of a way out for us. There's always a way out, but one won't come.
NOW, LADIES AND GENTLEMEN, I'M SURE WE CAN COME TO SOME ARRANGEMENT.
QUIET, ARTEMIS!
It takes a moment for my brain to process the fact that Butler just ordered me to be silent.
THESE PEOPLE ARE PROFESSIONALS. THEY ARE NOT TO BE BARGAINED WITH.
YOU GOT THAT RIGHT, BUTLER. WE'RE HERE TO KILL YOU. I CAN'T BELIEVE YOU TWO FELL FOR THIS, MAN. YOU MUST BE GETTING OLD.
Maybe Butler is getting old, but now there was an excellent chance he wouldn't be getting any older.
OKAY, BLUNT. YOU AND ME. ONE-ON-ONE.
VERY NOBLE. BUT IF YOU THINK I'M GOING TO RISK YOUR GETTING OUT OF HERE THEN YOU'RE CRAZY.
THIS IS AN UNCOMPLICATED DEAL. I SHOOT YOU. YOU DIE. NO FACE-OFF. NO DUEL.
My brain seems to shut down. The usual stream of ideas dries up. I'm going to die. We're going to die.
Butler's saying something. I decide to listen....
RICHARD OF YORK GAVE BATTLE IN VAIN...
I KNOW THAT. THAT'S ONE OF THOSE MEMORY TRICKS.
I know it too. It's virtually the entire verbal detonation code for the fairy sonix grenade underneath the table.
IT HELPS YOU REMEMBER THE COLORS OF THE...
I let my jaw go slack and relax my muscles.
...RAINBOW.

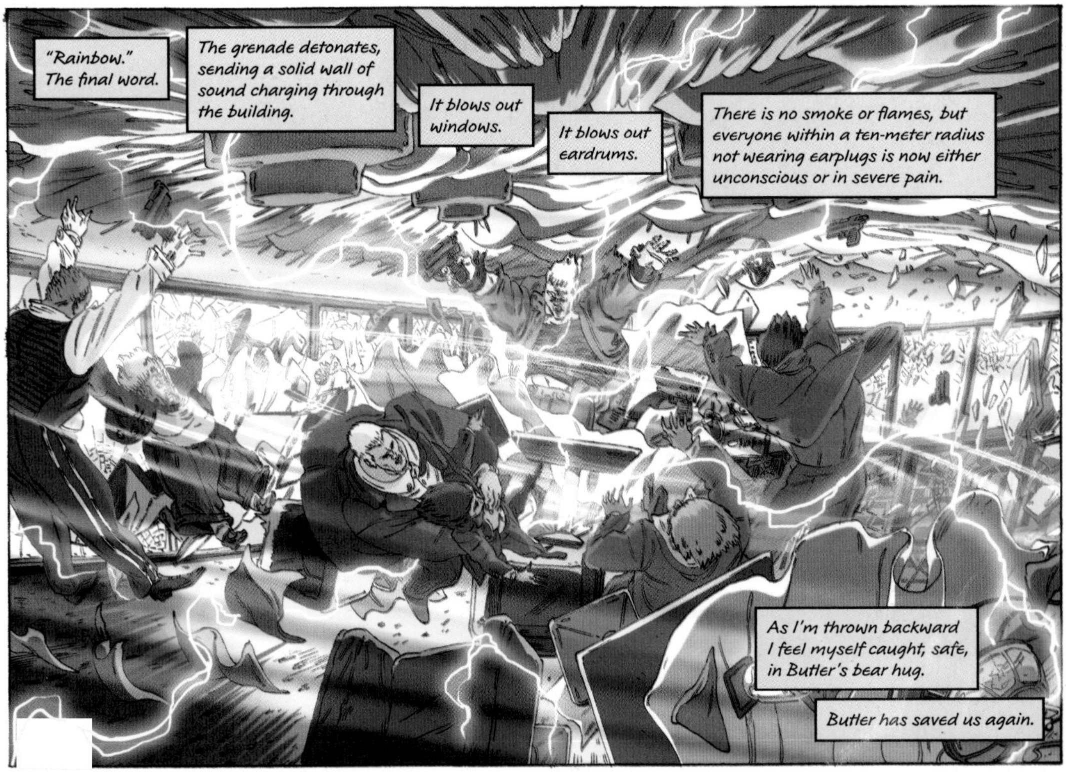
"Rainbow."
The final word.
The grenade detonates, sending a solid wall of sound charging through the building.
It blows out windows.
It blows out eardrums.
There is no smoke or flames, but everyone within a ten-meter radius not wearing earplugs is now either unconscious or in severe pain.
As I'm thrown backward I feel myself caught, safe, in Butler's bear hug.
Butler has saved us again.

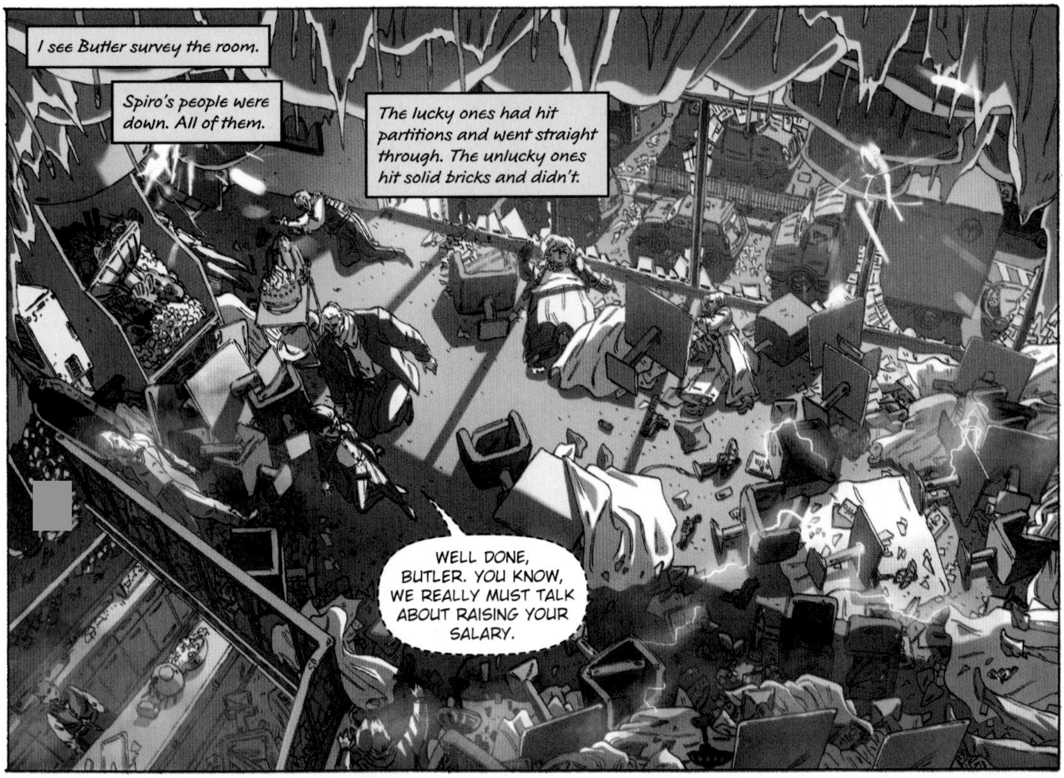
I see Butler survey the room.
Spiro's people were down. All of them.
The lucky ones had hit partitions and went straight through. The unlucky ones hit solid bricks and didn't.
WELL DONE, BUTLER. YOU KNOW, WE REALLY MUST TALK ABOUT RAISING YOUR SALARY.

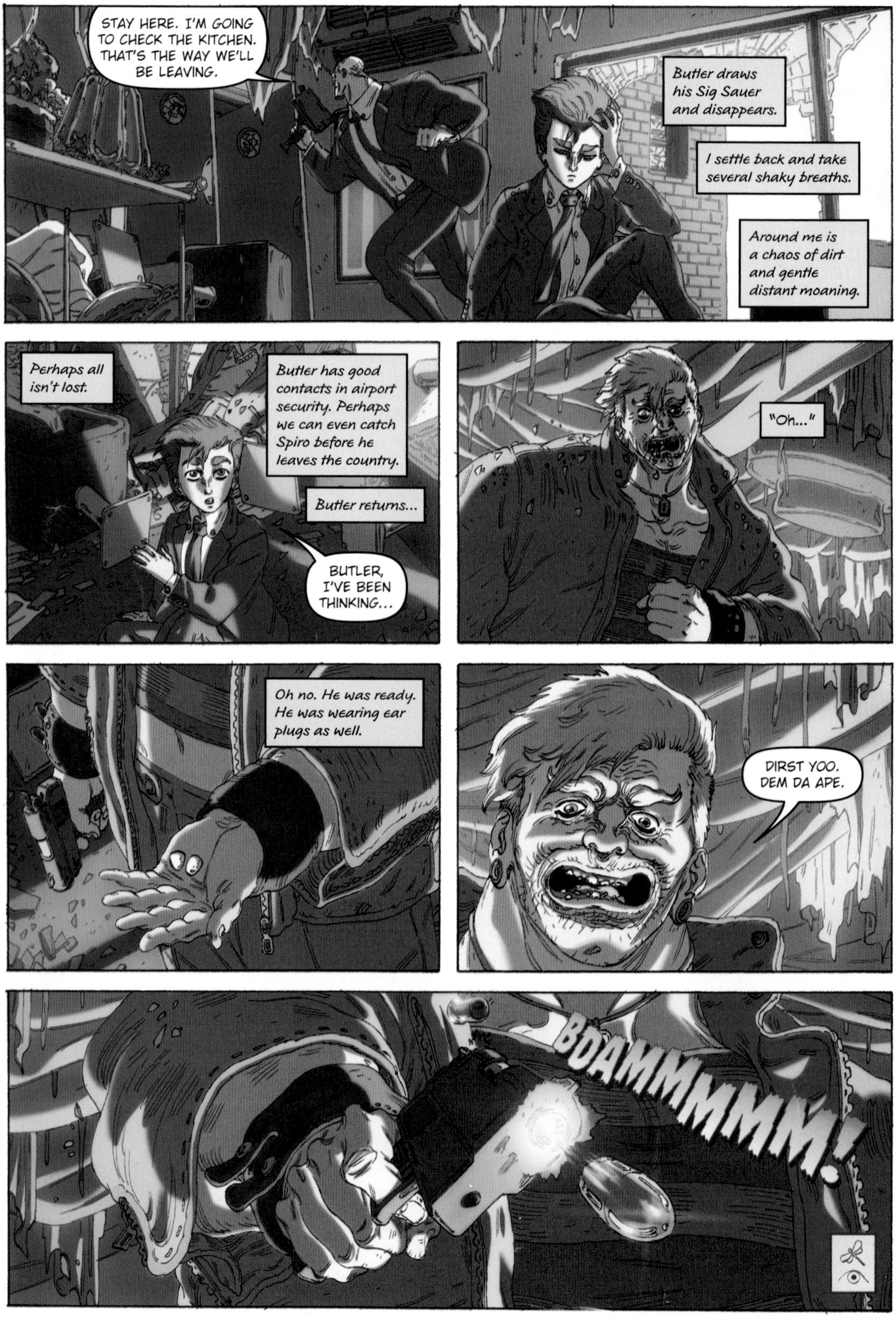
STAY HERE. I'M GOING TO CHECK THE KITCHEN. THAT'S THE WAY WE'LL BE LEAVING.
Butler draws his Sig Sauer and disappears.
I settle back and take several shaky breaths.
Around me is a chaos of dirt and gentle distant moaning.
Perhaps all isn't lost.
Butler has good contacts in airport security. Perhaps we can even catch Spiro before he leaves the country.
Butler returns...
BUTLER, I'VE BEEN THINKING...
"Oh..."
Oh no. He was ready. He was wearing ear plugs as well.
DIRST YOO. DEM DA APE.
BDAMMMMMM!

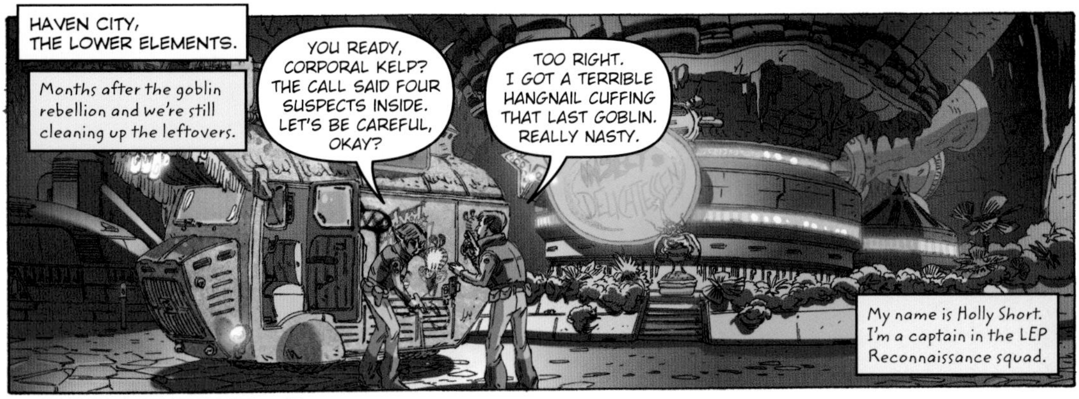
HAVEN CITY, THE LOWER ELEMENTS.
Months after the goblin rebellion and we're still cleaning up the leftovers.
YOU READY, CORPORAL KELP? THE CALL SAID FOUR SUSPECTS INSIDE. LET'S BE CAREFUL, OKAY?
TOO RIGHT. I GOT A TERRIBLE HANGNAIL CUFFING THAT LAST GOBLIN. REALLY NASTY.
DELICATESSEN
My name is Holly Short. I'm a captain in the LEP Reconnaissance squad.

CHAPTER 2: LOCKDOWN

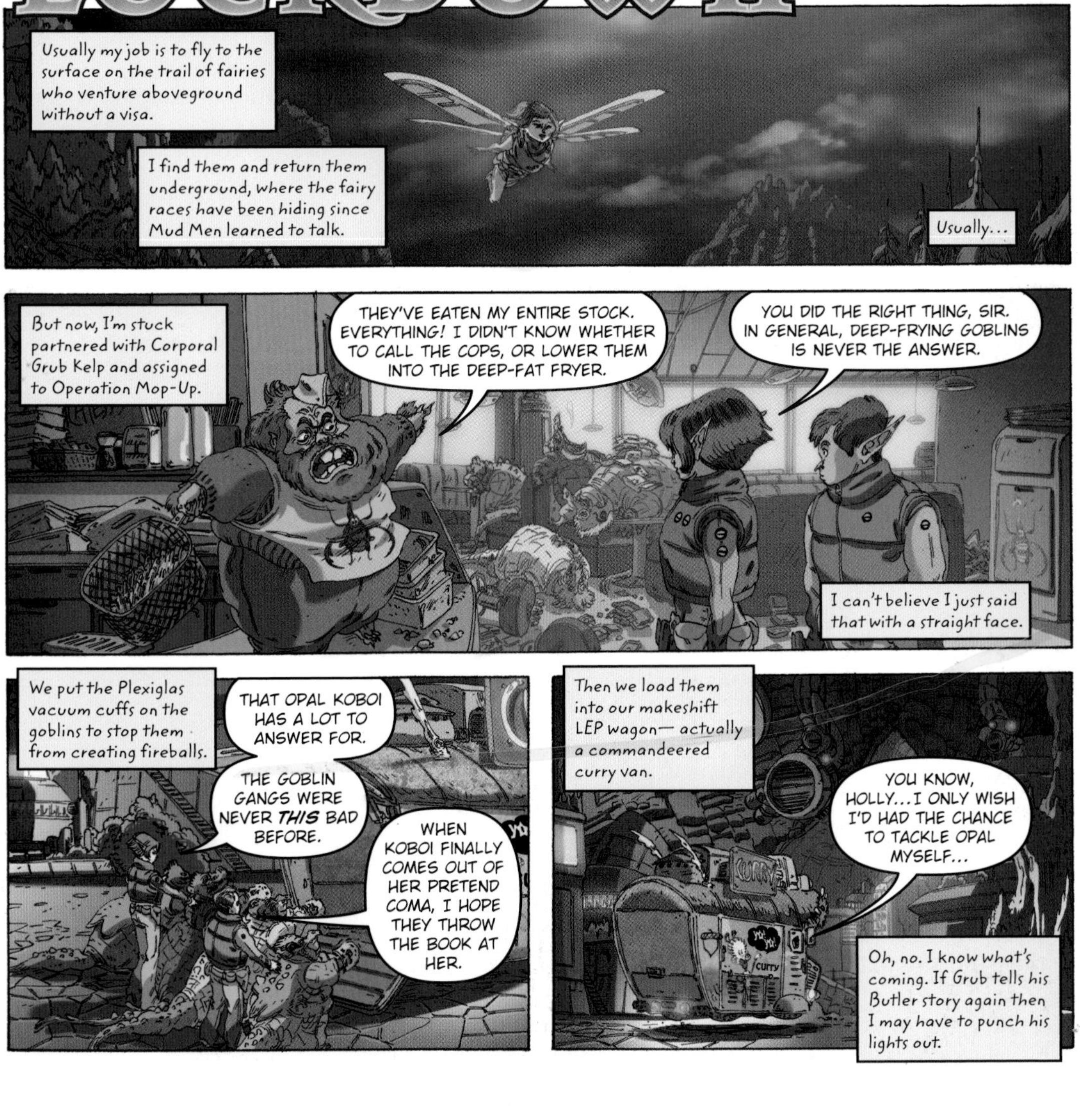
Usually my job is to fly to the surface on the trail of fairies who venture aboveground without a visa.
I find them and return them underground, where the fairy races have been hiding since Mud Men learned to talk.
Usually...
But now, I'm stuck partnered with Corporal Grub Kelp and assigned to Operation Mop-Up.
THEY'VE EATEN MY ENTIRE STOCK. EVERYTHING! I DIDN'T KNOW WHETHER TO CALL THE COPS, OR LOWER THEM INTO THE DEEP-FAT FRYER.
YOU DID THE RIGHT THING, SIR. IN GENERAL, DEEP-FRYING GOBLINS IS NEVER THE ANSWER.
I can't believe I just said that with a straight face.
We put the Plexiglas vacuum cuffs on the goblins to stop them from creating fireballs.
THAT OPAL KOBOI HAS A LOT TO ANSWER FOR.
THE GOBLIN GANGS WERE NEVER *THIS* BAD BEFORE.
WHEN KOBOI FINALLY COMES OUT OF HER PRETEND COMA, I HOPE THEY THROW THE BOOK AT HER.
Then we load them into our makeshift LEP wagon— actually a commandeered curry van.
YOU KNOW, HOLLY... I ONLY WISH I'D HAD THE CHANCE TO TACKLE OPAL MYSELF...
CURRY
Oh, no. I know what's coming. If Grub tells his Butler story again then I may have to punch his lights out.

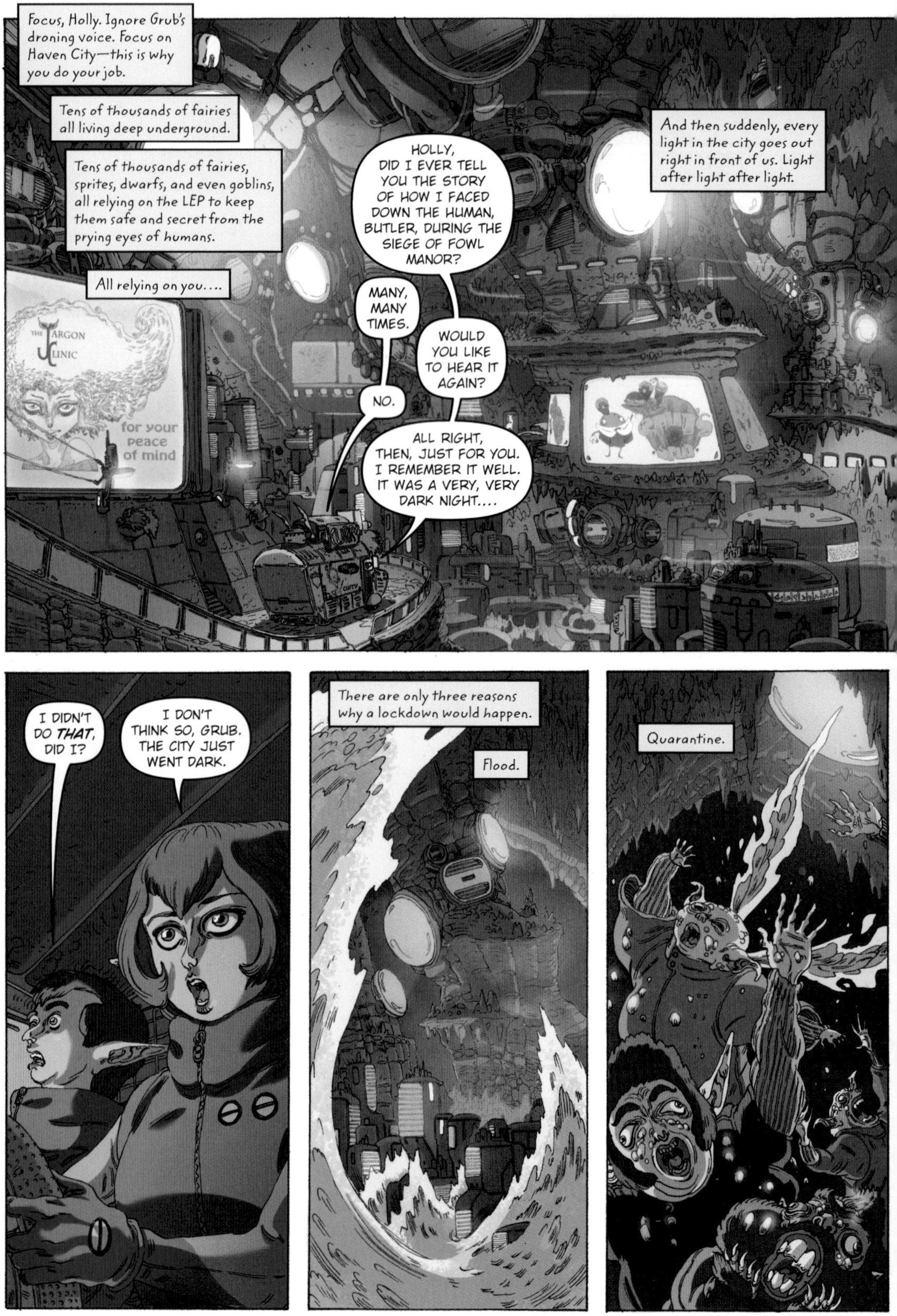

Focus, Holly. Ignore Grub's droning voice. Focus on Haven City—this is why you do your job.
Tens of thousands of fairies all living deep underground.
Tens of thousands of fairies, sprites, dwarfs, and even goblins, all relying on the LEP to keep them safe and secret from the prying eyes of humans.
All relying on you....
THE JARGON CLINIC
for your peace of mind
HOLLY, DID I EVER TELL YOU THE STORY OF HOW I FACED DOWN THE HUMAN, BUTLER, DURING THE SIEGE OF FOWL MANOR?
MANY, MANY TIMES.
WOULD YOU LIKE TO HEAR IT AGAIN?
NO.
ALL RIGHT, THEN, JUST FOR YOU. I REMEMBER IT WELL. IT WAS A VERY, VERY DARK NIGHT....
And then suddenly, every light in the city goes out right in front of us. Light after light after light.
I DIDN'T DO *THAT*, DID I?
I DON'T THINK SO, GRUB. THE CITY JUST WENT DARK.
There are only three reasons why a lockdown would happen.
Flood.
Quarantine.

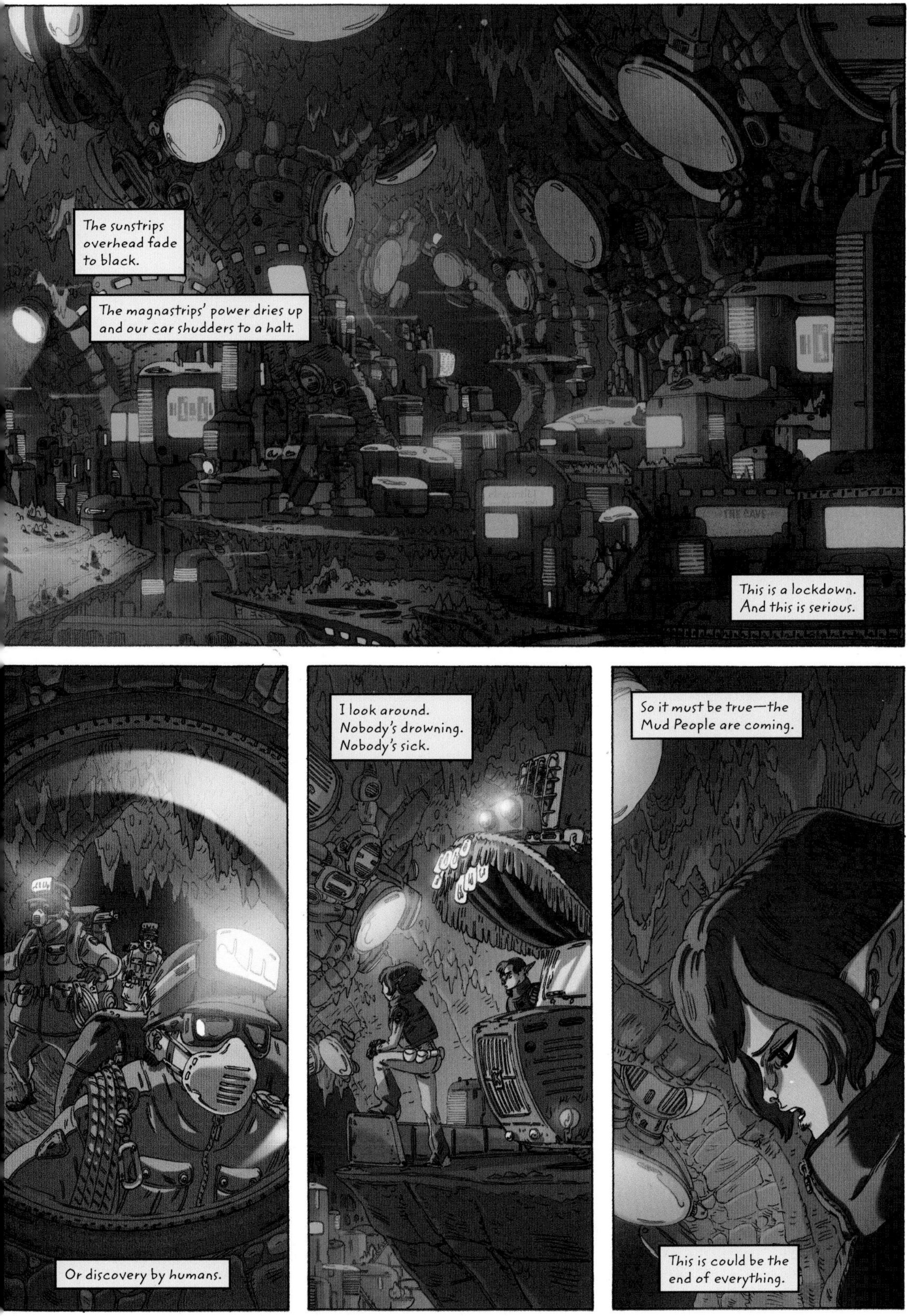
The sunstrips overhead fade to black.
The magnastrips' power dries up and our car shudders to a halt.
This is a lockdown. And this is serious.
Or discovery by humans.
I look around. Nobody's drowning. Nobody's sick.
So it must be true—the Mud People are coming.
This is could be the end of everything.

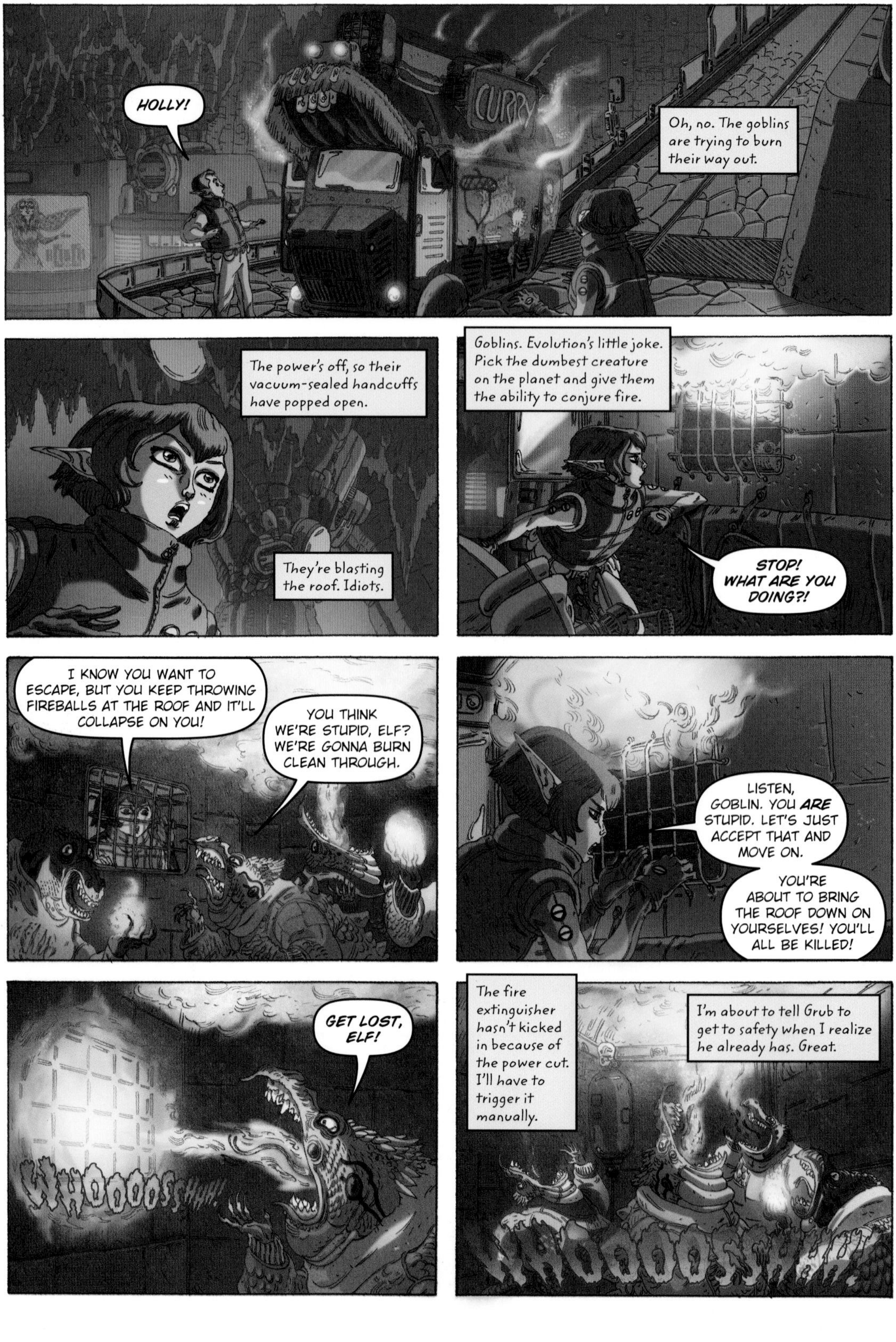
HOLLY!
Oh, no. The goblins are trying to burn their way out.
The power's off, so their vacuum-sealed handcuffs have popped open.
They're blasting the roof. Idiots.
Goblins. Evolution's little joke. Pick the dumbest creature on the planet and give them the ability to conjure fire.
STOP! WHAT ARE YOU DOING?!
I KNOW YOU WANT TO ESCAPE, BUT YOU KEEP THROWING FIREBALLS AT THE ROOF AND IT'LL COLLAPSE ON YOU!
YOU THINK WE'RE STUPID, ELF? WE'RE GONNA BURN CLEAN THROUGH.
LISTEN, GOBLIN. YOU ARE STUPID. LET'S JUST ACCEPT THAT AND MOVE ON.
YOU'RE ABOUT TO BRING THE ROOF DOWN ON YOURSELVES! YOU'LL ALL BE KILLED!
GET LOST, ELF!
WHOOOOSHHH!
The fire extinguisher hasn't kicked in because of the power cut. I'll have to trigger it manually.
I'm about to tell Grub to get to safety when I realize he already has. Great.

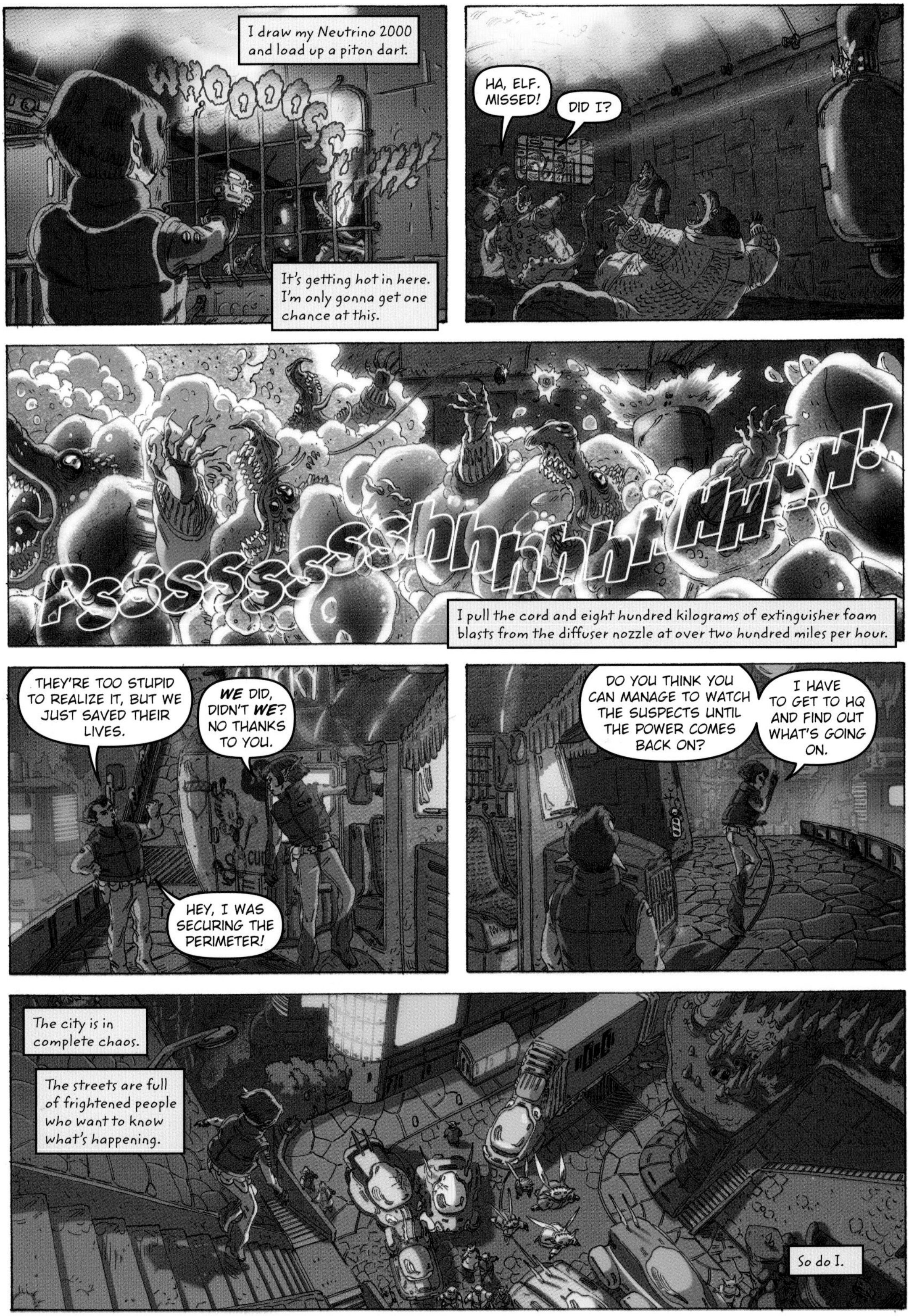
I draw my Neutrino 2000 and load up a piton dart.
It's getting hot in here. I'm only gonna get one chance at this.
HA, ELF. MISSED!
DID I?
I pull the cord and eight hundred kilograms of extinguisher foam blasts from the diffuser nozzle at over two hundred miles per hour.
THEY'RE TOO STUPID TO REALIZE IT, BUT WE JUST SAVED THEIR LIVES.
WE DID, DIDN'T WE? NO THANKS TO YOU.
HEY, I WAS SECURING THE PERIMETER!
DO YOU THINK YOU CAN MANAGE TO WATCH THE SUSPECTS UNTIL THE POWER COMES BACK ON?
I HAVE TO GET TO HQ AND FIND OUT WHAT'S GOING ON.
The city is in complete chaos.
The streets are full of frightened people who want to know what's happening.
So do I.

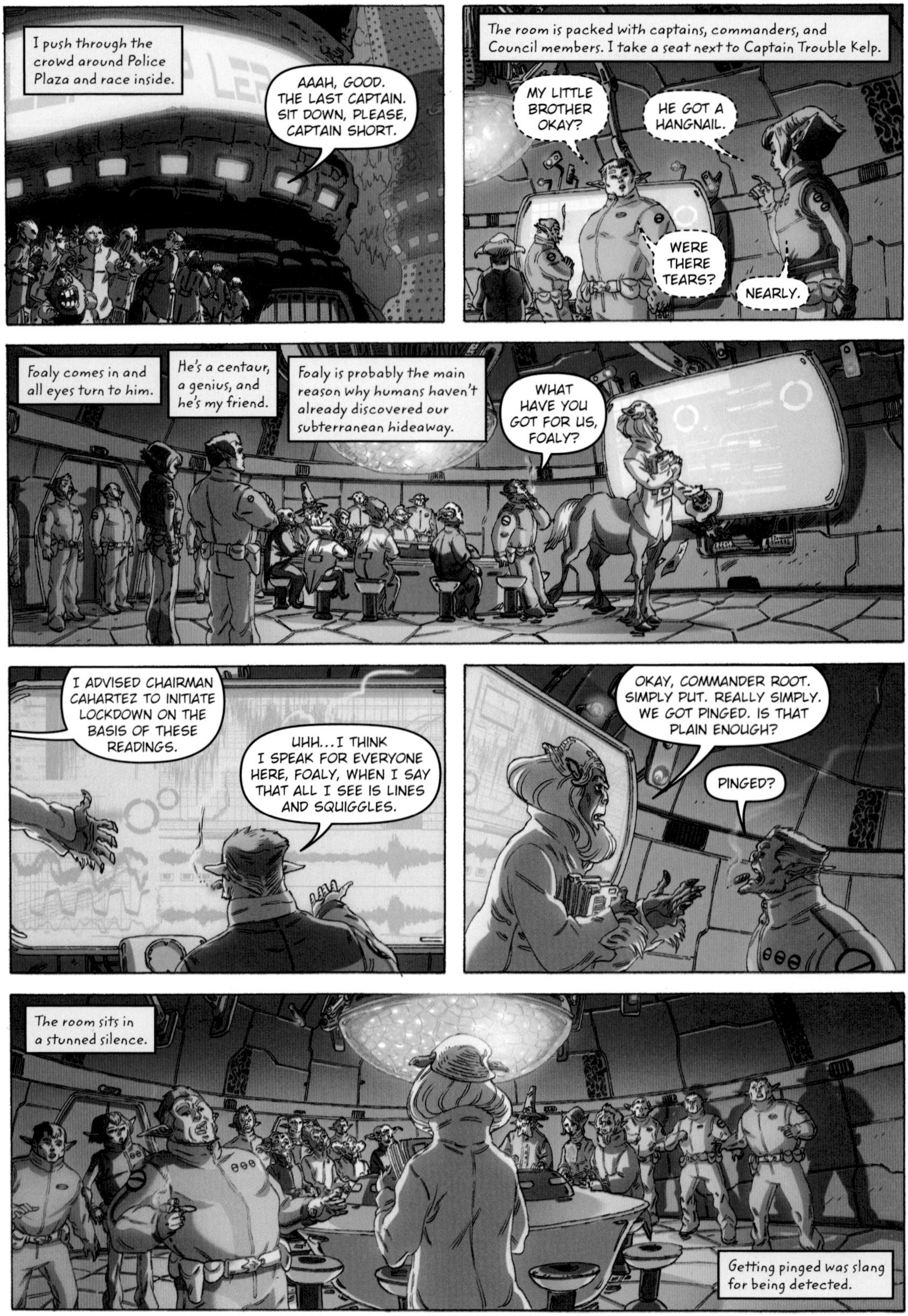
I push through the crowd around Police Plaza and race inside.
AAAH, GOOD. THE LAST CAPTAIN. SIT DOWN, PLEASE, CAPTAIN SHORT.
The room is packed with captains, commanders, and Council members. I take a seat next to Captain Trouble Kelp.
MY LITTLE BROTHER OKAY?
HE GOT A HANGNAIL.
WERE THERE TEARS?
NEARLY.
Foaly comes in and all eyes turn to him.
He's a centaur, a genius, and he's my friend.
Foaly is probably the main reason why humans haven't already discovered our subterranean hideaway.
WHAT HAVE YOU GOT FOR US, FOALY?
I ADVISED CHAIRMAN CAHARTEZ TO INITIATE LOCKDOWN ON THE BASIS OF THESE READINGS.
UHH... I THINK I SPEAK FOR EVERYONE HERE, FOALY, WHEN I SAY THAT ALL I SEE IS LINES AND SQUIGGLES.
OKAY, COMMANDER ROOT. SIMPLY PUT. REALLY SIMPLY. WE GOT PINGED. IS THAT PLAIN ENOUGH?
PINGED?
The room sits in a stunned silence.
Getting pinged was slang for being detected.

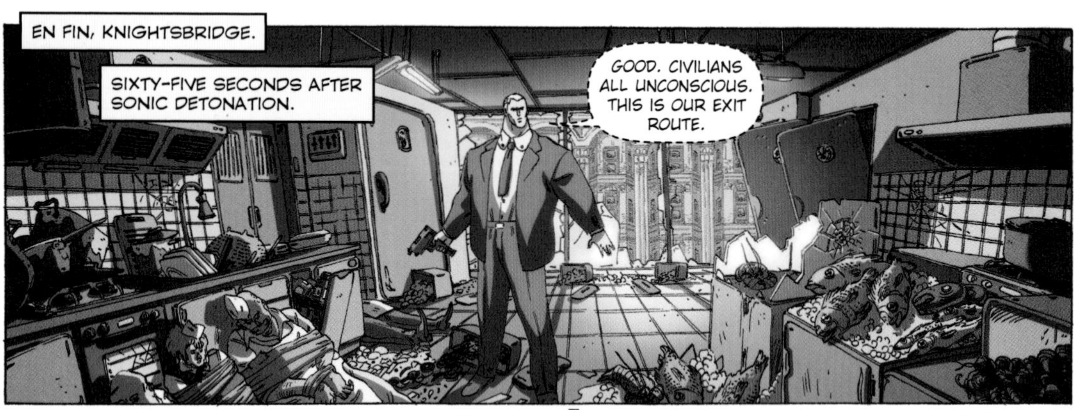
EN FIN, KNIGHTSBRIDGE.
SIXTY-FIVE SECONDS AFTER SONIC DETONATION.
GOOD. CIVILIANS ALL UNCONSCIOUS. THIS IS OUR EXIT ROUTE.

CHAPTER 3: ON ICE

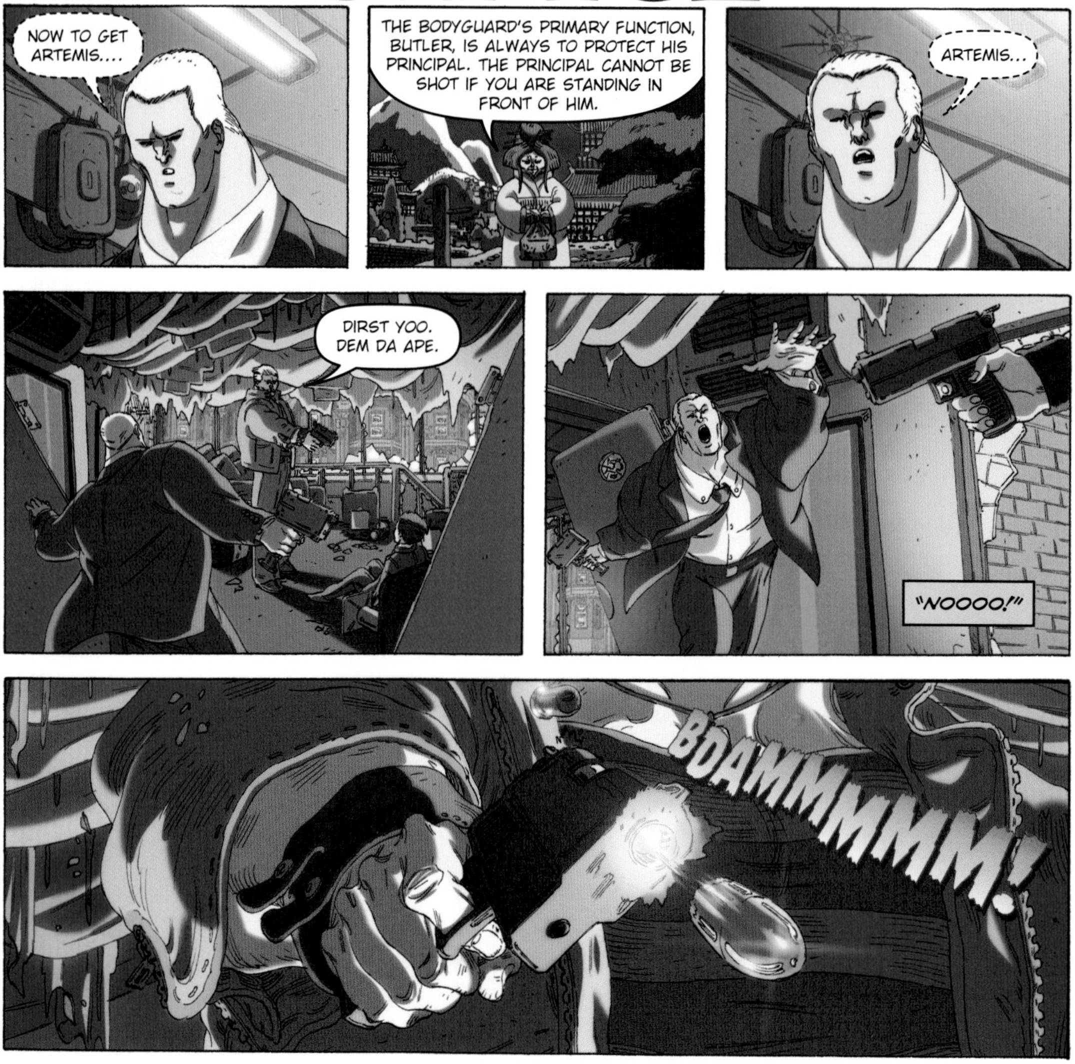
NOW TO GET ARTEMIS....
THE BODYGUARD'S PRIMARY FUNCTION, BUTLER, IS ALWAYS TO PROTECT HIS PRINCIPAL. THE PRINCIPAL CANNOT BE SHOT IF YOU ARE STANDING IN FRONT OF HIM.
ARTEMIS...
DIRST YOO. DEM DA APE.
"NOOOO!"
BDAMMMMMM!

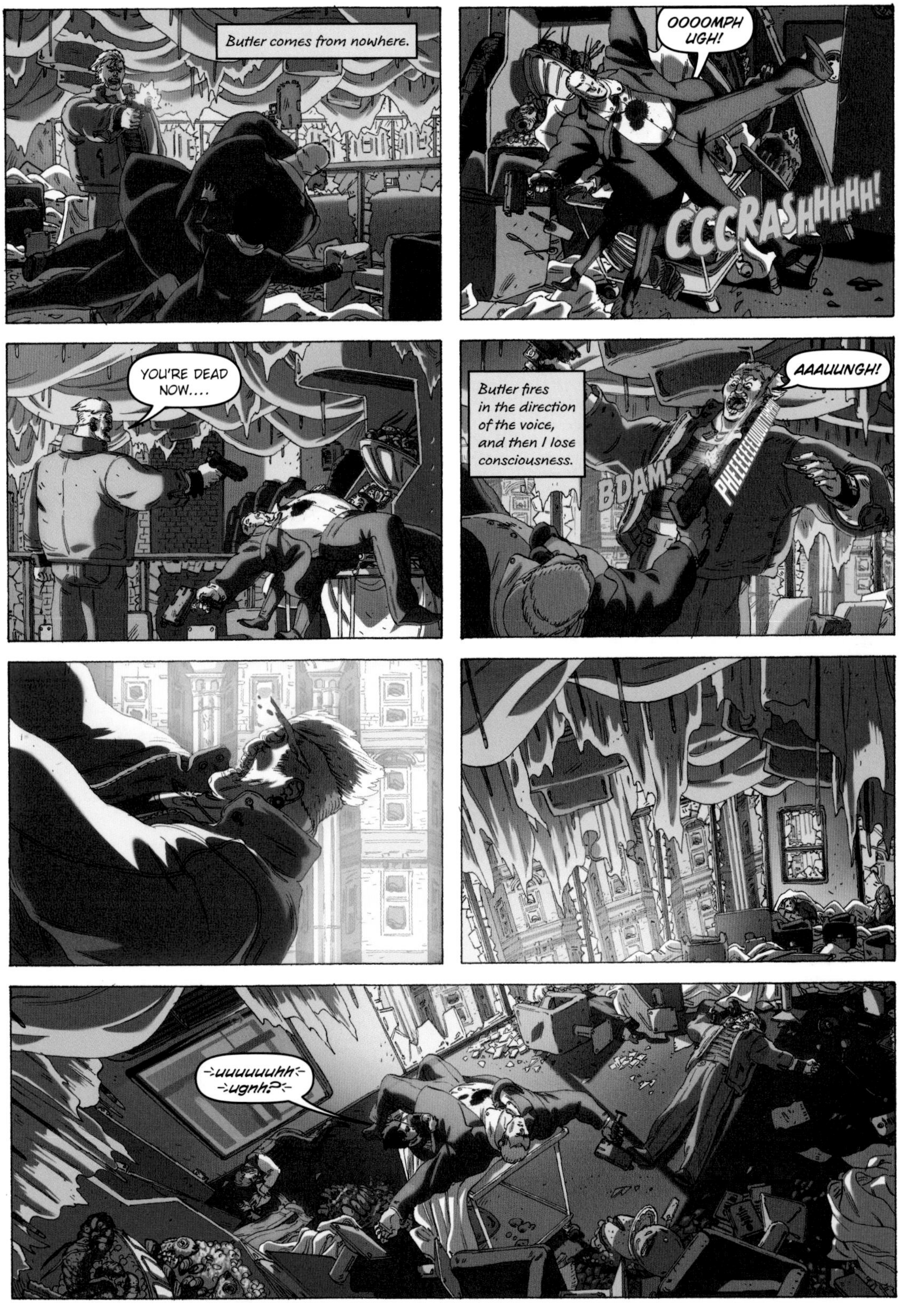
Butler comes from nowhere.
OOOOMPH UGH!
CCCRASHHHHH!
YOU'RE DEAD NOW....
Butler fires in the direction of the voice, and then I lose consciousness.
AAAUUNGH!
BDAM!
-uuuuuuhh- -ugnh?-

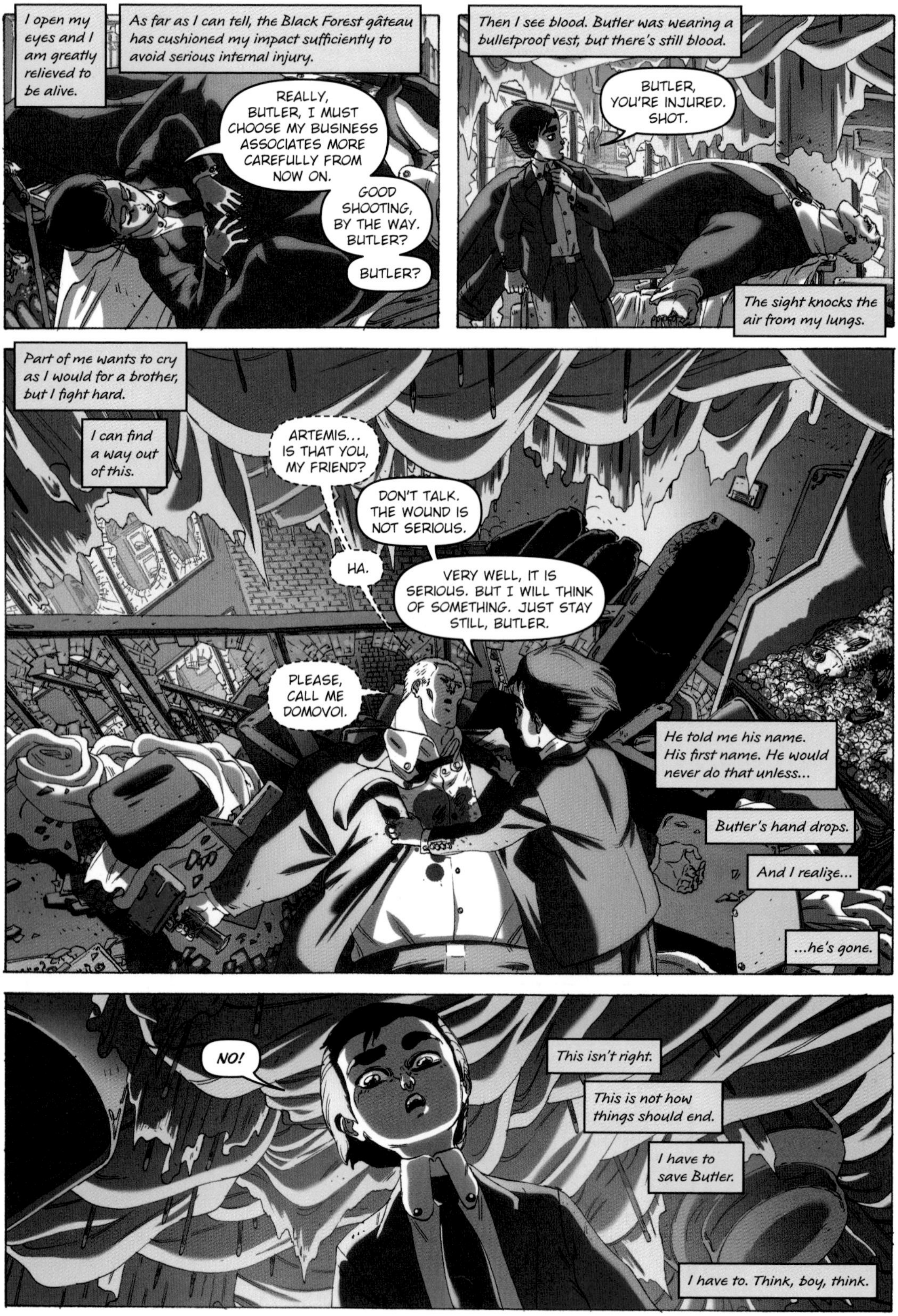
I open my eyes and I am greatly relieved to be alive.
As far as I can tell, the Black Forest gâteau has cushioned my impact sufficiently to avoid serious internal injury.
REALLY, BUTLER, I MUST CHOOSE MY BUSINESS ASSOCIATES MORE CAREFULLY FROM NOW ON.
GOOD SHOOTING, BY THE WAY. BUTLER?
BUTLER?
Then I see blood. Butler was wearing a bulletproof vest, but there's still blood.
BUTLER, YOU'RE INJURED. SHOT.
The sight knocks the air from my lungs.
Part of me wants to cry as I would for a brother, but I fight hard.
I can find a way out of this.
ARTEMIS... IS THAT YOU, MY FRIEND?
DON'T TALK. THE WOUND IS NOT SERIOUS.
HA.
VERY WELL, IT IS SERIOUS. BUT I WILL THINK OF SOMETHING. JUST STAY STILL, BUTLER.
PLEASE, CALL ME DOMOVOI.
He told me his name. His first name. He would never do that unless...
Butler's hand drops.
And I realize...
...he's gone.
NO!
This isn't right.
This is not how things should end.
I have to save Butler.
I have to. Think, boy, think.

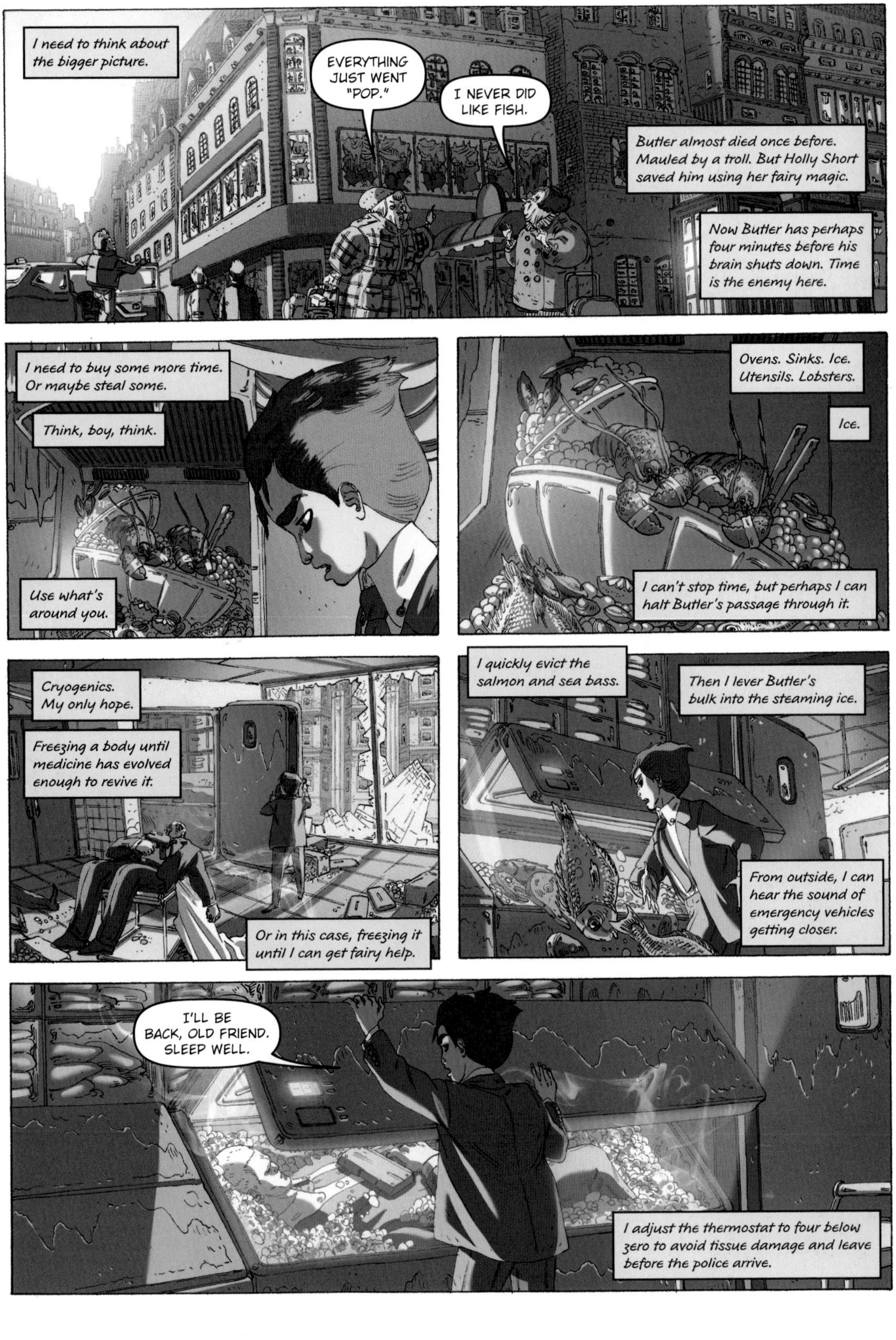
I need to think about the bigger picture.
EVERYTHING JUST WENT "POP."
I NEVER DID LIKE FISH.
Butler almost died once before. Mauled by a troll. But Holly Short saved him using her fairy magic.
Now Butler has perhaps four minutes before his brain shuts down. Time is the enemy here.
I need to buy some more time. Or maybe steal some.
Think, boy, think.
Use what's around you.
Ovens. Sinks. Ice. Utensils. Lobsters.
Ice.
I can't stop time, but perhaps I can halt Butler's passage through it.
Cryogenics. My only hope.
Freezing a body until medicine has evolved enough to revive it.
Or in this case, freezing it until I can get fairy help.
I quickly evict the salmon and sea bass.
Then I lever Butler's bulk into the steaming ice.
From outside, I can hear the sound of emergency vehicles getting closer.
I'LL BE BACK, OLD FRIEND. SLEEP WELL.
I adjust the thermostat to four below zero to avoid tissue damage and leave before the police arrive.

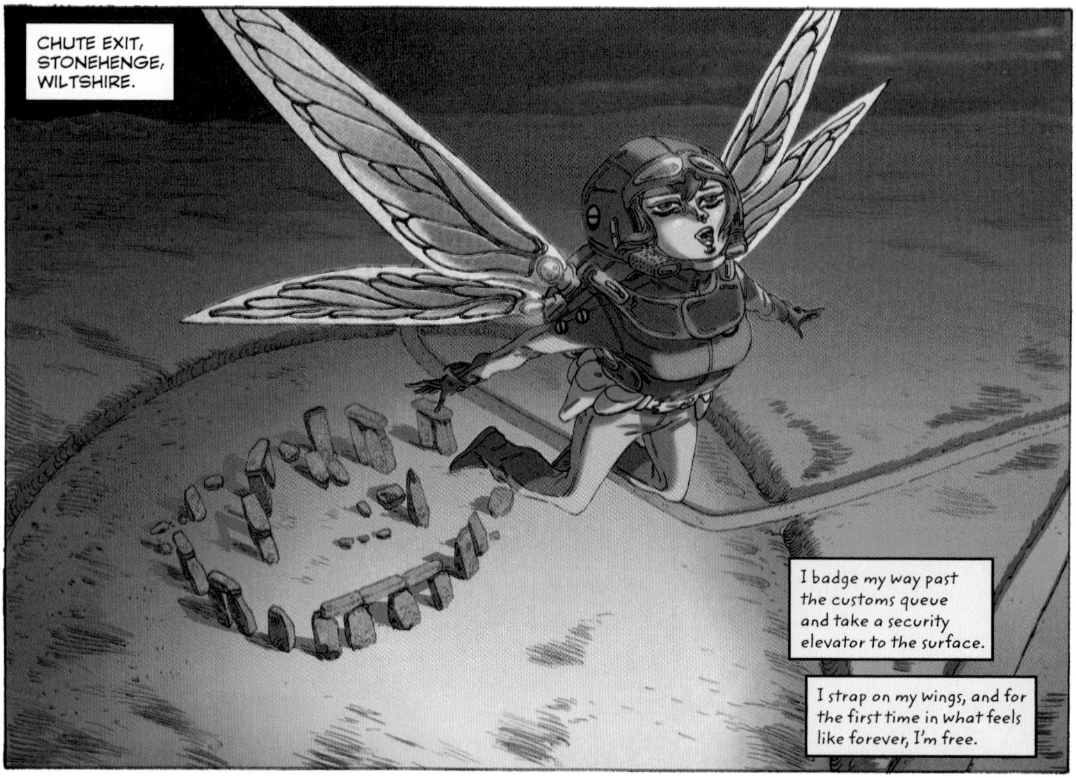
CHUTE EXIT, STONEHENGE, WILTSHIRE.
I badge my way past the customs queue and take a security elevator to the surface.
I strap on my wings, and for the first time in what feels like forever, I'm free.

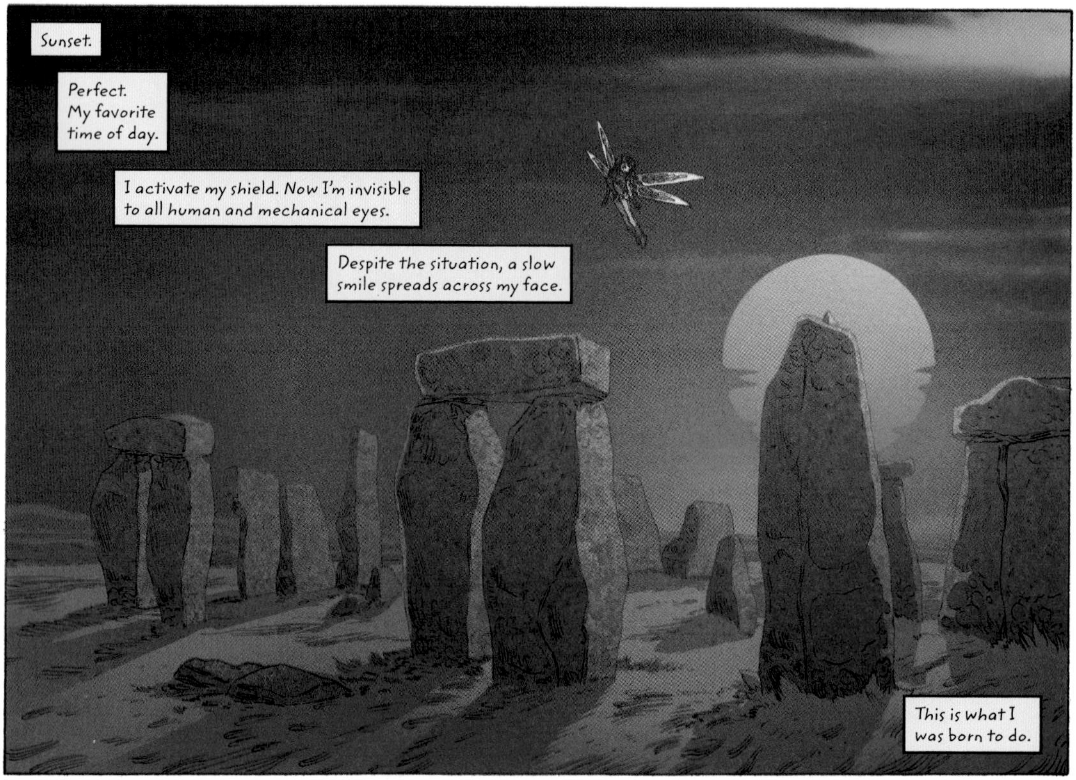
Sunset.
Perfect. My favorite time of day.
I activate my shield. Now I'm invisible to all human and mechanical eyes.
Despite the situation, a slow smile spreads across my face.
This is what I was born to do.

I head for London.

Doctor Lane prepares Butler.

I slip into Doctor Lane's office and make a very important phone call.

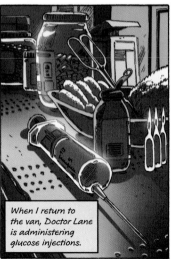

When I return to the van, Doctor Lane is administering glucose injections.

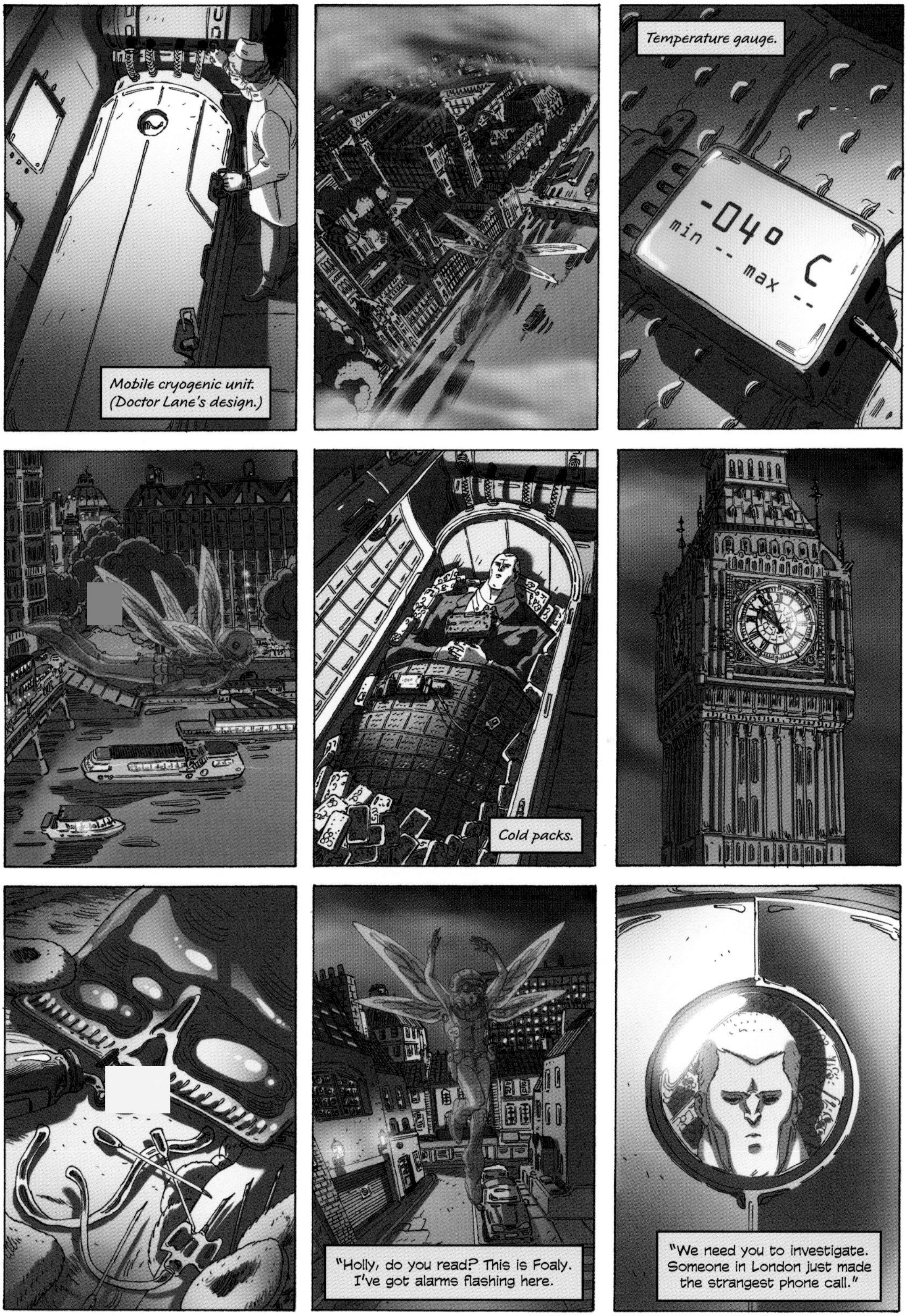
Mobile cryogenic unit.
(Doctor Lane's design.)
Temperature gauge.
-04º C
min -- max --
Cold packs.
"Holly, do you read? This is Foaly.
I've got alarms flashing here.
"We need you to investigate.
Someone in London just made
the strangest phone call."

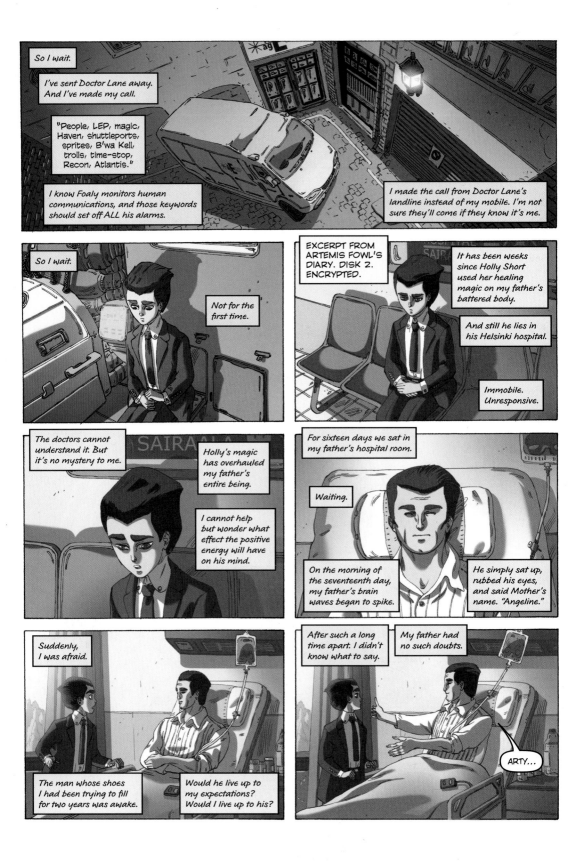

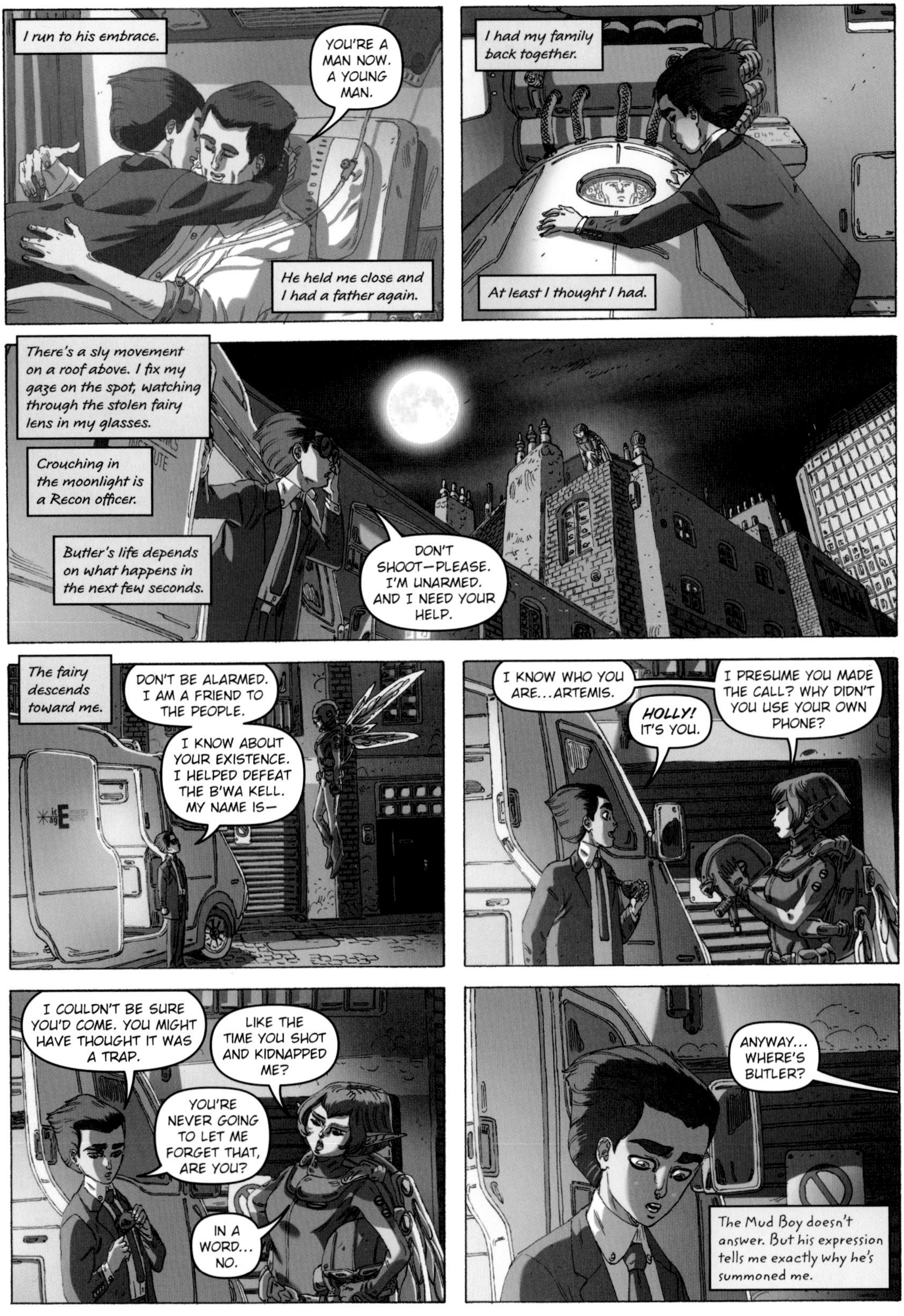
I run to his embrace.
YOU'RE A MAN NOW. A YOUNG MAN.
He held me close and I had a father again.
I had my family back together.
At least I thought I had.
There's a sly movement on a roof above. I fix my gaze on the spot, watching through the stolen fairy lens in my glasses.
Crouching in the moonlight is a Recon officer.
Butler's life depends on what happens in the next few seconds.
DON'T SHOOT—PLEASE. I'M UNARMED. AND I NEED YOUR HELP.
The fairy descends toward me.
DON'T BE ALARMED. I AM A FRIEND TO THE PEOPLE.
I KNOW ABOUT YOUR EXISTENCE. I HELPED DEFEAT THE B'WA KELL. MY NAME IS—
I KNOW WHO YOU ARE... ARTEMIS.
HOLLY! IT'S YOU.
I PRESUME YOU MADE THE CALL? WHY DIDN'T YOU USE YOUR OWN PHONE?
I COULDN'T BE SURE YOU'D COME. YOU MIGHT HAVE THOUGHT IT WAS A TRAP.
LIKE THE TIME YOU SHOT AND KIDNAPPED ME?
YOU'RE NEVER GOING TO LET ME FORGET THAT, ARE YOU?
IN A WORD... NO.
ANYWAY... WHERE'S BUTLER?
The Mud Boy doesn't answer. But his expression tells me exactly why he's summoned me.

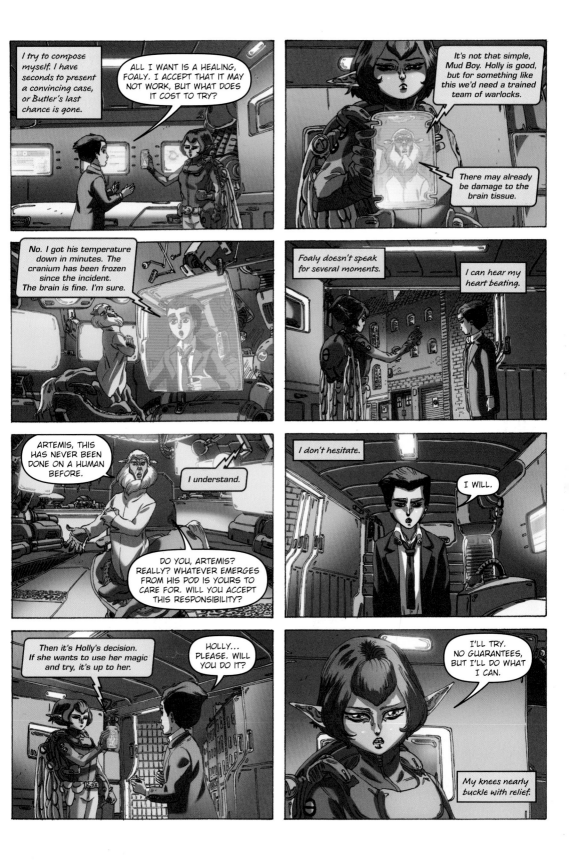

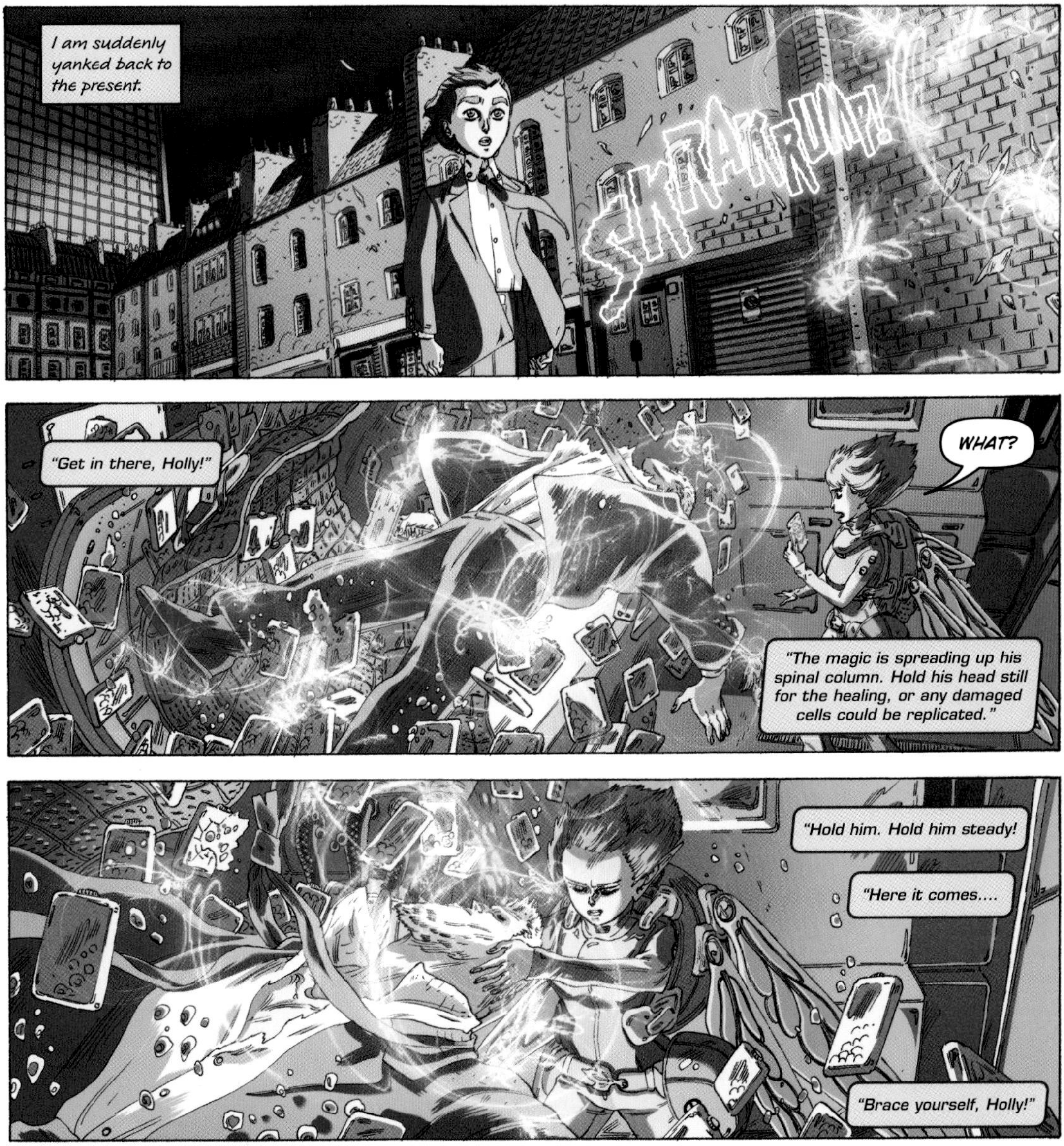
I am suddenly yanked back to the present.
SKRATTRUMP!
"Get in there, Holly!"
WHAT?
"The magic is spreading up his spinal column. Hold his head still for the healing, or any damaged cells could be replicated."
"Hold him. Hold him steady!
"Here it comes....
"Brace yourself, Holly!"
KA-BOOOOOOM!

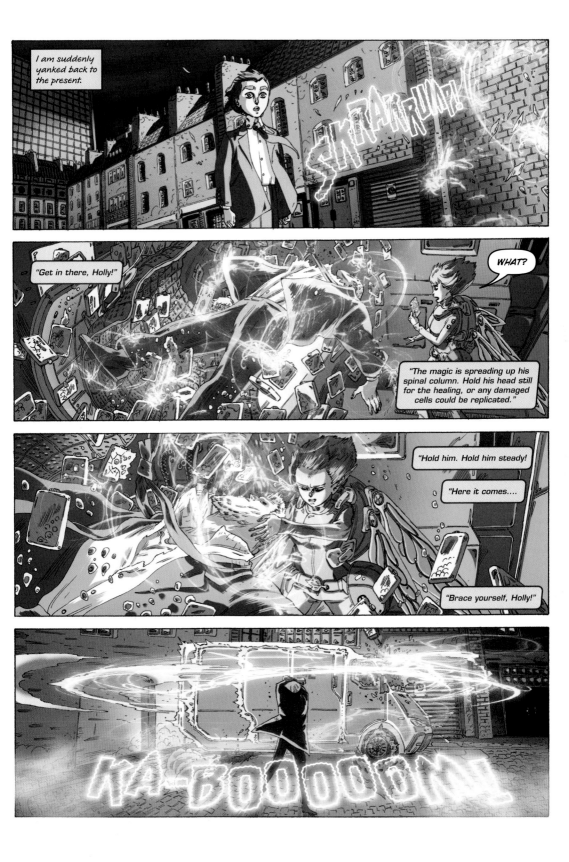

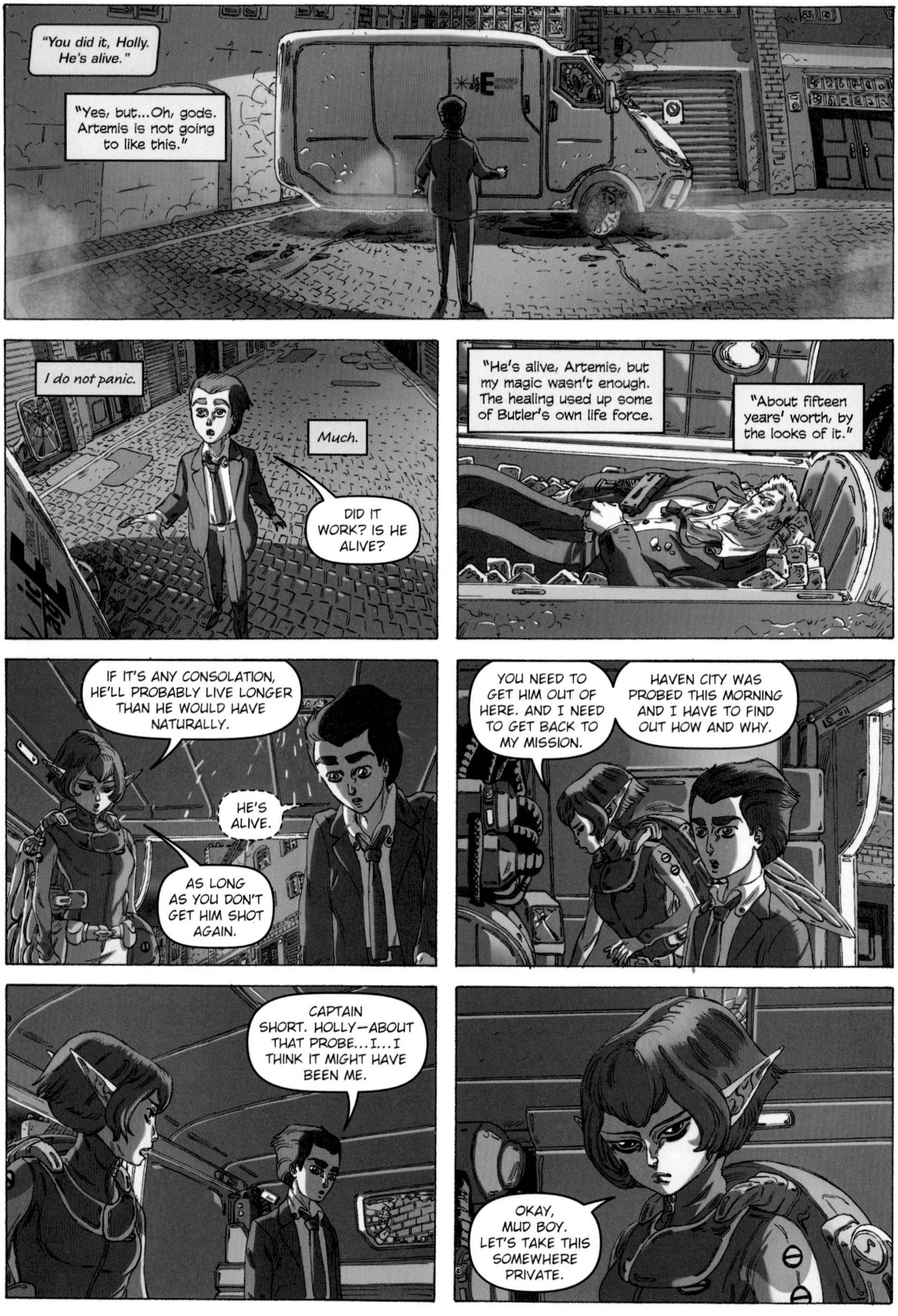
"You did it, Holly. He's alive."
"Yes, but...Oh, gods. Artemis is not going to like this."
I do not panic.
Much.
DID IT WORK? IS HE ALIVE?
"He's alive, Artemis, but my magic wasn't enough. The healing used up some of Butler's own life force.
"About fifteen years' worth, by the looks of it."
IF IT'S ANY CONSOLATION, HE'LL PROBABLY LIVE LONGER THAN HE WOULD HAVE NATURALLY.
HE'S ALIVE.
AS LONG AS YOU DON'T GET HIM SHOT AGAIN.
YOU NEED TO GET HIM OUT OF HERE. AND I NEED TO GET BACK TO MY MISSION.
HAVEN CITY WAS PROBED THIS MORNING AND I HAVE TO FIND OUT HOW AND WHY.
CAPTAIN SHORT. HOLLY—ABOUT THAT PROBE...I...I THINK IT MIGHT HAVE BEEN ME.
OKAY, MUD BOY. LET'S TAKE THIS SOMEWHERE PRIVATE.

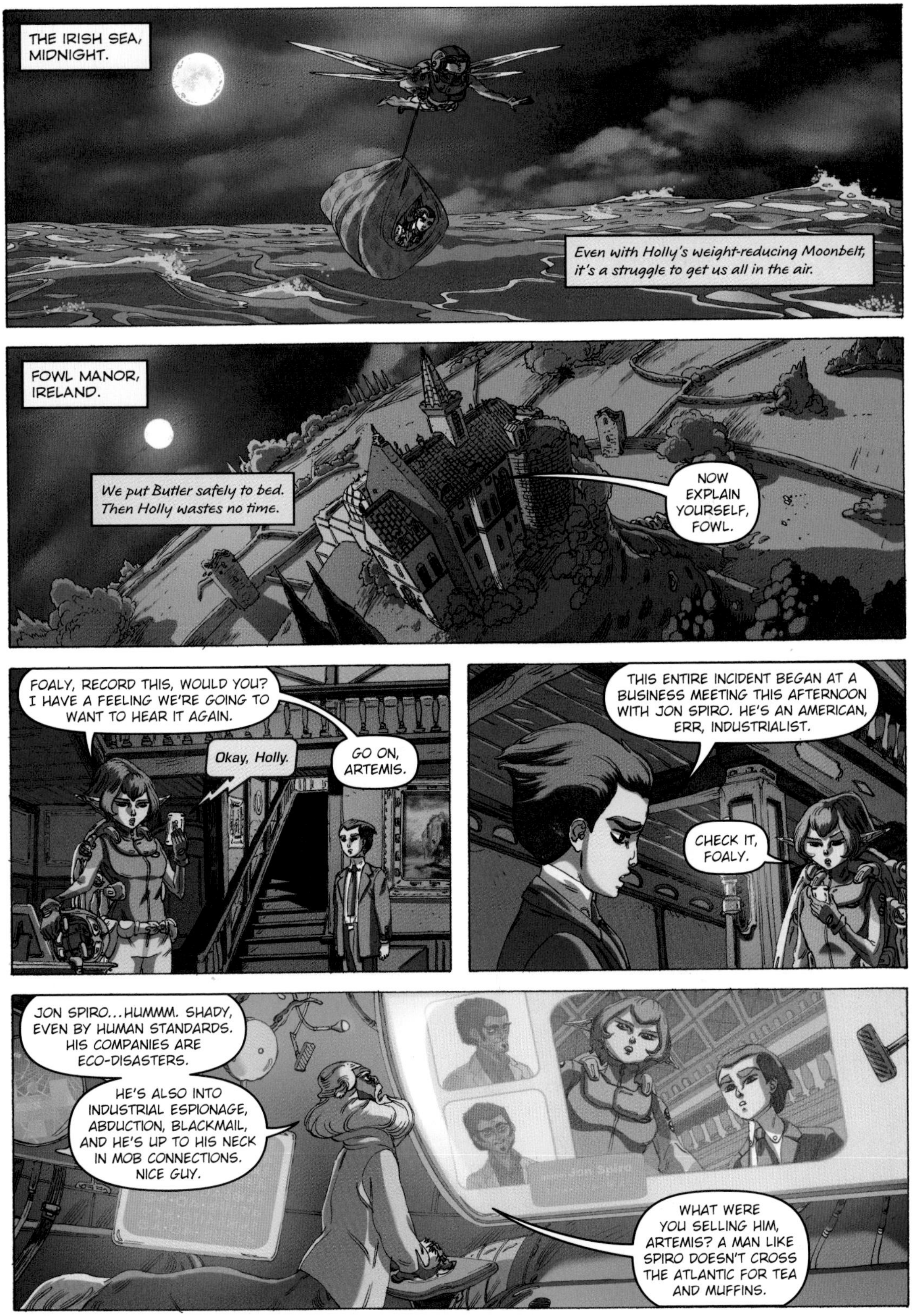
THE IRISH SEA, MIDNIGHT.
Even with Holly's weight-reducing Moonbelt, it's a struggle to get us all in the air.
FOWL MANOR, IRELAND.
We put Butler safely to bed. Then Holly wastes no time.
NOW EXPLAIN YOURSELF, FOWL.
FOALY, RECORD THIS, WOULD YOU? I HAVE A FEELING WE'RE GOING TO WANT TO HEAR IT AGAIN.
Okay, Holly.
GO ON, ARTEMIS.
THIS ENTIRE INCIDENT BEGAN AT A BUSINESS MEETING THIS AFTERNOON WITH JON SPIRO. HE'S AN AMERICAN, ERR, INDUSTRIALIST.
CHECK IT, FOALY.
JON SPIRO... HUMMM. SHADY, EVEN BY HUMAN STANDARDS. HIS COMPANIES ARE ECO-DISASTERS.
HE'S ALSO INTO INDUSTRIAL ESPIONAGE, ABDUCTION, BLACKMAIL, AND HE'S UP TO HIS NECK IN MOB CONNECTIONS. NICE GUY.
WHAT WERE YOU SELLING HIM, ARTEMIS? A MAN LIKE SPIRO DOESN'T CROSS THE ATLANTIC FOR TEA AND MUFFINS.

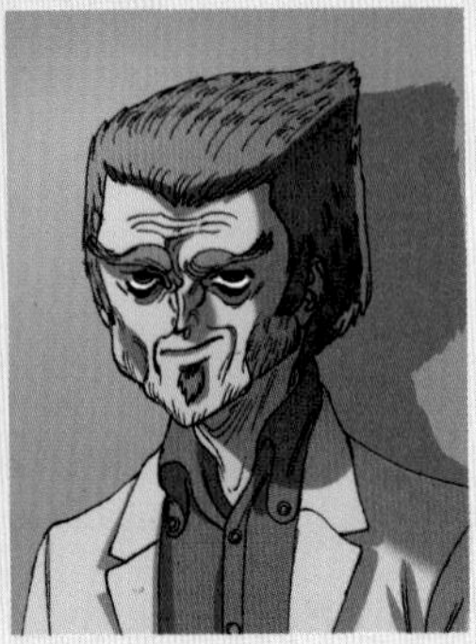

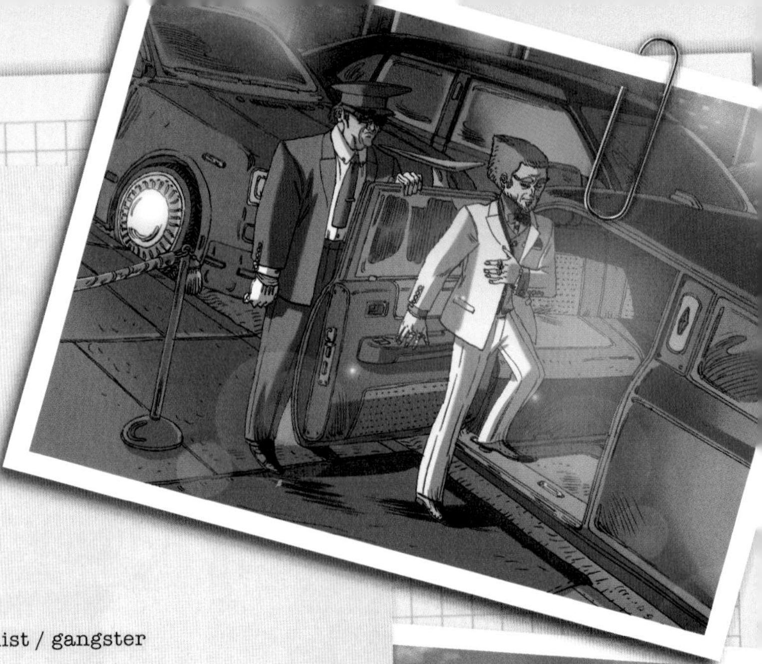

NAME: Jon Spiro

OCCUPATION: Industrialist / gangster

NUMBER OF PREVIOUS ARRESTS: 10

NUMBER OF PREVIOUS CONVICTIONS: None

LIKES: Money, dressing in white, gold jewelry, and more money.

DISLIKES: Rival company Phonetix, the FBI, the police, the CIA, the entire American justice system, etc., etc.

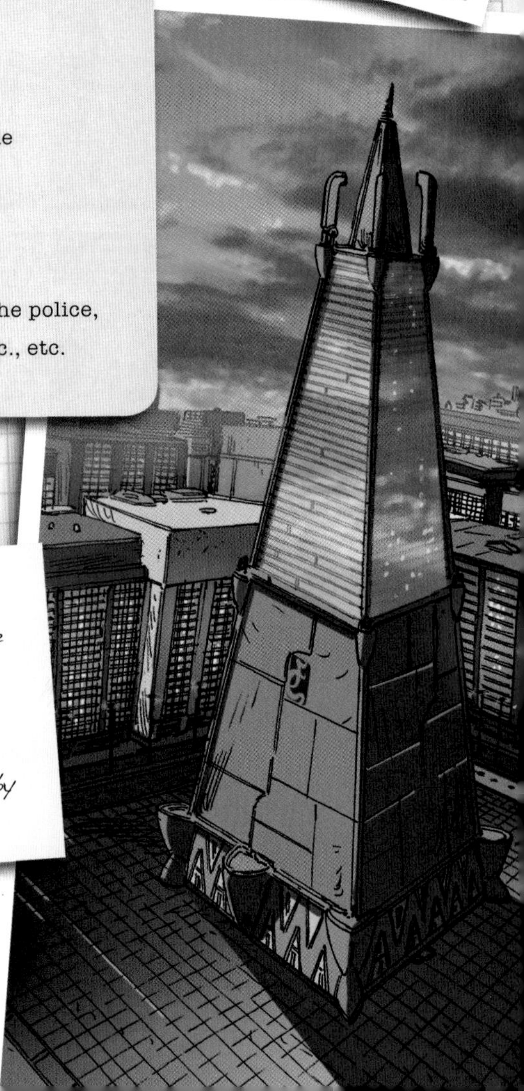

The Spiro Needle, a sliver of steel and glass rising eighty-six stories on the Chicago skyline. Spiro Industries is located on floors fifty through eighty-five. The eighty-sixth floor is Spiro's personal residence, accessible by either private elevator or heliport.

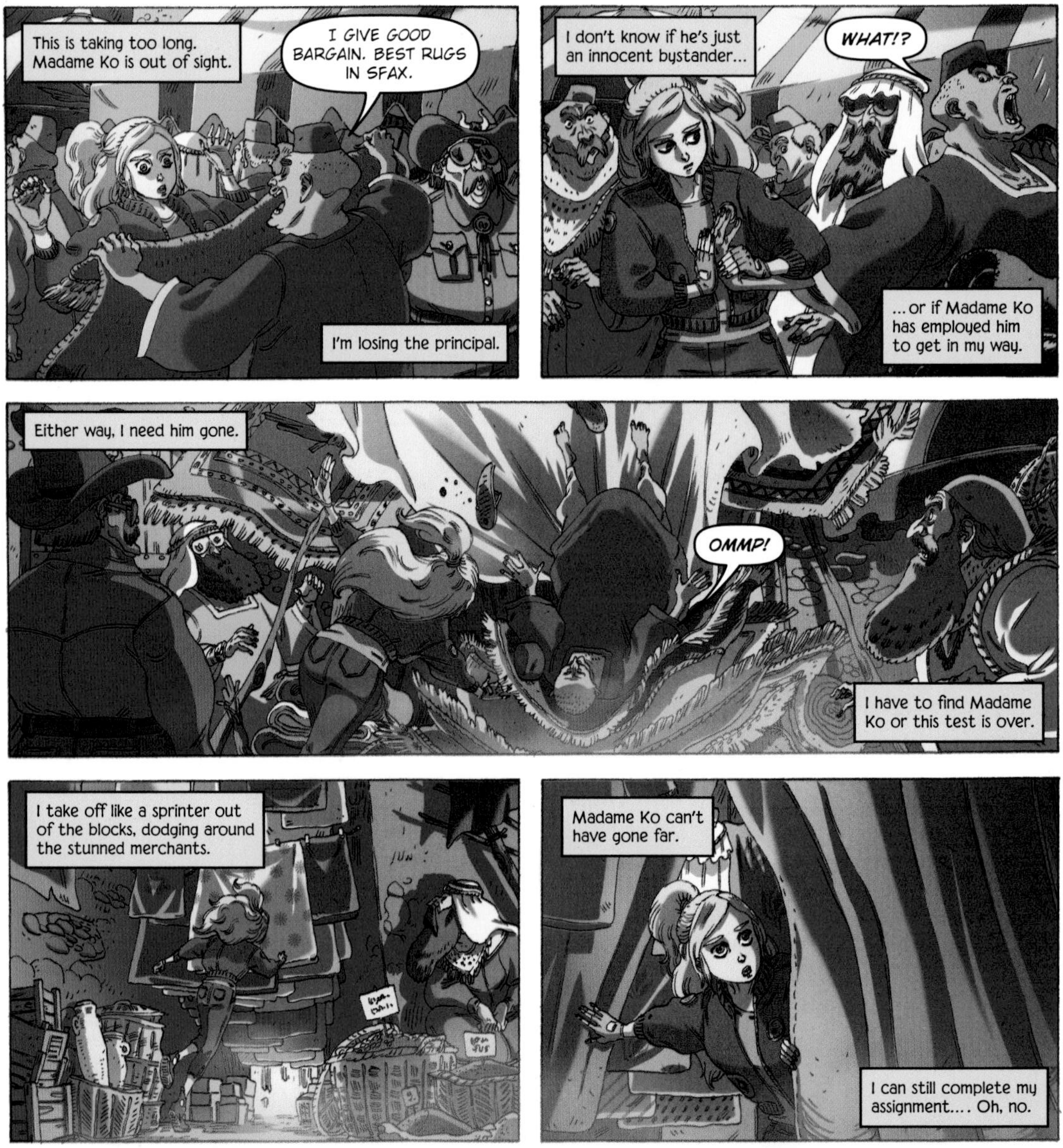
This is taking too long.
Madame Ko is out of sight.
I GIVE GOOD BARGAIN. BEST RUGS IN SFAX.
I'm losing the principal.
I don't know if he's just an innocent bystander...
WHAT!?
...or if Madame Ko has employed him to get in my way.
Either way, I need him gone.
OMMP!
I have to find Madame Ko or this test is over.
I take off like a sprinter out of the blocks, dodging around the stunned merchants.
Madame Ko can't have gone far.
I can still complete my assignment.... Oh, no.
These aren't merchants.
This is no test.
These men are trying to kill my sensei.

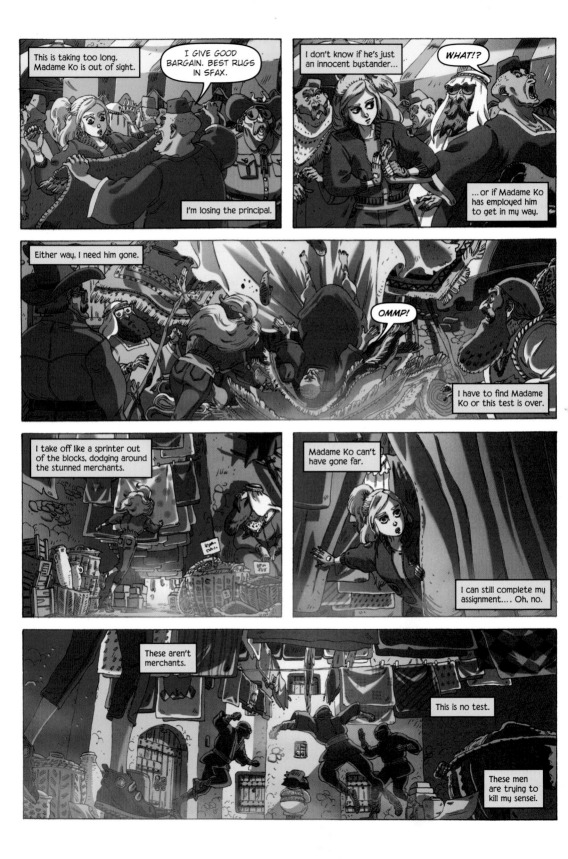

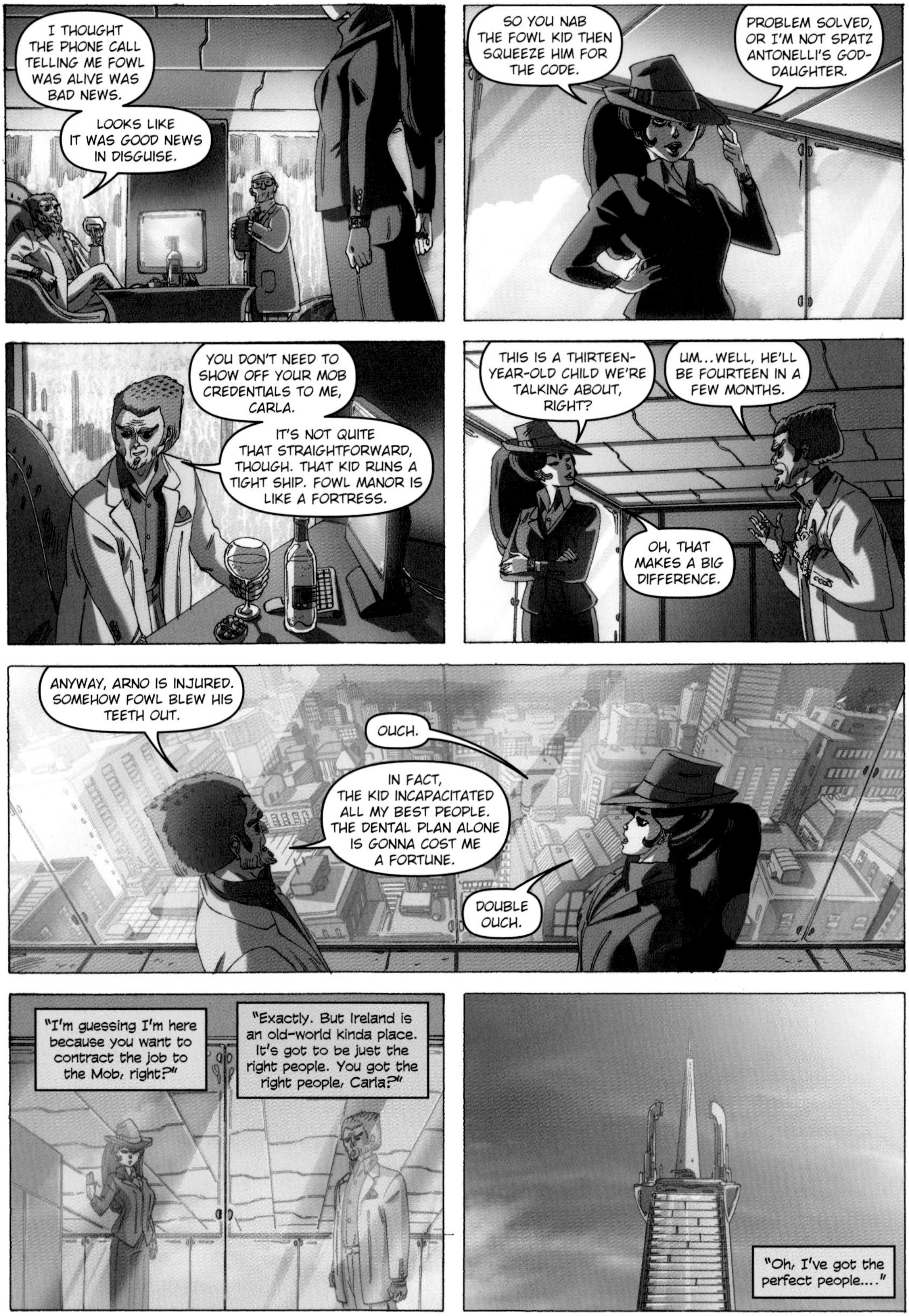
I THOUGHT THE PHONE CALL TELLING ME FOWL WAS ALIVE WAS BAD NEWS.
LOOKS LIKE IT WAS GOOD NEWS IN DISGUISE.
SO YOU NAB THE FOWL KID THEN SQUEEZE HIM FOR THE CODE.
PROBLEM SOLVED, OR I'M NOT SPATZ ANTONELLI'S GOD-DAUGHTER.
YOU DON'T NEED TO SHOW OFF YOUR MOB CREDENTIALS TO ME, CARLA.
IT'S NOT QUITE THAT STRAIGHTFORWARD, THOUGH. THAT KID RUNS A TIGHT SHIP. FOWL MANOR IS LIKE A FORTRESS.
THIS IS A THIRTEEN-YEAR-OLD CHILD WE'RE TALKING ABOUT, RIGHT?
UM...WELL, HE'LL BE FOURTEEN IN A FEW MONTHS.
OH, THAT MAKES A BIG DIFFERENCE.
ANYWAY, ARNO IS INJURED. SOMEHOW FOWL BLEW HIS TEETH OUT.
OUCH.
IN FACT, THE KID INCAPACITATED ALL MY BEST PEOPLE. THE DENTAL PLAN ALONE IS GONNA COST ME A FORTUNE.
DOUBLE OUCH.
"I'm guessing I'm here because you want to contract the job to the Mob, right?"
"Exactly. But Ireland is an old-world kinda place. It's got to be just the right people. You got the right people, Carla?"
"Oh, I've got the perfect people...."

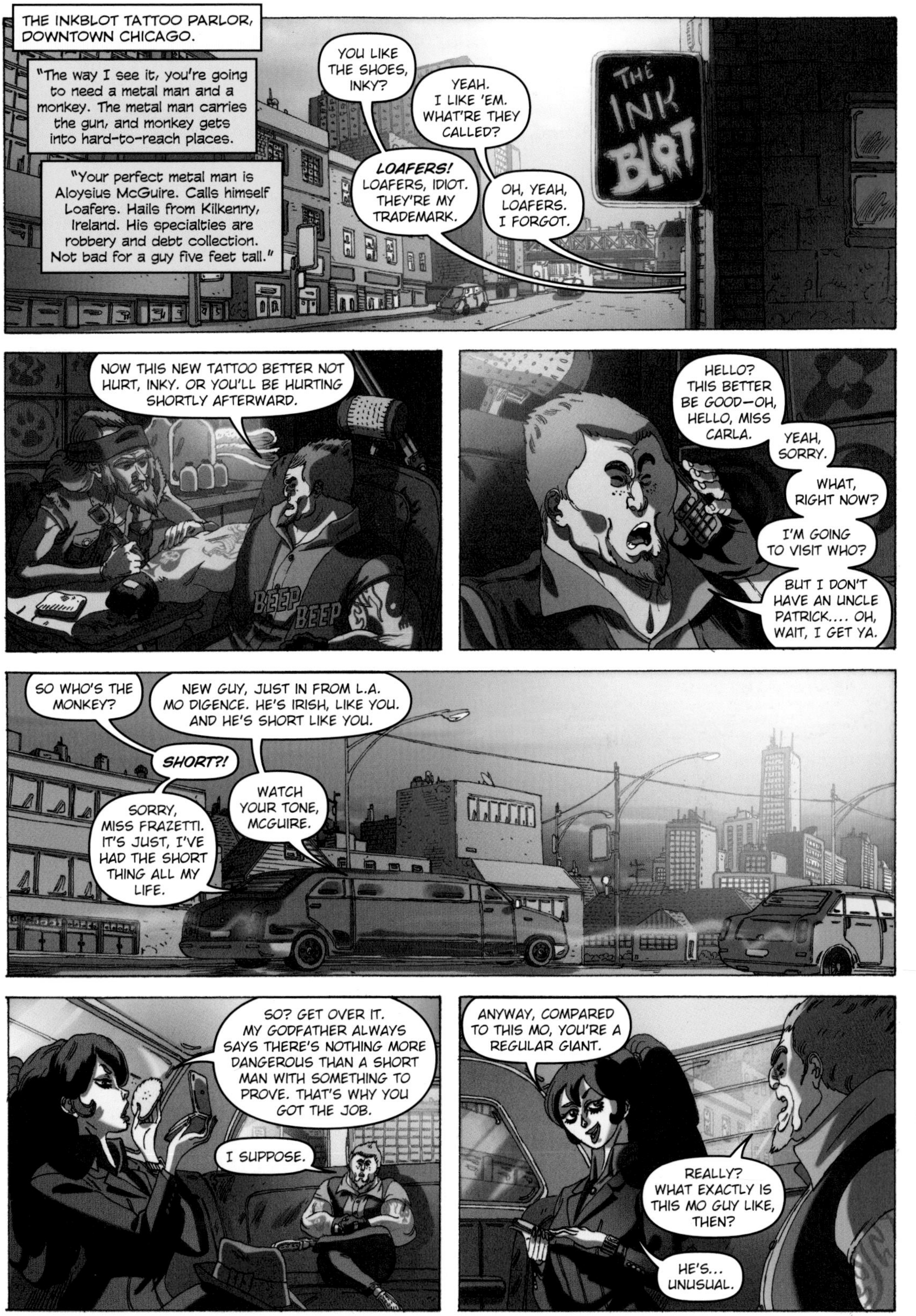
THE INKBLOT TATTOO PARLOR, DOWNTOWN CHICAGO.
"The way I see it, you're going to need a metal man and a monkey. The metal man carries the gun, and monkey gets into hard-to-reach places.
"Your perfect metal man is Aloysius McGuire. Calls himself Loafers. Hails from Kilkenny, Ireland. His specialties are robbery and debt collection. Not bad for a guy five feet tall."
YOU LIKE THE SHOES, INKY?
YEAH. I LIKE 'EM. WHAT'RE THEY CALLED?
LOAFERS! LOAFERS, IDIOT. THEY'RE MY TRADEMARK.
OH, YEAH, LOAFERS. I FORGOT.
THE INK BLOT
NOW THIS NEW TATTOO BETTER NOT HURT, INKY. OR YOU'LL BE HURTING SHORTLY AFTERWARD.
BEEP BEEP
HELLO? THIS BETTER BE GOOD—OH, HELLO, MISS CARLA.
YEAH, SORRY.
WHAT, RIGHT NOW?
I'M GOING TO VISIT WHO?
BUT I DON'T HAVE AN UNCLE PATRICK.... OH, WAIT, I GET YA.
SO WHO'S THE MONKEY?
NEW GUY, JUST IN FROM L.A. MO DIGENCE. HE'S IRISH, LIKE YOU. AND HE'S SHORT LIKE YOU.
SHORT?!
SORRY, MISS FRAZETTI. IT'S JUST, I'VE HAD THE SHORT THING ALL MY LIFE.
WATCH YOUR TONE, MCGUIRE.
SO? GET OVER IT. MY GODFATHER ALWAYS SAYS THERE'S NOTHING MORE DANGEROUS THAN A SHORT MAN WITH SOMETHING TO PROVE. THAT'S WHY YOU GOT THE JOB.
I SUPPOSE.
ANYWAY, COMPARED TO THIS MO, YOU'RE A REGULAR GIANT.
REALLY? WHAT EXACTLY IS THIS MO GUY LIKE, THEN?
HE'S... UNUSUAL.

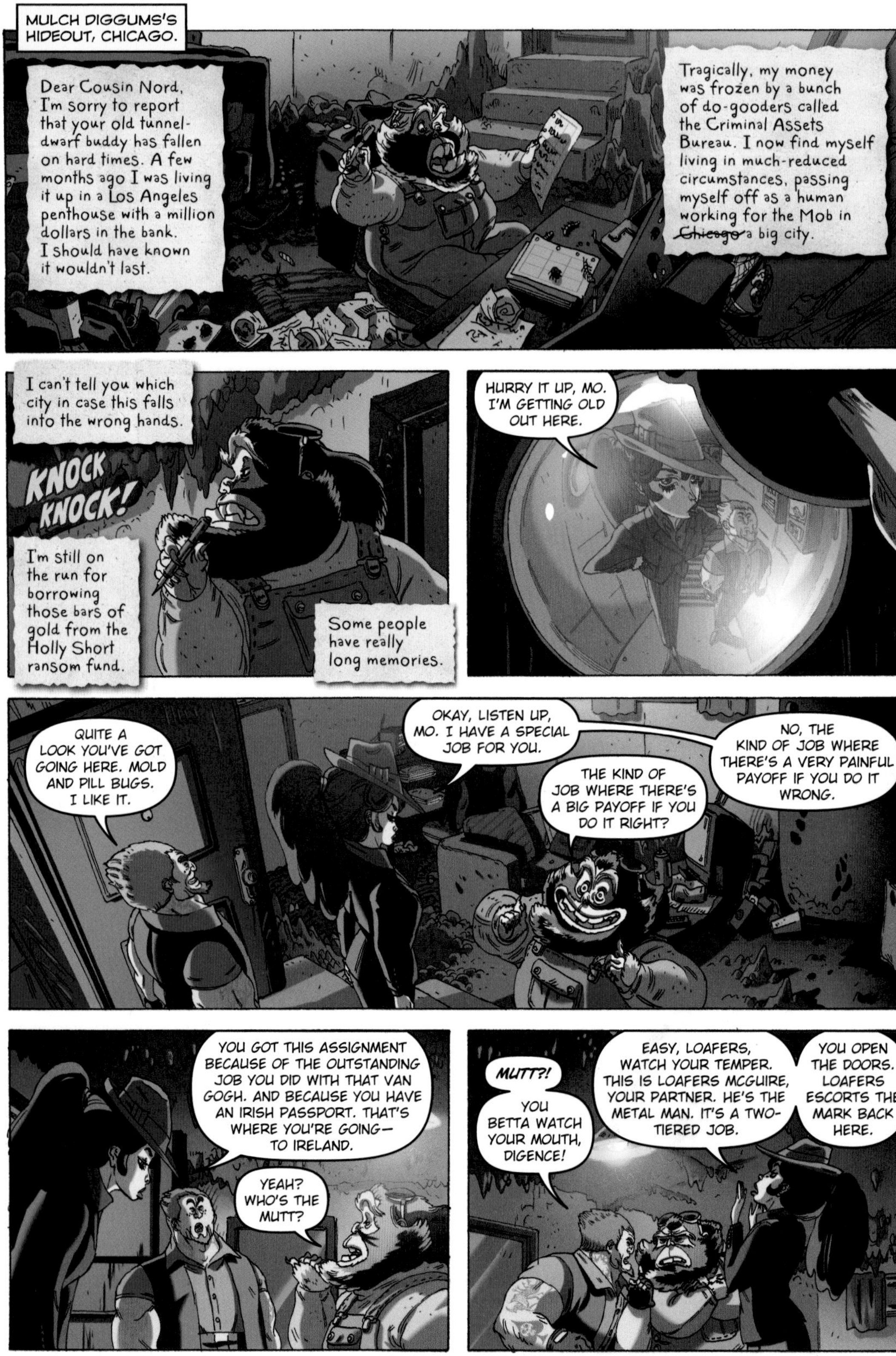
MULCH DIGGUMS'S HIDEOUT, CHICAGO.
Dear Cousin Nord, I'm sorry to report that your old tunnel-dwarf buddy has fallen on hard times. A few months ago I was living it up in a Los Angeles penthouse with a million dollars in the bank. I should have known it wouldn't last.
Tragically, my money was frozen by a bunch of do-gooders called the Criminal Assets Bureau. I now find myself living in much-reduced circumstances, passing myself off as a human working for the Mob in ~~Chicago~~ a big city.
I can't tell you which city in case this falls into the wrong hands.
KNOCK KNOCK!
I'm still on the run for borrowing those bars of gold from the Holly Short ransom fund.
Some people have really long memories.
HURRY IT UP, MO. I'M GETTING OLD OUT HERE.
QUITE A LOOK YOU'VE GOT GOING HERE. MOLD AND PILL BUGS. I LIKE IT.
OKAY, LISTEN UP, MO. I HAVE A SPECIAL JOB FOR YOU.
THE KIND OF JOB WHERE THERE'S A BIG PAYOFF IF YOU DO IT RIGHT?
NO, THE KIND OF JOB WHERE THERE'S A VERY PAINFUL PAYOFF IF YOU DO IT WRONG.
YOU GOT THIS ASSIGNMENT BECAUSE OF THE OUTSTANDING JOB YOU DID WITH THAT VAN GOGH. AND BECAUSE YOU HAVE AN IRISH PASSPORT. THAT'S WHERE YOU'RE GOING— TO IRELAND.
YEAH? WHO'S THE MUTT?
MUTT?!
YOU BETTA WATCH YOUR MOUTH, DIGENCE!
EASY, LOAFERS, WATCH YOUR TEMPER. THIS IS LOAFERS MCGUIRE, YOUR PARTNER. HE'S THE METAL MAN. IT'S A TWO-TIERED JOB.
YOU OPEN THE DOORS. LOAFERS ESCORTS THE MARK BACK HERE.

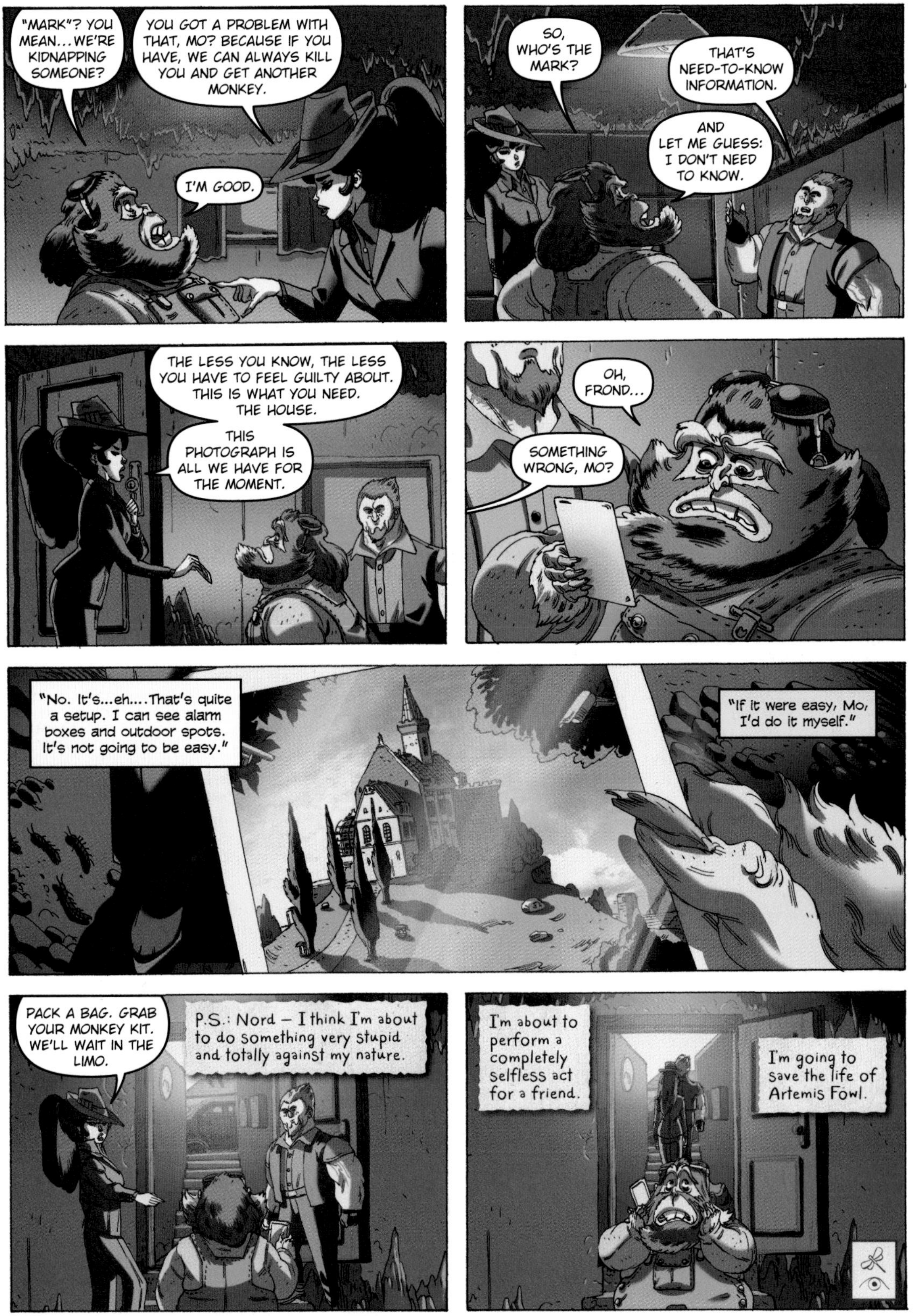
"MARK"? YOU MEAN...WE'RE KIDNAPPING SOMEONE?
YOU GOT A PROBLEM WITH THAT, MO? BECAUSE IF YOU HAVE, WE CAN ALWAYS KILL YOU AND GET ANOTHER MONKEY.
I'M GOOD.
SO, WHO'S THE MARK?
THAT'S NEED-TO-KNOW INFORMATION.
AND LET ME GUESS: I DON'T NEED TO KNOW.
THE LESS YOU KNOW, THE LESS YOU HAVE TO FEEL GUILTY ABOUT. THIS IS WHAT YOU NEED. THE HOUSE.
THIS PHOTOGRAPH IS ALL WE HAVE FOR THE MOMENT.
OH, FROND...
SOMETHING WRONG, MO?
"No. It's...eh....That's quite a setup. I can see alarm boxes and outdoor spots. It's not going to be easy."
"If it were easy, Mo, I'd do it myself."
PACK A BAG. GRAB YOUR MONKEY KIT. WE'LL WAIT IN THE LIMO.
P.S.: Nord — I think I'm about to do something very stupid and totally against my nature.
I'm about to perform a completely selfless act for a friend.
I'm going to save the life of Artemis Fowl.

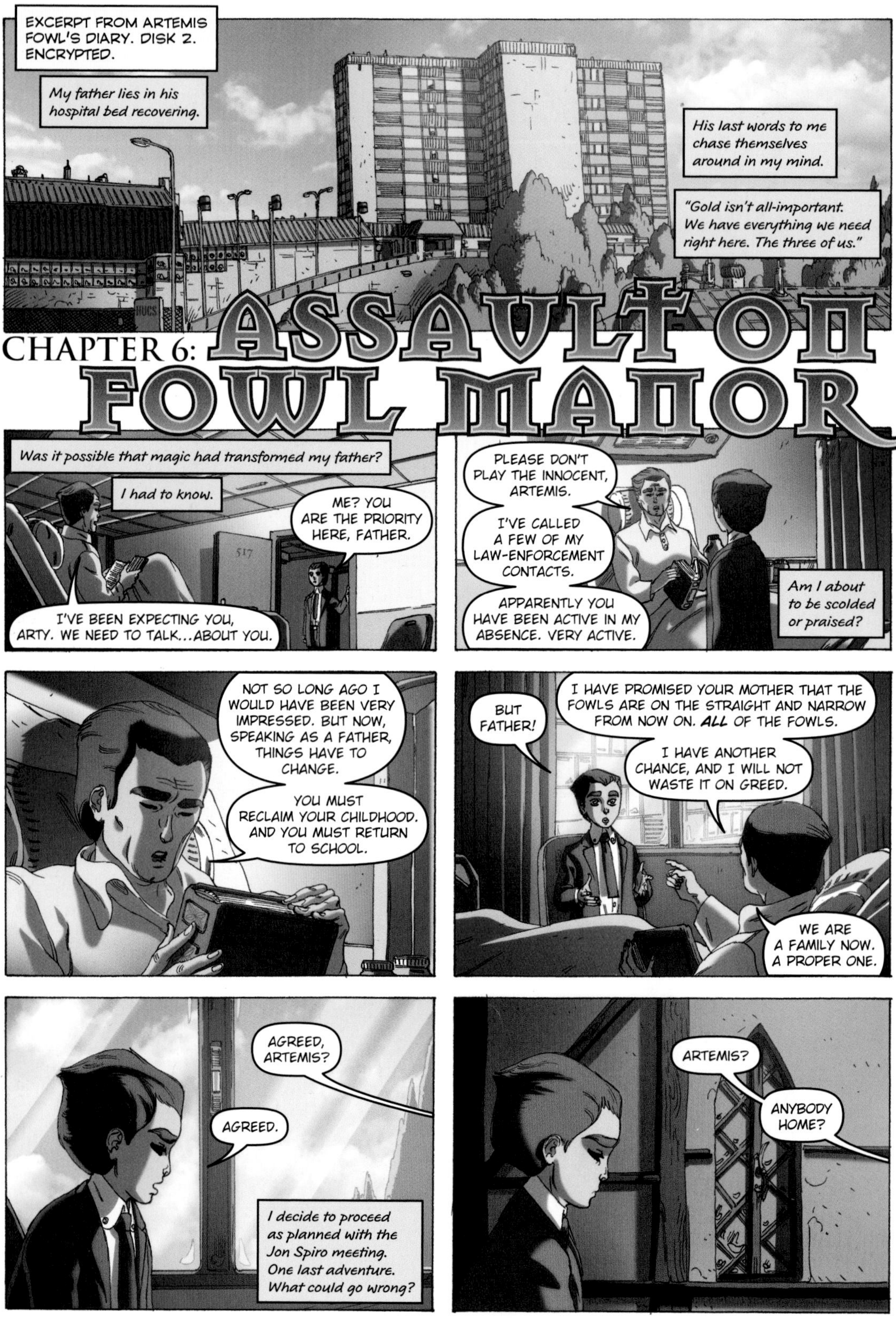

EXCERPT FROM ARTEMIS FOWL'S DIARY. DISK 2. ENCRYPTED.
My father lies in his hospital bed recovering.
His last words to me chase themselves around in my mind.
"Gold isn't all-important. We have everything we need right here. The three of us."
CHAPTER 6: ASSAULT ON FOWL MANOR
Was it possible that magic had transformed my father?
I had to know.
I'VE BEEN EXPECTING YOU, ARTY. WE NEED TO TALK...ABOUT YOU.
ME? YOU ARE THE PRIORITY HERE, FATHER.
PLEASE DON'T PLAY THE INNOCENT, ARTEMIS.
I'VE CALLED A FEW OF MY LAW-ENFORCEMENT CONTACTS.
APPARENTLY YOU HAVE BEEN ACTIVE IN MY ABSENCE. VERY ACTIVE.
Am I about to be scolded or praised?
NOT SO LONG AGO I WOULD HAVE BEEN VERY IMPRESSED. BUT NOW, SPEAKING AS A FATHER, THINGS HAVE TO CHANGE.
YOU MUST RECLAIM YOUR CHILDHOOD. AND YOU MUST RETURN TO SCHOOL.
BUT FATHER!
I HAVE PROMISED YOUR MOTHER THAT THE FOWLS ARE ON THE STRAIGHT AND NARROW FROM NOW ON. ALL OF THE FOWLS.
I HAVE ANOTHER CHANCE, AND I WILL NOT WASTE IT ON GREED.
WE ARE A FAMILY NOW. A PROPER ONE.
AGREED, ARTEMIS?
AGREED.
I decide to proceed as planned with the Jon Spiro meeting. One last adventure. What could go wrong?
ARTEMIS?
ANYBODY HOME?

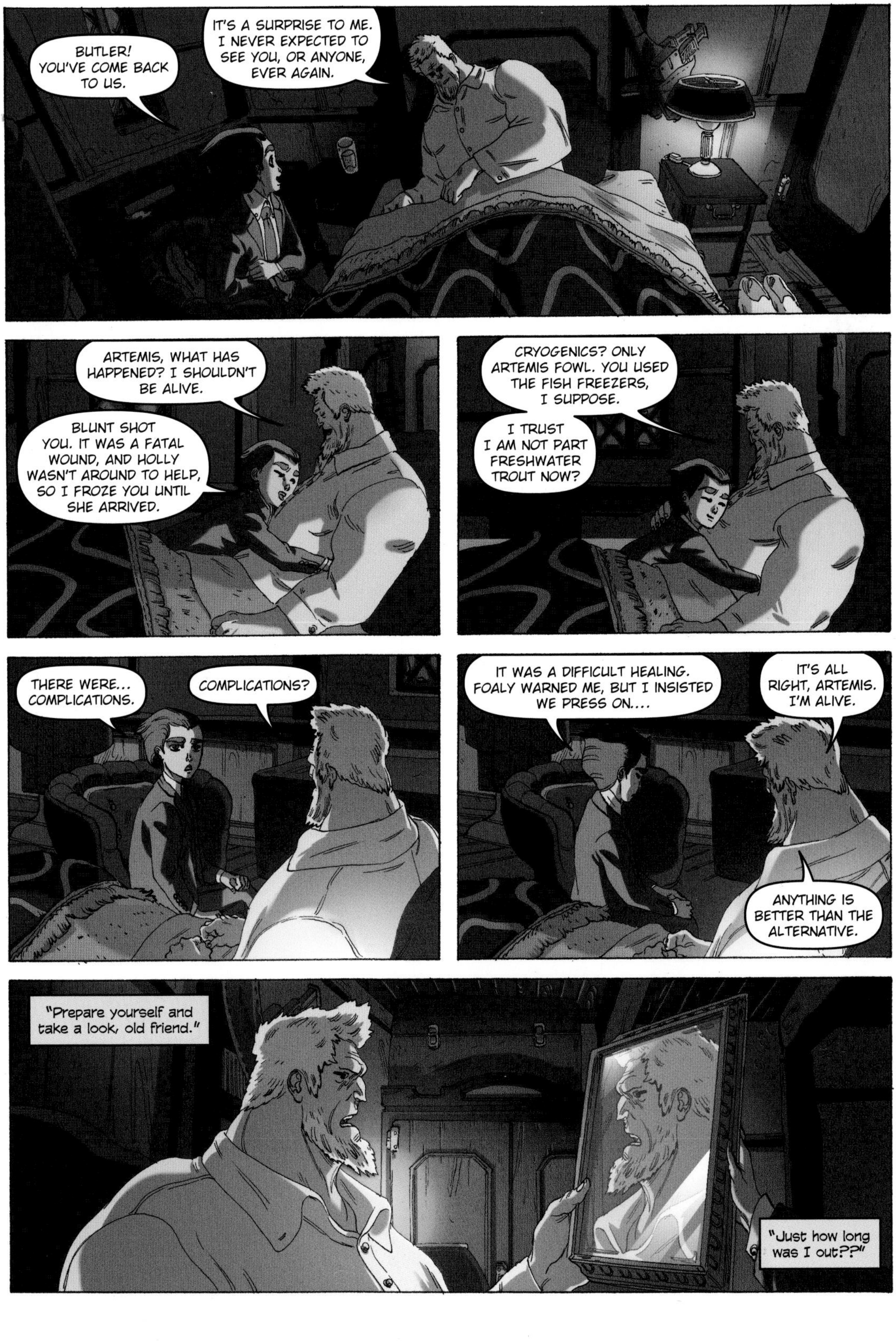
BUTLER! YOU'VE COME BACK TO US.
IT'S A SURPRISE TO ME. I NEVER EXPECTED TO SEE YOU, OR ANYONE, EVER AGAIN.
ARTEMIS, WHAT HAS HAPPENED? I SHOULDN'T BE ALIVE.
BLUNT SHOT YOU. IT WAS A FATAL WOUND, AND HOLLY WASN'T AROUND TO HELP, SO I FROZE YOU UNTIL SHE ARRIVED.
CRYOGENICS? ONLY ARTEMIS FOWL. YOU USED THE FISH FREEZERS, I SUPPOSE.
I TRUST I AM NOT PART FRESHWATER TROUT NOW?
THERE WERE... COMPLICATIONS.
COMPLICATIONS?
IT WAS A DIFFICULT HEALING. FOALY WARNED ME, BUT I INSISTED WE PRESS ON....
IT'S ALL RIGHT, ARTEMIS. I'M ALIVE.
ANYTHING IS BETTER THAN THE ALTERNATIVE.
"Prepare yourself and take a look, old friend."
"Just how long was I out??"

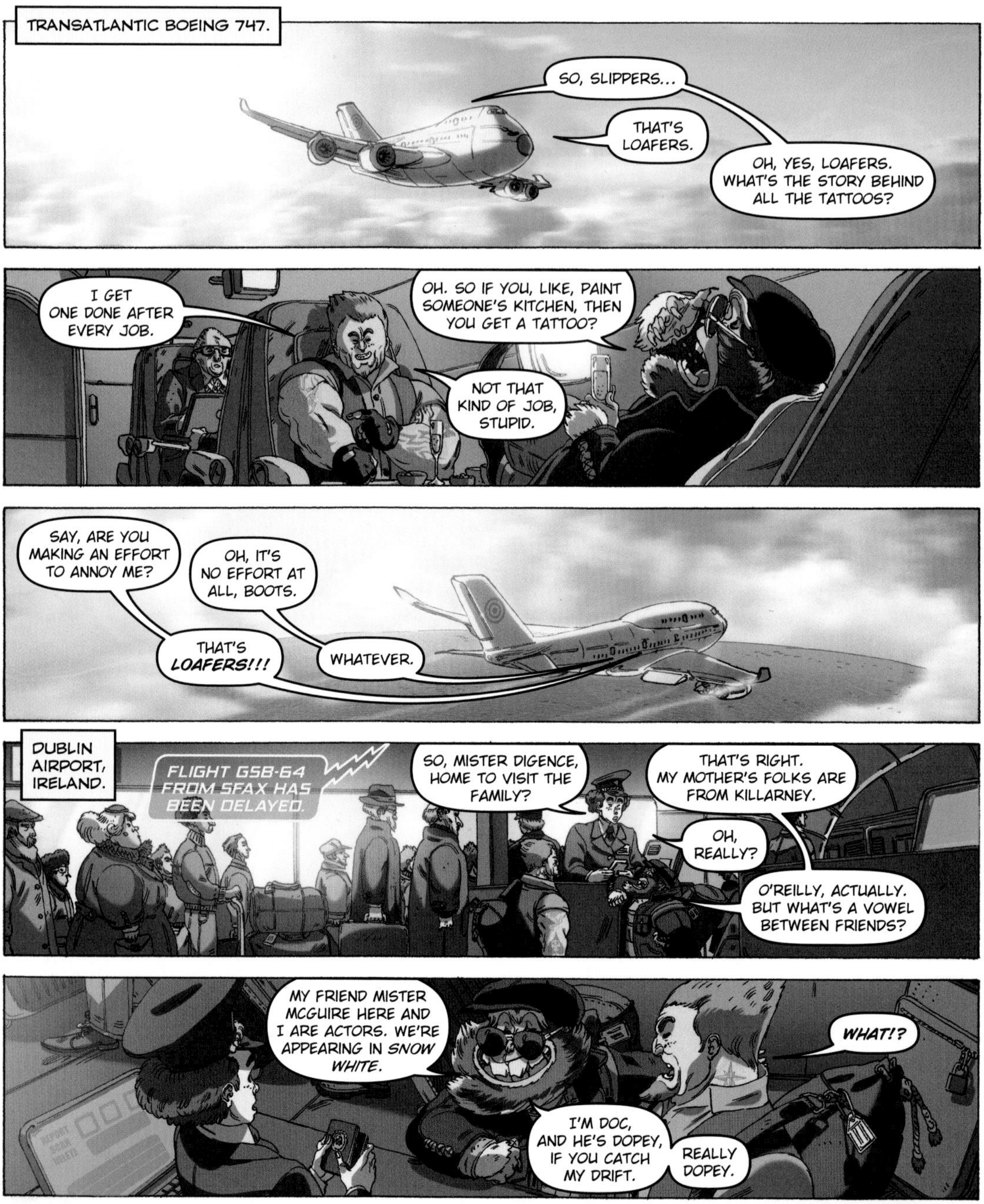
TRANSATLANTIC BOEING 747.
SO, SLIPPERS...
THAT'S LOAFERS.
OH, YES, LOAFERS. WHAT'S THE STORY BEHIND ALL THE TATTOOS?
I GET ONE DONE AFTER EVERY JOB.
OH. SO IF YOU, LIKE, PAINT SOMEONE'S KITCHEN, THEN YOU GET A TATTOO?
NOT THAT KIND OF JOB, STUPID.
SAY, ARE YOU MAKING AN EFFORT TO ANNOY ME?
OH, IT'S NO EFFORT AT ALL, BOOTS.
THAT'S *LOAFERS!!!*
WHATEVER.
DUBLIN AIRPORT, IRELAND.
FLIGHT GSB-64 FROM SFAX HAS BEEN DELAYED.
SO, MISTER DIGENCE, HOME TO VISIT THE FAMILY?
THAT'S RIGHT. MY MOTHER'S FOLKS ARE FROM KILLARNEY.
OH, REALLY?
O'REILLY, ACTUALLY. BUT WHAT'S A VOWEL BETWEEN FRIENDS?
MY FRIEND MISTER MCGUIRE HERE AND I ARE ACTORS. WE'RE APPEARING IN *SNOW WHITE*.
WHAT!?
I'M DOC, AND HE'S DOPEY, IF YOU CATCH MY DRIFT.
REALLY DOPEY.
YOU LITTLE FREAK! HOW DARE YOU? I'LL KILL YOU! YOU'LL BE MY NEXT TATTOO!
SECURITY!

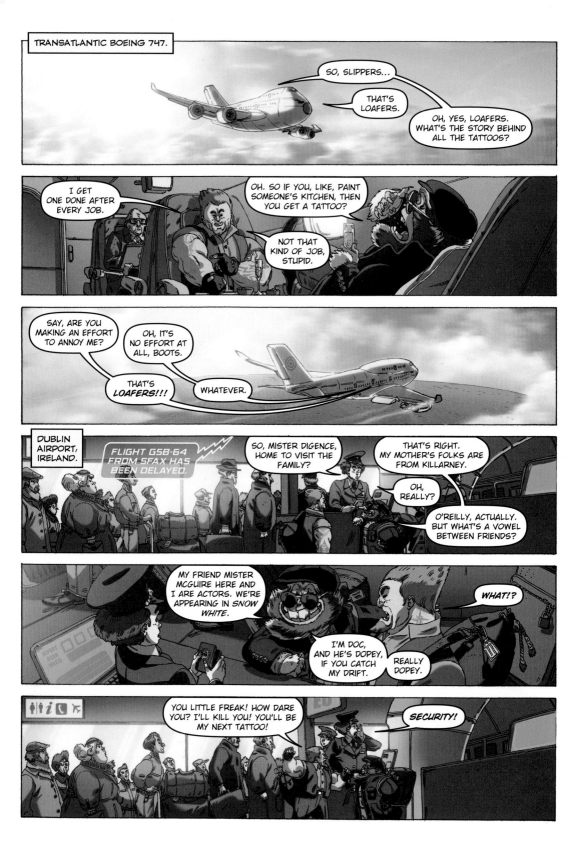

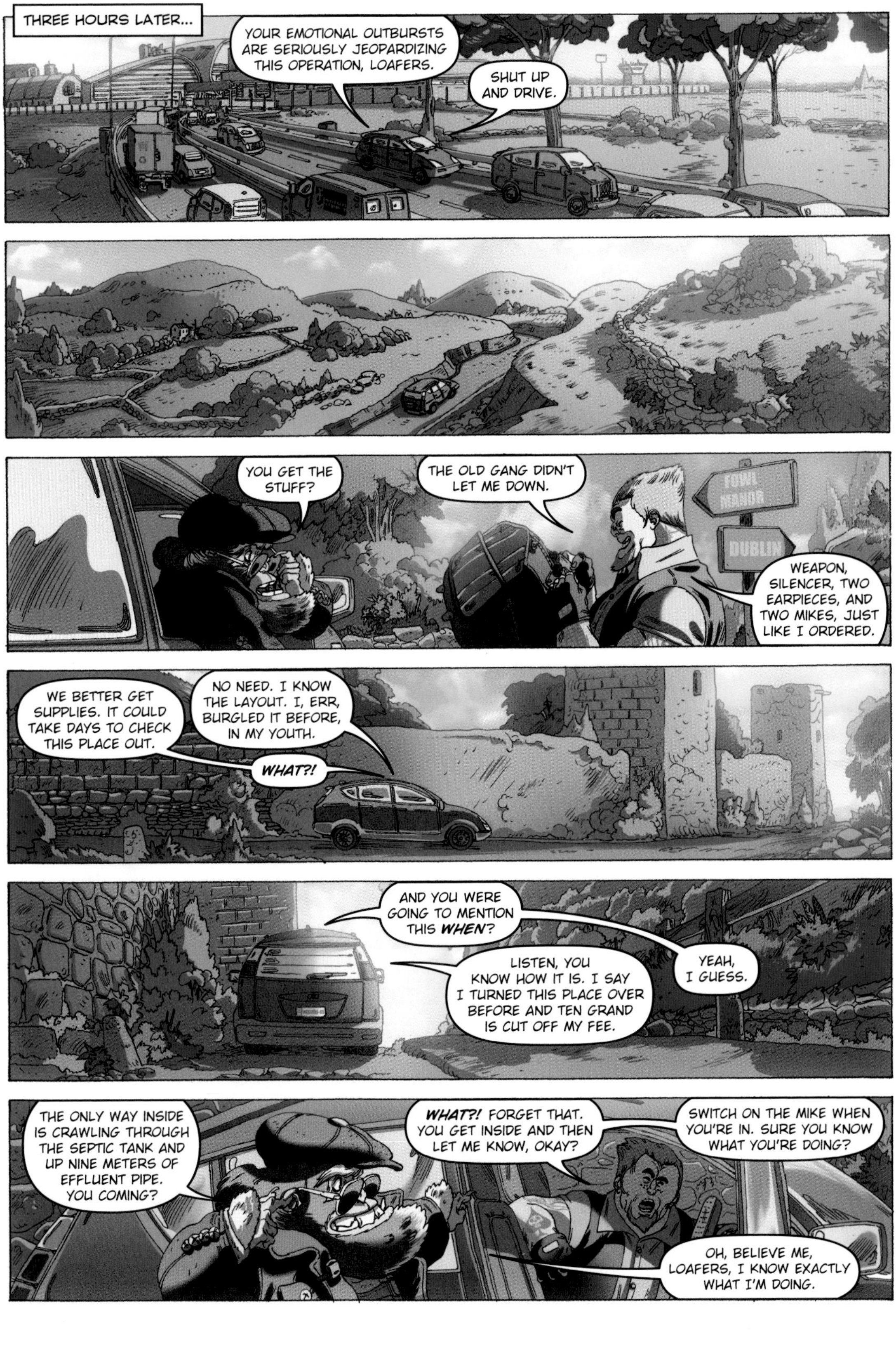
THREE HOURS LATER...
YOUR EMOTIONAL OUTBURSTS ARE SERIOUSLY JEOPARDIZING THIS OPERATION, LOAFERS.
SHUT UP AND DRIVE.
YOU GET THE STUFF?
THE OLD GANG DIDN'T LET ME DOWN.
FOWL MANOR
DUBLIN
WEAPON, SILENCER, TWO EARPIECES, AND TWO MIKES, JUST LIKE I ORDERED.
WE BETTER GET SUPPLIES. IT COULD TAKE DAYS TO CHECK THIS PLACE OUT.
NO NEED. I KNOW THE LAYOUT. I, ERR, BURGLED IT BEFORE, IN MY YOUTH.
WHAT?!
AND YOU WERE GOING TO MENTION THIS WHEN?
LISTEN, YOU KNOW HOW IT IS. I SAY I TURNED THIS PLACE OVER BEFORE AND TEN GRAND IS CUT OFF MY FEE.
YEAH, I GUESS.
THE ONLY WAY INSIDE IS CRAWLING THROUGH THE SEPTIC TANK AND UP NINE METERS OF EFFLUENT PIPE. YOU COMING?
WHAT?! FORGET THAT. YOU GET INSIDE AND THEN LET ME KNOW, OKAY?
SWITCH ON THE MIKE WHEN YOU'RE IN. SURE YOU KNOW WHAT YOU'RE DOING?
OH, BELIEVE ME, LOAFERS, I KNOW EXACTLY WHAT I'M DOING.

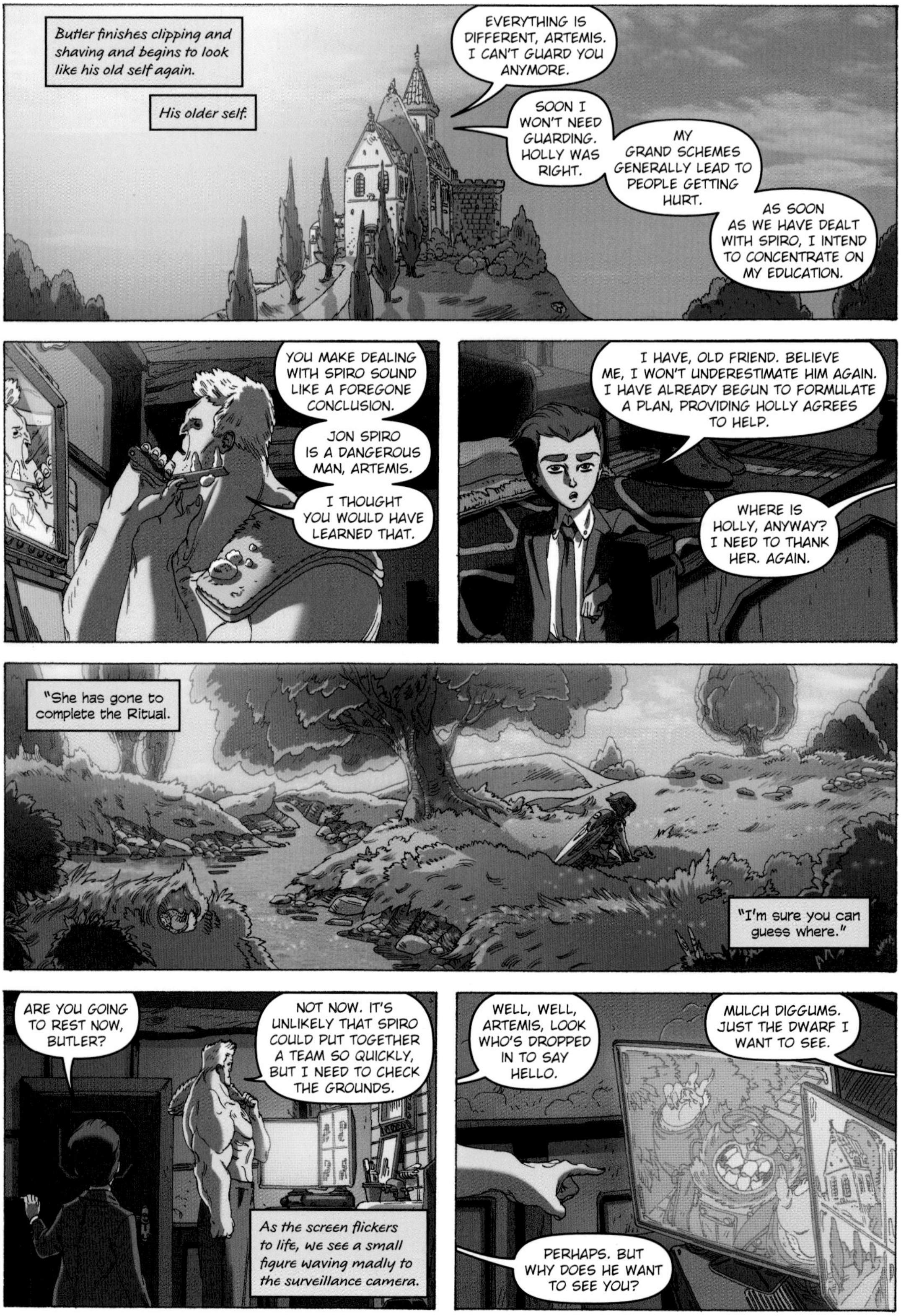
Butler finishes clipping and shaving and begins to look like his old self again.
His older self.
EVERYTHING IS DIFFERENT, ARTEMIS. I CAN'T GUARD YOU ANYMORE.
SOON I WON'T NEED GUARDING. HOLLY WAS RIGHT.
MY GRAND SCHEMES GENERALLY LEAD TO PEOPLE GETTING HURT.
AS SOON AS WE HAVE DEALT WITH SPIRO, I INTEND TO CONCENTRATE ON MY EDUCATION.
YOU MAKE DEALING WITH SPIRO SOUND LIKE A FOREGONE CONCLUSION.
JON SPIRO IS A DANGEROUS MAN, ARTEMIS.
I THOUGHT YOU WOULD HAVE LEARNED THAT.
I HAVE, OLD FRIEND. BELIEVE ME, I WON'T UNDERESTIMATE HIM AGAIN. I HAVE ALREADY BEGUN TO FORMULATE A PLAN, PROVIDING HOLLY AGREES TO HELP.
WHERE IS HOLLY, ANYWAY? I NEED TO THANK HER. AGAIN.
"She has gone to complete the Ritual.
"I'm sure you can guess where."
ARE YOU GOING TO REST NOW, BUTLER?
NOT NOW. IT'S UNLIKELY THAT SPIRO COULD PUT TOGETHER A TEAM SO QUICKLY, BUT I NEED TO CHECK THE GROUNDS.
As the screen flickers to life, we see a small figure waving madly to the surveillance camera.
WELL, WELL, ARTEMIS, LOOK WHO'S DROPPED IN TO SAY HELLO.
MULCH DIGGUMS. JUST THE DWARF I WANT TO SEE.
PERHAPS. BUT WHY DOES HE WANT TO SEE YOU?

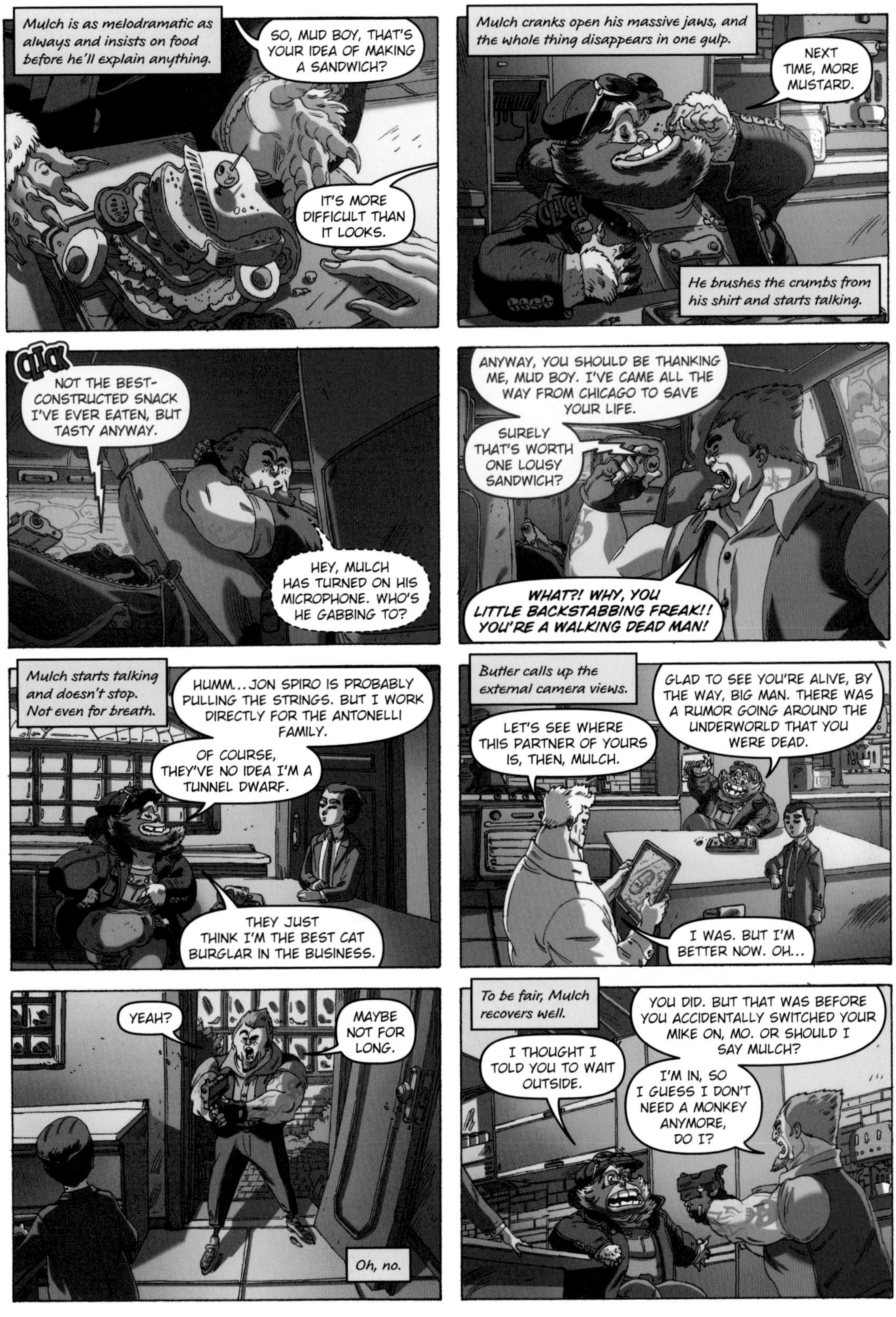
Mulch is as melodramatic as always and insists on food before he'll explain anything.
SO, MUD BOY, THAT'S YOUR IDEA OF MAKING A SANDWICH?
IT'S MORE DIFFICULT THAN IT LOOKS.
Mulch cranks open his massive jaws, and the whole thing disappears in one gulp.
NEXT TIME, MORE MUSTARD.
CLICK
He brushes the crumbs from his shirt and starts talking.
CLICK
NOT THE BEST-CONSTRUCTED SNACK I'VE EVER EATEN, BUT TASTY ANYWAY.
HEY, MULCH HAS TURNED ON HIS MICROPHONE. WHO'S HE GABBING TO?
ANYWAY, YOU SHOULD BE THANKING ME, MUD BOY. I'VE CAME ALL THE WAY FROM CHICAGO TO SAVE YOUR LIFE.
SURELY THAT'S WORTH ONE LOUSY SANDWICH?
WHAT?! WHY, YOU LITTLE BACKSTABBING FREAK!! YOU'RE A WALKING DEAD MAN!
Mulch starts talking and doesn't stop. Not even for breath.
HUMM...JON SPIRO IS PROBABLY PULLING THE STRINGS. BUT I WORK DIRECTLY FOR THE ANTONELLI FAMILY.
OF COURSE, THEY'VE NO IDEA I'M A TUNNEL DWARF.
THEY JUST THINK I'M THE BEST CAT BURGLAR IN THE BUSINESS.
Butler calls up the external camera views.
GLAD TO SEE YOU'RE ALIVE, BY THE WAY, BIG MAN. THERE WAS A RUMOR GOING AROUND THE UNDERWORLD THAT YOU WERE DEAD.
LET'S SEE WHERE THIS PARTNER OF YOURS IS, THEN, MULCH.
I WAS. BUT I'M BETTER NOW. OH...
YEAH?
MAYBE NOT FOR LONG.
Oh, no.
To be fair, Mulch recovers well.
YOU DID. BUT THAT WAS BEFORE YOU ACCIDENTALLY SWITCHED YOUR MIKE ON, MO. OR SHOULD I SAY MULCH?
I THOUGHT I TOLD YOU TO WAIT OUTSIDE.
I'M IN, SO I GUESS I DON'T NEED A MONKEY ANYMORE, DO I?

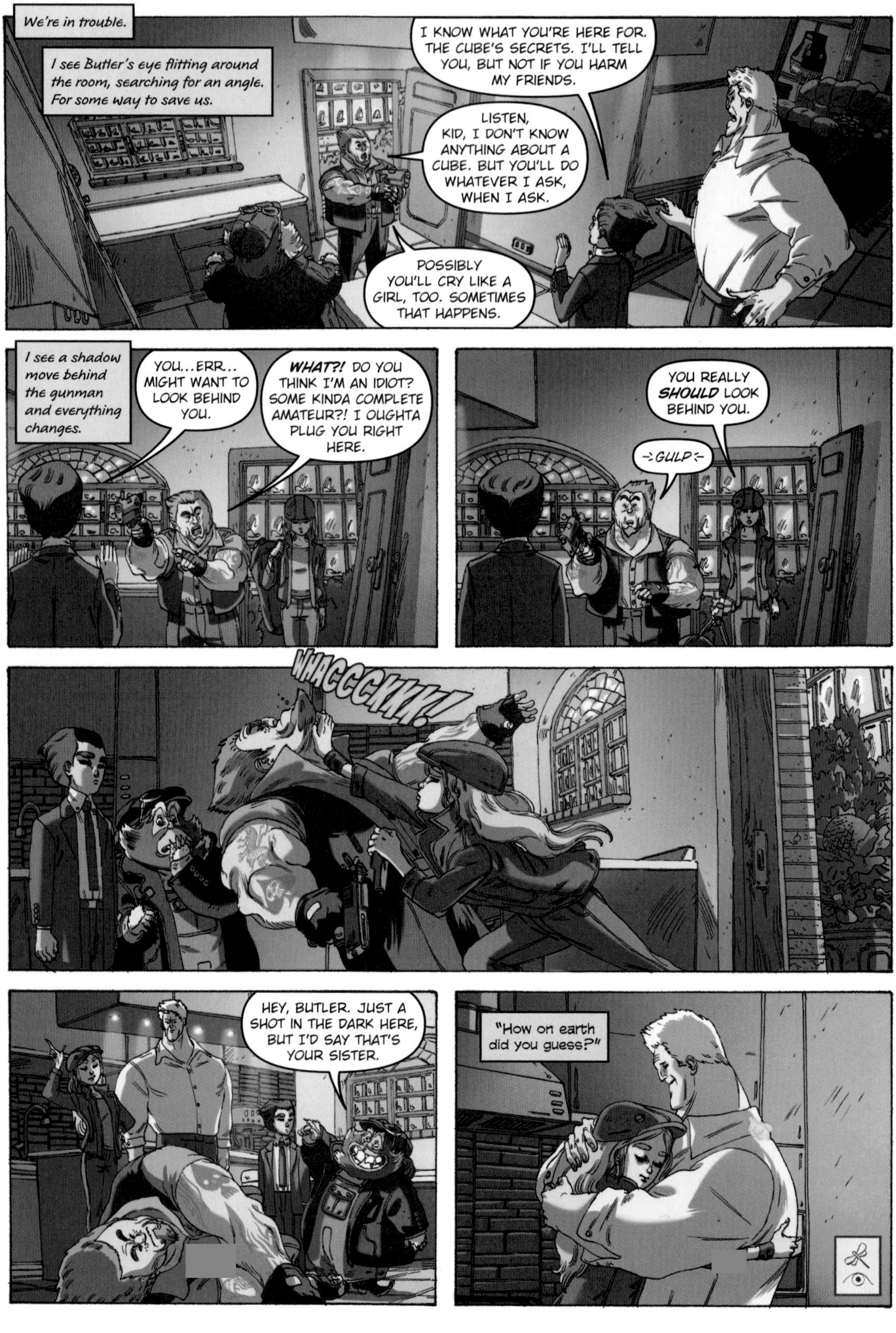
We're in trouble.
I see Butler's eye flitting around the room, searching for an angle. For some way to save us.
I KNOW WHAT YOU'RE HERE FOR. THE CUBE'S SECRETS. I'LL TELL YOU, BUT NOT IF YOU HARM MY FRIENDS.
LISTEN, KID, I DON'T KNOW ANYTHING ABOUT A CUBE. BUT YOU'LL DO WHATEVER I ASK, WHEN I ASK.
POSSIBLY YOU'LL CRY LIKE A GIRL, TOO. SOMETIMES THAT HAPPENS.
I see a shadow move behind the gunman and everything changes.
YOU...ERR... MIGHT WANT TO LOOK BEHIND YOU.
WHAT?! DO YOU THINK I'M AN IDIOT? SOME KINDA COMPLETE AMATEUR?! I OUGHTA PLUG YOU RIGHT HERE.
YOU REALLY SHOULD LOOK BEHIND YOU.
GULP
WHACCCKKK!
HEY, BUTLER. JUST A SHOT IN THE DARK HERE, BUT I'D SAY THAT'S YOUR SISTER.
"How on earth did you guess?"

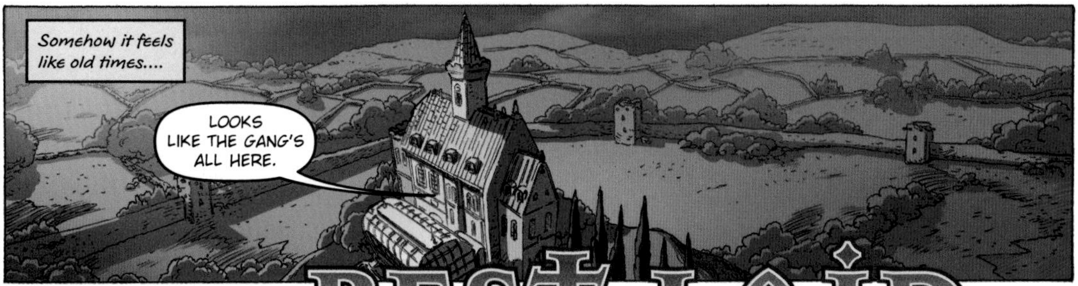
Somehow it feels like old times....
LOOKS LIKE THE GANG'S ALL HERE.

CHAPTER 7: BEST-LAID PLANS

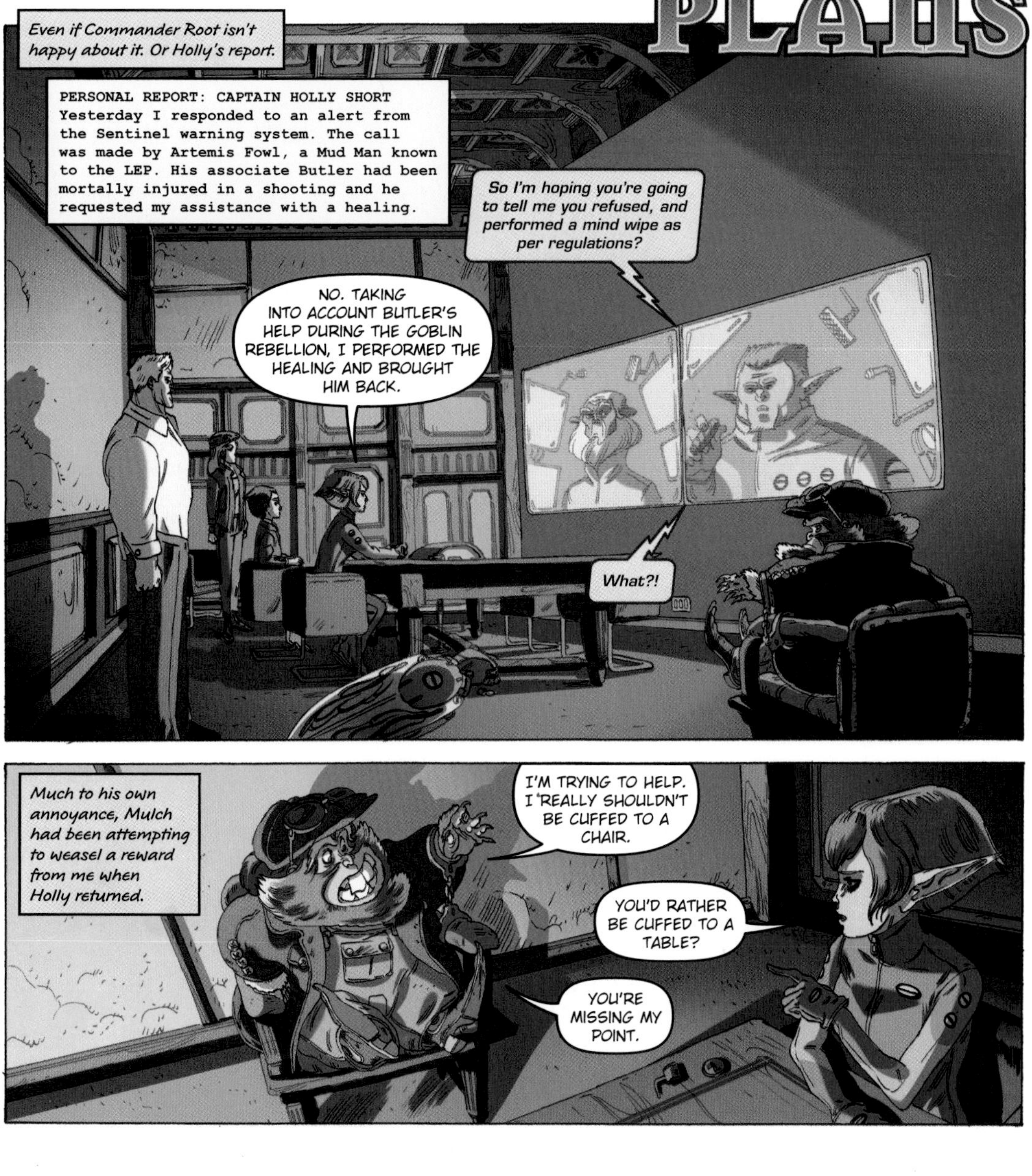
Even if Commander Root isn't happy about it. Or Holly's report.
PERSONAL REPORT: CAPTAIN HOLLY SHORT
Yesterday I responded to an alert from the Sentinel warning system. The call was made by Artemis Fowl, a Mud Man known to the LEP. His associate Butler had been mortally injured in a shooting and he requested my assistance with a healing.
So I'm hoping you're going to tell me you refused, and performed a mind wipe as per regulations?
NO. TAKING INTO ACCOUNT BUTLER'S HELP DURING THE GOBLIN REBELLION, I PERFORMED THE HEALING AND BROUGHT HIM BACK.
What?!
Much to his own annoyance, Mulch had been attempting to weasel a reward from me when Holly returned.
I'M TRYING TO HELP. I REALLY SHOULDN'T BE CUFFED TO A CHAIR.
YOU'D RATHER BE CUFFED TO A TABLE?
YOU'RE MISSING MY POINT.

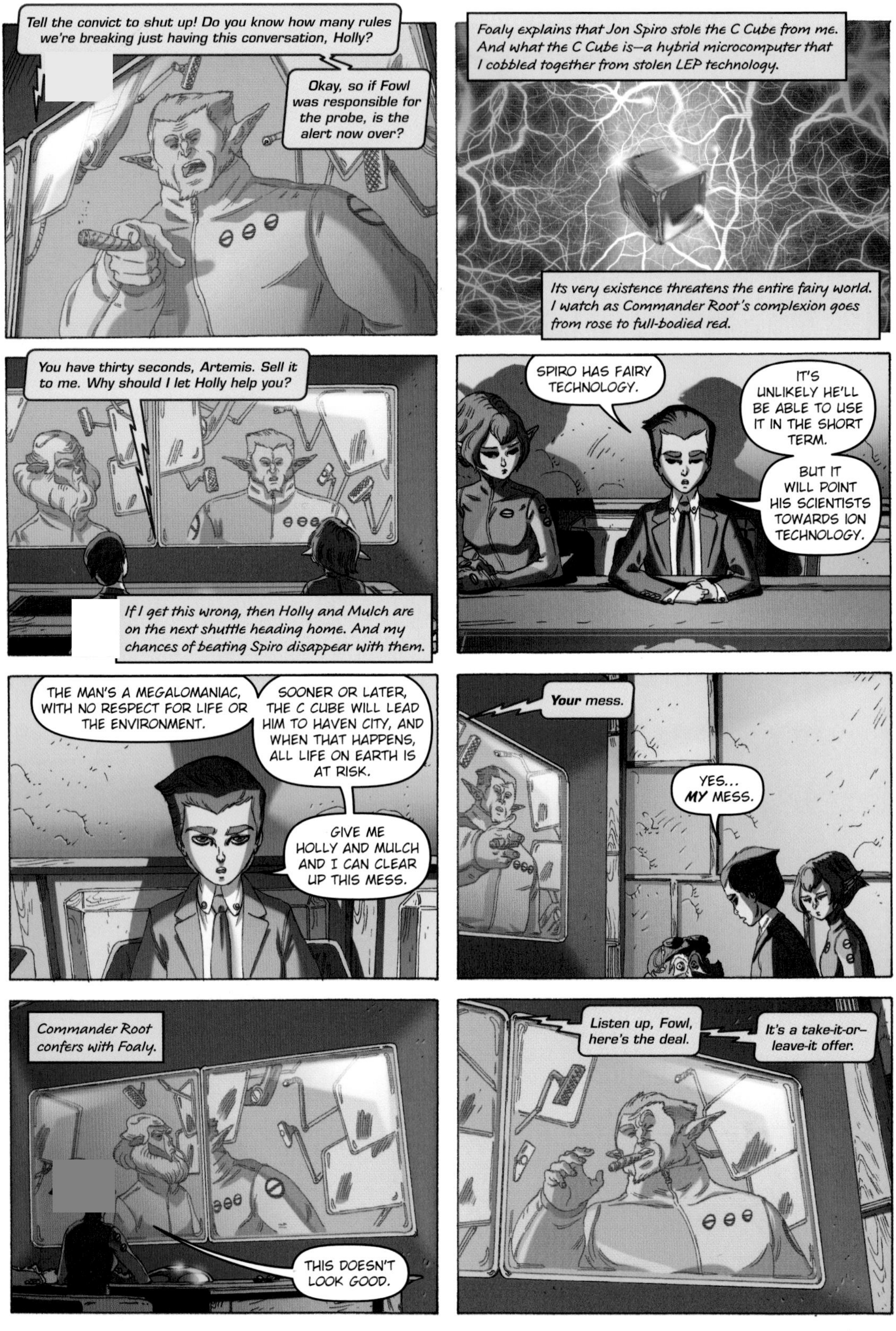
Tell the convict to shut up! Do you know how many rules we're breaking just having this conversation, Holly?
Okay, so if Fowl was responsible for the probe, is the alert now over?
Foaly explains that Jon Spiro stole the C Cube from me. And what the C Cube is—a hybrid microcomputer that I cobbled together from stolen LEP technology.
Its very existence threatens the entire fairy world. I watch as Commander Root's complexion goes from rose to full-bodied red.
You have thirty seconds, Artemis. Sell it to me. Why should I let Holly help you?
If I get this wrong, then Holly and Mulch are on the next shuttle heading home. And my chances of beating Spiro disappear with them.
SPIRO HAS FAIRY TECHNOLOGY.
IT'S UNLIKELY HE'LL BE ABLE TO USE IT IN THE SHORT TERM.
BUT IT WILL POINT HIS SCIENTISTS TOWARDS ION TECHNOLOGY.
THE MAN'S A MEGALOMANIAC, WITH NO RESPECT FOR LIFE OR THE ENVIRONMENT.
SOONER OR LATER, THE C CUBE WILL LEAD HIM TO HAVEN CITY, AND WHEN THAT HAPPENS, ALL LIFE ON EARTH IS AT RISK.
GIVE ME HOLLY AND MULCH AND I CAN CLEAR UP THIS MESS.
Your mess.
YES... MY MESS.
Commander Root confers with Foaly.
THIS DOESN'T LOOK GOOD.
Listen up, Fowl, here's the deal.
It's a take-it-or-leave-it offer.

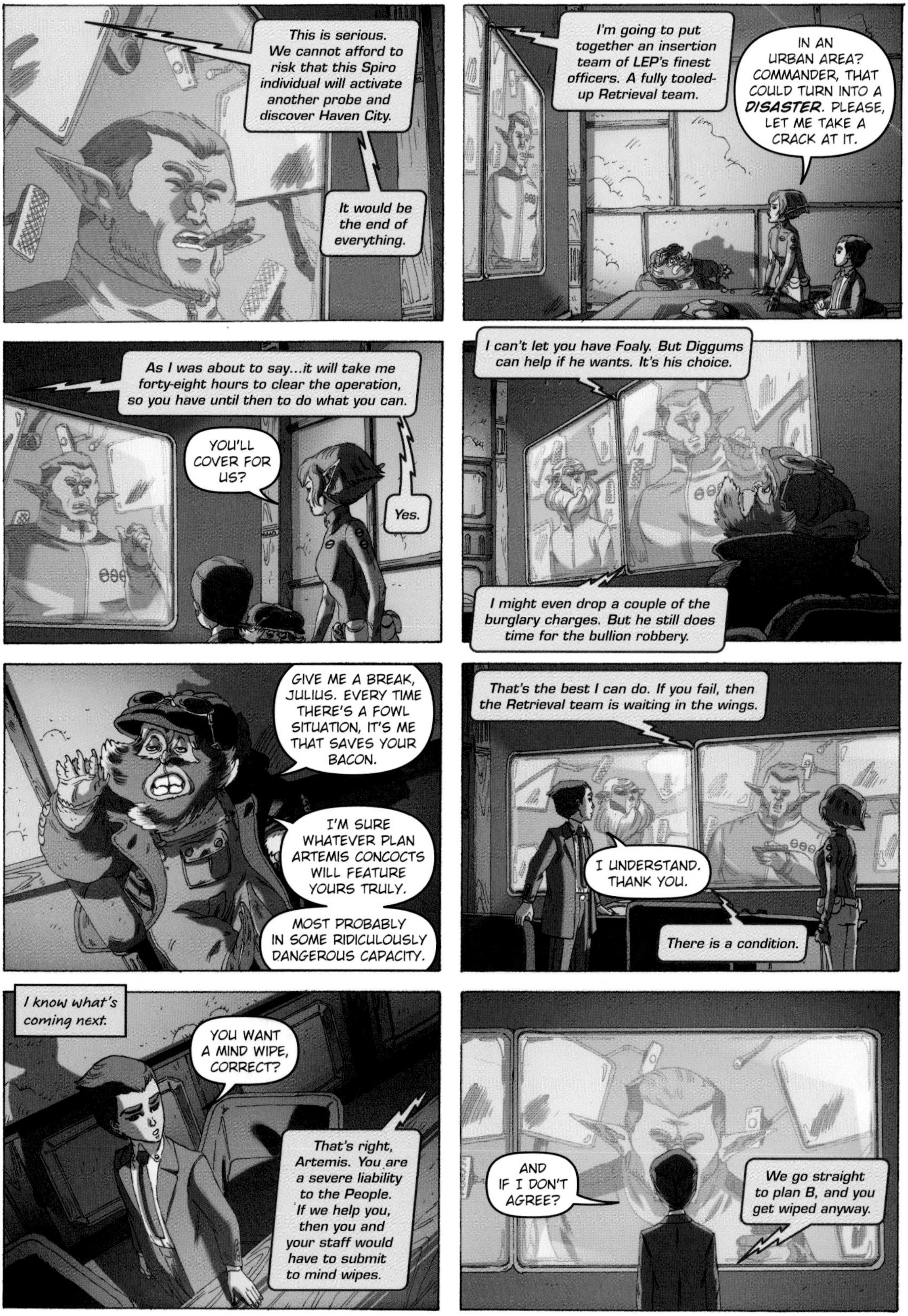
This is serious. We cannot afford to risk that this Spiro individual will activate another probe and discover Haven City.
It would be the end of everything.
I'm going to put together an insertion team of LEP's finest officers. A fully tooled-up Retrieval team.
IN AN URBAN AREA? COMMANDER, THAT COULD TURN INTO A *DISASTER*. PLEASE, LET ME TAKE A CRACK AT IT.
As I was about to say...it will take me forty-eight hours to clear the operation, so you have until then to do what you can.
YOU'LL COVER FOR US?
Yes.
I can't let you have Foaly. But Diggums can help if he wants. It's his choice.
I might even drop a couple of the burglary charges. But he still does time for the bullion robbery.
GIVE ME A BREAK, JULIUS. EVERY TIME THERE'S A FOWL SITUATION, IT'S ME THAT SAVES YOUR BACON.
I'M SURE WHATEVER PLAN ARTEMIS CONCOCTS WILL FEATURE YOURS TRULY.
MOST PROBABLY IN SOME RIDICULOUSLY DANGEROUS CAPACITY.
That's the best I can do. If you fail, then the Retrieval team is waiting in the wings.
I UNDERSTAND. THANK YOU.
There is a condition.
I know what's coming next.
YOU WANT A MIND WIPE, CORRECT?
That's right, Artemis. You are a severe liability to the People. If we help you, then you and your staff would have to submit to mind wipes.
AND IF I DON'T AGREE?
We go straight to plan B, and you get wiped anyway.

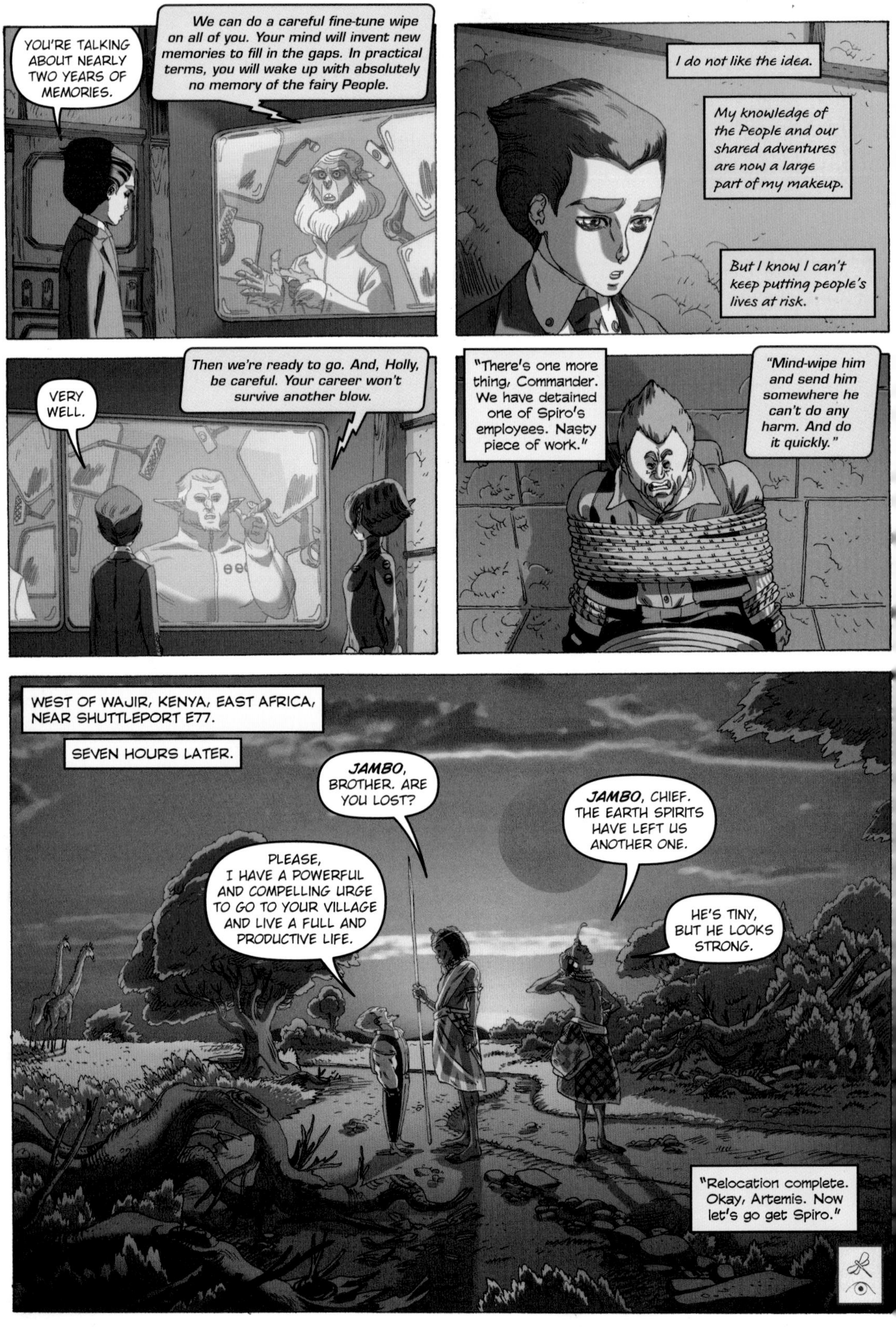
YOU'RE TALKING ABOUT NEARLY TWO YEARS OF MEMORIES.
We can do a careful fine-tune wipe on all of you. Your mind will invent new memories to fill in the gaps. In practical terms, you will wake up with absolutely no memory of the fairy People.
I do not like the idea.
My knowledge of the People and our shared adventures are now a large part of my makeup.
But I know I can't keep putting people's lives at risk.
VERY WELL.
Then we're ready to go. And, Holly, be careful. Your career won't survive another blow.
"There's one more thing, Commander. We have detained one of Spiro's employees. Nasty piece of work."
"Mind-wipe him and send him somewhere he can't do any harm. And do it quickly."
WEST OF WAJIR, KENYA, EAST AFRICA, NEAR SHUTTLEPORT E77.
SEVEN HOURS LATER.
JAMBO, BROTHER. ARE YOU LOST?
PLEASE, I HAVE A POWERFUL AND COMPELLING URGE TO GO TO YOUR VILLAGE AND LIVE A FULL AND PRODUCTIVE LIFE.
JAMBO, CHIEF. THE EARTH SPIRITS HAVE LEFT US ANOTHER ONE.
HE'S TINY, BUT HE LOOKS STRONG.
"Relocation complete. Okay, Artemis. Now let's go get Spiro."

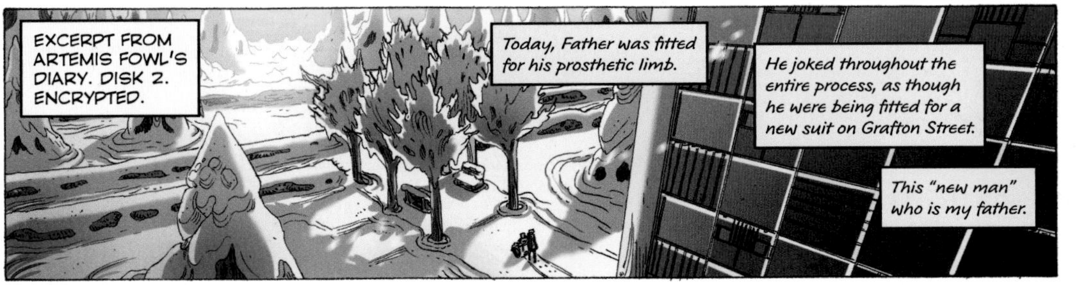
EXCERPT FROM ARTEMIS FOWL'S DIARY. DISK 2. ENCRYPTED.
Today, Father was fitted for his prosthetic limb.
He joked throughout the entire process, as though he were being fitted for a new suit on Grafton Street.
This "new man" who is my father.

CHAPTER 8: HOOKS, LINES, AND SINKERS

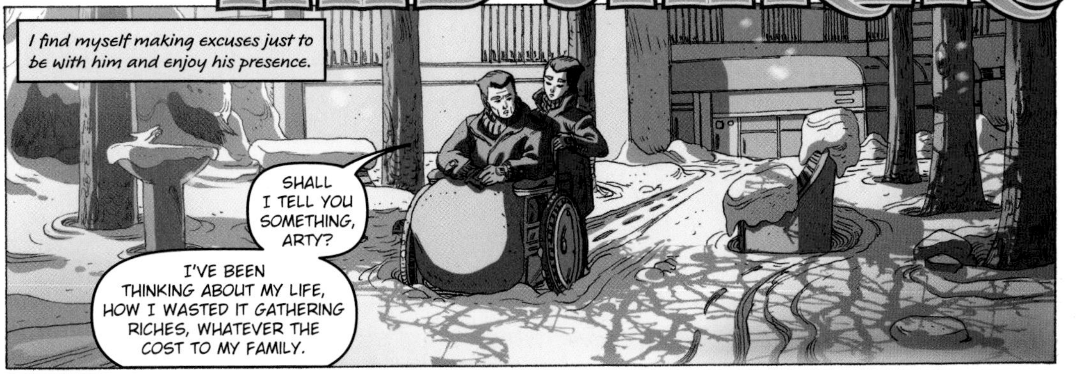
I find myself making excuses just to be with him and enjoy his presence.
SHALL I TELL YOU SOMETHING, ARTY?
I'VE BEEN THINKING ABOUT MY LIFE, HOW I WASTED IT GATHERING RICHES, WHATEVER THE COST TO MY FAMILY.

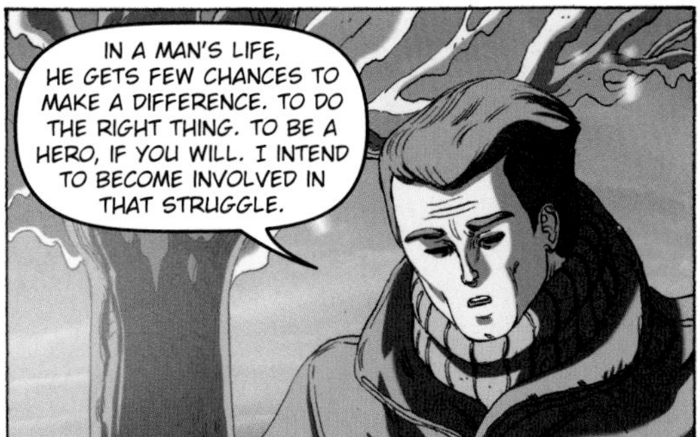
IN A MAN'S LIFE, HE GETS FEW CHANCES TO MAKE A DIFFERENCE. TO DO THE RIGHT THING. TO BE A HERO, IF YOU WILL. I INTEND TO BECOME INVOLVED IN THAT STRUGGLE.

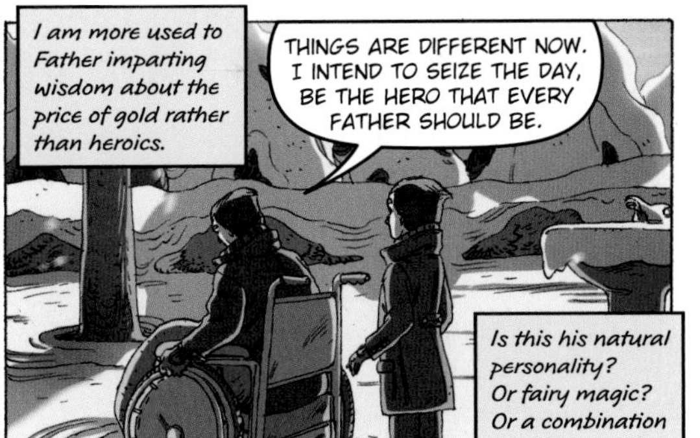
I am more used to Father imparting wisdom about the price of gold rather than heroics.
THINGS ARE DIFFERENT NOW. I INTEND TO SEIZE THE DAY, BE THE HERO THAT EVERY FATHER SHOULD BE.
Is this his natural personality? Or fairy magic? Or a combination of both?

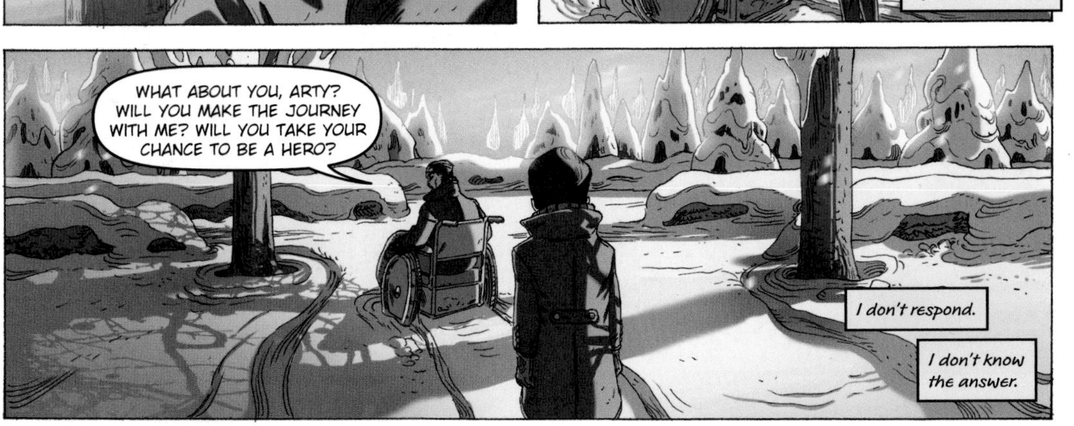
WHAT ABOUT YOU, ARTY? WILL YOU MAKE THE JOURNEY WITH ME? WILL YOU TAKE YOUR CHANCE TO BE A HERO?
I don't respond.
I don't know the answer.

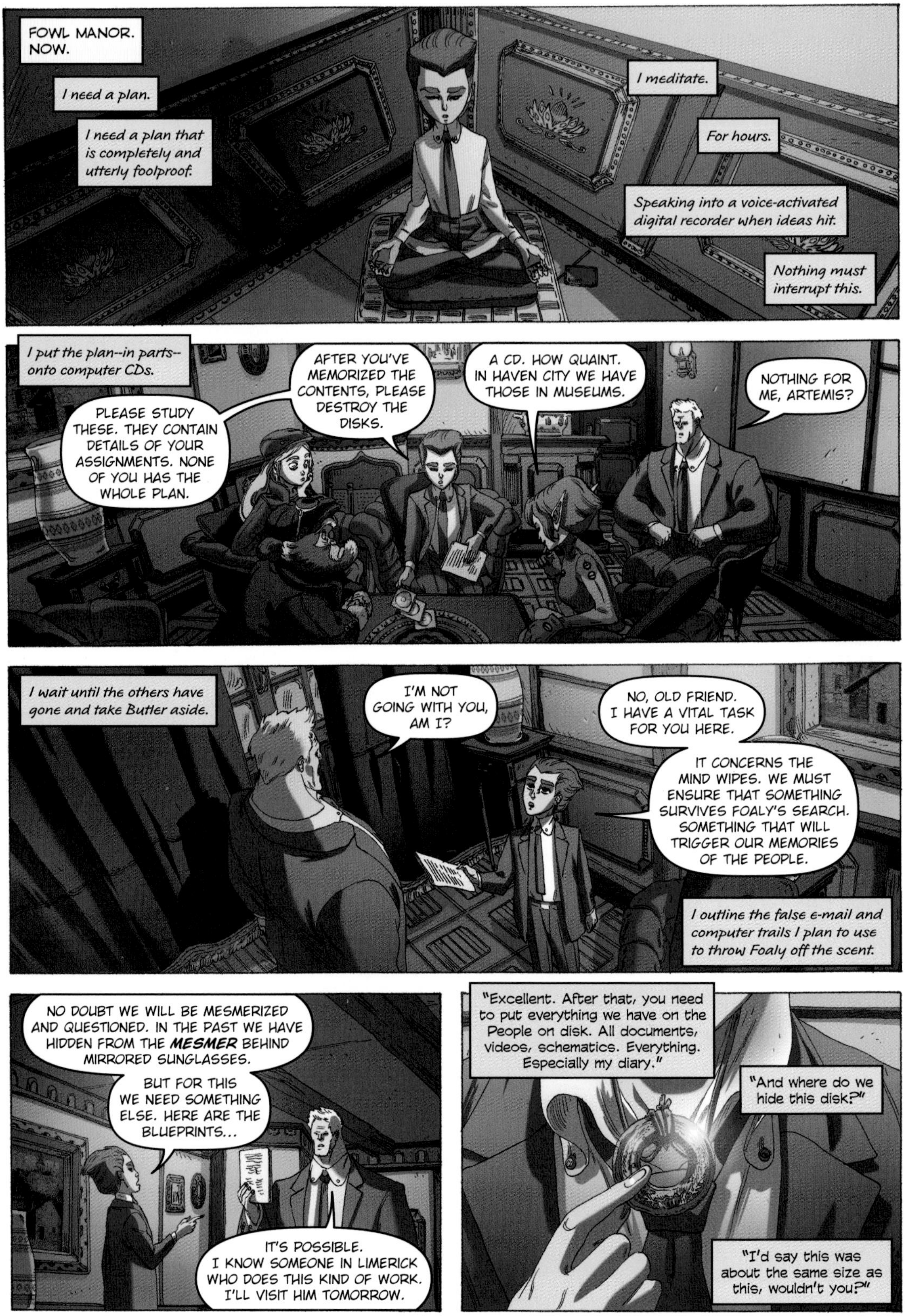

FOWL MANOR. NOW.
I need a plan.
I need a plan that is completely and utterly foolproof.
I meditate.
For hours.
Speaking into a voice-activated digital recorder when ideas hit.
Nothing must interrupt this.
I put the plan--in parts--onto computer CDs.
PLEASE STUDY THESE. THEY CONTAIN DETAILS OF YOUR ASSIGNMENTS. NONE OF YOU HAS THE WHOLE PLAN.
AFTER YOU'VE MEMORIZED THE CONTENTS, PLEASE DESTROY THE DISKS.
A CD. HOW QUAINT. IN HAVEN CITY WE HAVE THOSE IN MUSEUMS.
NOTHING FOR ME, ARTEMIS?
I wait until the others have gone and take Butter aside.
I'M NOT GOING WITH YOU, AM I?
NO, OLD FRIEND. I HAVE A VITAL TASK FOR YOU HERE.
IT CONCERNS THE MIND WIPES. WE MUST ENSURE THAT SOMETHING SURVIVES FOALY'S SEARCH. SOMETHING THAT WILL TRIGGER OUR MEMORIES OF THE PEOPLE.
I outline the false e-mail and computer trails I plan to use to throw Foaly off the scent.
NO DOUBT WE WILL BE MESMERIZED AND QUESTIONED. IN THE PAST WE HAVE HIDDEN FROM THE MESMER BEHIND MIRRORED SUNGLASSES.
BUT FOR THIS WE NEED SOMETHING ELSE. HERE ARE THE BLUEPRINTS...
IT'S POSSIBLE. I KNOW SOMEONE IN LIMERICK WHO DOES THIS KIND OF WORK. I'LL VISIT HIM TOMORROW.
"Excellent. After that, you need to put everything we have on the People on disk. All documents, videos, schematics. Everything. Especially my diary."
"And where do we hide this disk?"
"I'd say this was about the same size as this, wouldn't you?"

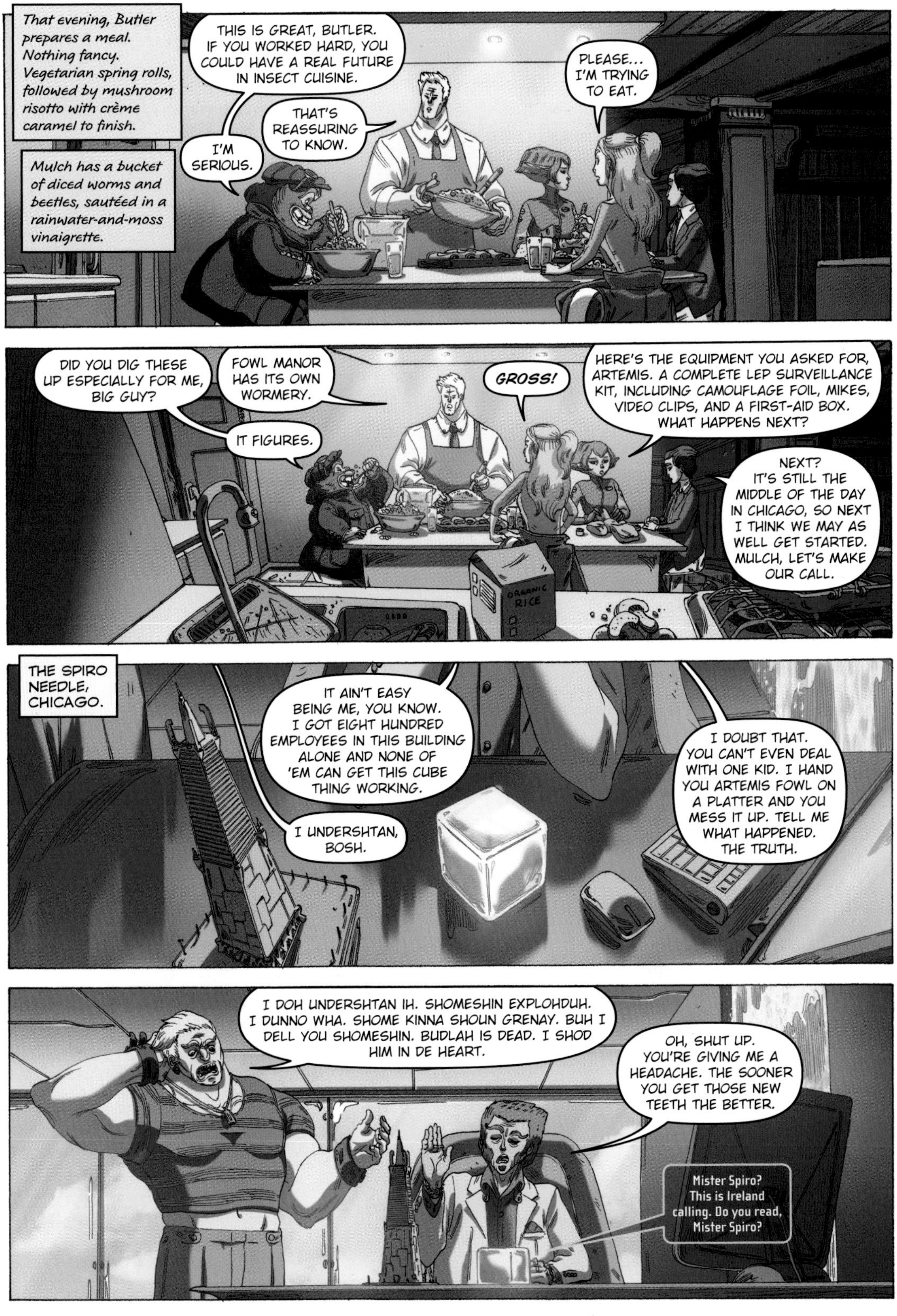
That evening, Butler prepares a meal. Nothing fancy. Vegetarian spring rolls, followed by mushroom risotto with crème caramel to finish.
Mulch has a bucket of diced worms and beetles, sautéed in a rainwater-and-moss vinaigrette.
THIS IS GREAT, BUTLER. IF YOU WORKED HARD, YOU COULD HAVE A REAL FUTURE IN INSECT CUISINE.
THAT'S REASSURING TO KNOW.
I'M SERIOUS.
PLEASE... I'M TRYING TO EAT.
DID YOU DIG THESE UP ESPECIALLY FOR ME, BIG GUY?
FOWL MANOR HAS ITS OWN WORMERY.
IT FIGURES.
GROSS!
HERE'S THE EQUIPMENT YOU ASKED FOR, ARTEMIS. A COMPLETE LEP SURVEILLANCE KIT, INCLUDING CAMOUFLAGE FOIL, MIKES, VIDEO CLIPS, AND A FIRST-AID BOX. WHAT HAPPENS NEXT?
NEXT? IT'S STILL THE MIDDLE OF THE DAY IN CHICAGO, SO NEXT I THINK WE MAY AS WELL GET STARTED. MULCH, LET'S MAKE OUR CALL.
ORGANIC RICE
THE SPIRO NEEDLE, CHICAGO.
IT AIN'T EASY BEING ME, YOU KNOW. I GOT EIGHT HUNDRED EMPLOYEES IN THIS BUILDING ALONE AND NONE OF 'EM CAN GET THIS CUBE THING WORKING.
I UNDERSHTAN, BOSH.
I DOUBT THAT. YOU CAN'T EVEN DEAL WITH ONE KID. I HAND YOU ARTEMIS FOWL ON A PLATTER AND YOU MESS IT UP. TELL ME WHAT HAPPENED. THE TRUTH.
I DOH UNDERSHTAN IH. SHOMESHIN EXPLOHDUH. I DUNNO WHA. SHOME KINNA SHOUN GRENAY. BUH I DELL YOU SHOMESHIN. BUDLAH IS DEAD. I SHOD HIM IN DE HEART.
OH, SHUT UP. YOU'RE GIVING ME A HEADACHE. THE SOONER YOU GET THOSE NEW TEETH THE BETTER.
Mister Spiro? This is Ireland calling. Do you read, Mister Spiro?

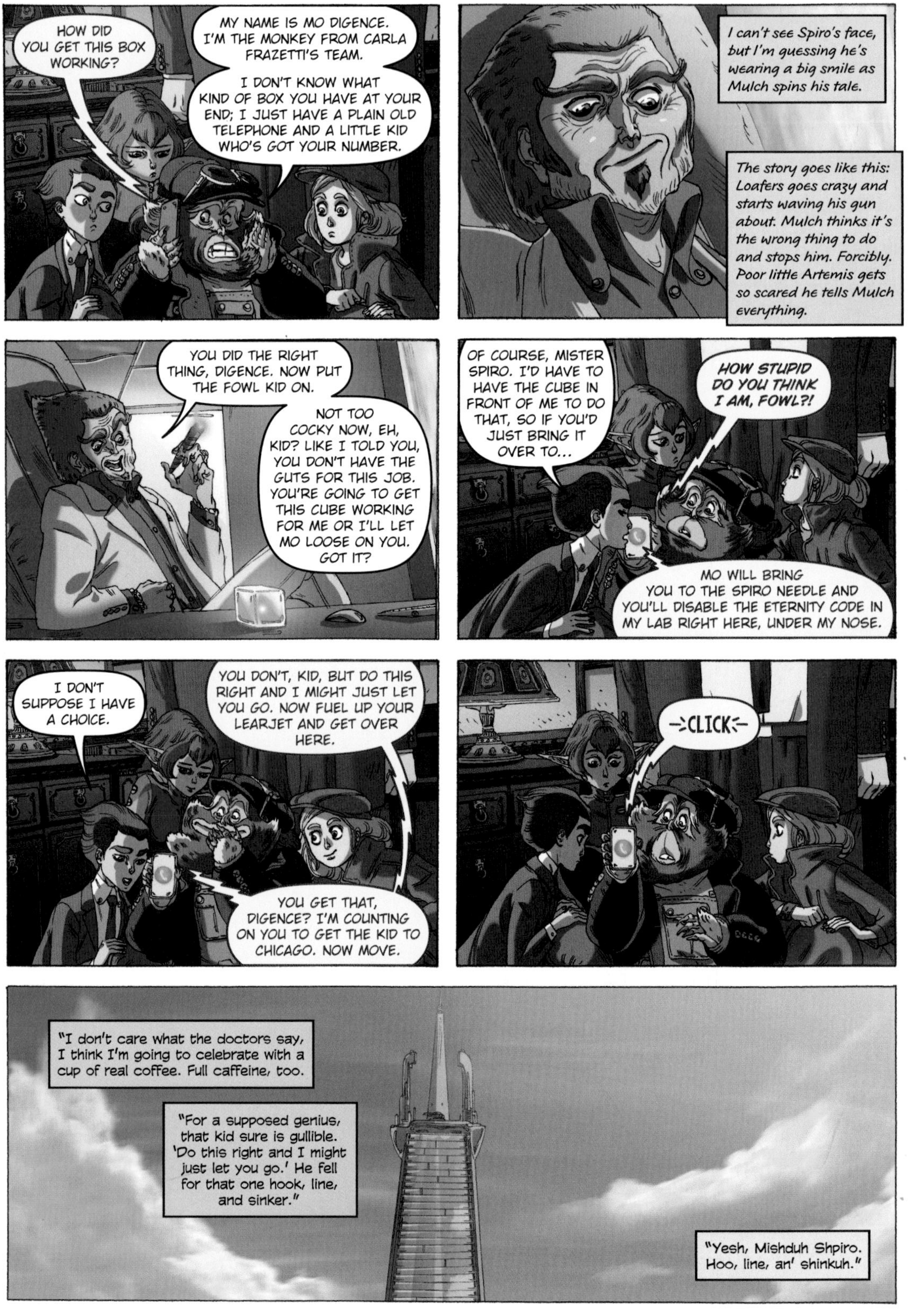
HOW DID YOU GET THIS BOX WORKING?
MY NAME IS MO DIGENCE. I'M THE MONKEY FROM CARLA FRAZETTI'S TEAM.
I DON'T KNOW WHAT KIND OF BOX YOU HAVE AT YOUR END; I JUST HAVE A PLAIN OLD TELEPHONE AND A LITTLE KID WHO'S GOT YOUR NUMBER.
I can't see Spiro's face, but I'm guessing he's wearing a big smile as Mulch spins his tale.
The story goes like this: Loafers goes crazy and starts waving his gun about. Mulch thinks it's the wrong thing to do and stops him. Forcibly. Poor little Artemis gets so scared he tells Mulch everything.
YOU DID THE RIGHT THING, DIGENCE. NOW PUT THE FOWL KID ON.
NOT TOO COCKY NOW, EH, KID? LIKE I TOLD YOU, YOU DON'T HAVE THE GUTS FOR THIS JOB. YOU'RE GOING TO GET THIS CUBE WORKING FOR ME OR I'LL LET MO LOOSE ON YOU. GOT IT?
OF COURSE, MISTER SPIRO. I'D HAVE TO HAVE THE CUBE IN FRONT OF ME TO DO THAT, SO IF YOU'D JUST BRING IT OVER TO...
HOW STUPID DO YOU THINK I AM, FOWL?!
MO WILL BRING YOU TO THE SPIRO NEEDLE AND YOU'LL DISABLE THE ETERNITY CODE IN MY LAB RIGHT HERE, UNDER MY NOSE.
I DON'T SUPPOSE I HAVE A CHOICE.
YOU DON'T, KID, BUT DO THIS RIGHT AND I MIGHT JUST LET YOU GO. NOW FUEL UP YOUR LEARJET AND GET OVER HERE.
YOU GET THAT, DIGENCE? I'M COUNTING ON YOU TO GET THE KID TO CHICAGO. NOW MOVE.
CLICK
"I don't care what the doctors say, I think I'm going to celebrate with a cup of real coffee. Full caffeine, too.
"For a supposed genius, that kid sure is gullible. 'Do this right and I might just let you go.' He fell for that one hook, line, and sinker."
"Yesh, Mishduh Shpiro. Hoo, line, an' shinkuh."

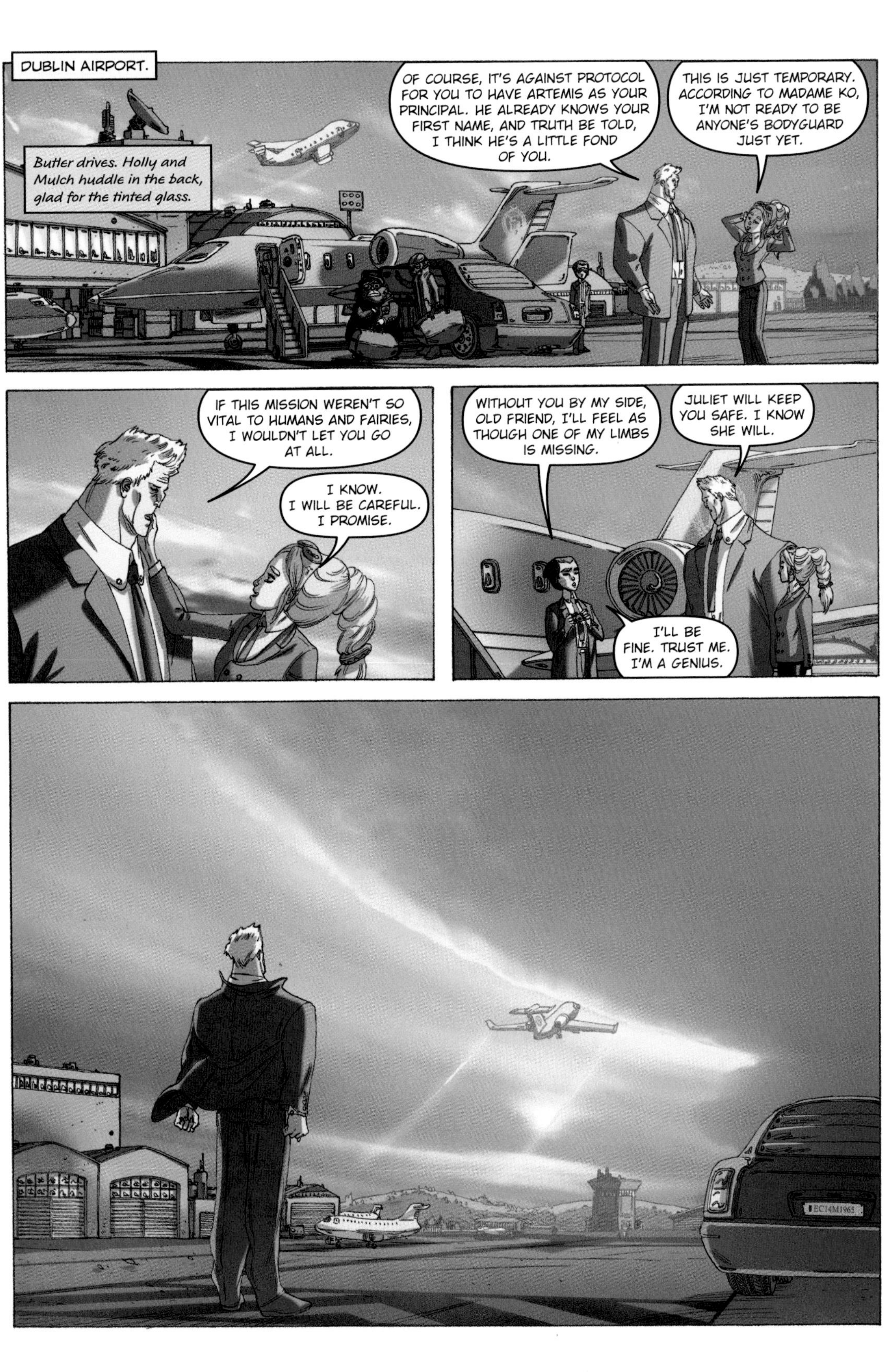
DUBLIN AIRPORT.
Butler drives. Holly and Mulch huddle in the back, glad for the tinted glass.
OF COURSE, IT'S AGAINST PROTOCOL FOR YOU TO HAVE ARTEMIS AS YOUR PRINCIPAL. HE ALREADY KNOWS YOUR FIRST NAME, AND TRUTH BE TOLD, I THINK HE'S A LITTLE FOND OF YOU.
THIS IS JUST TEMPORARY. ACCORDING TO MADAME KO, I'M NOT READY TO BE ANYONE'S BODYGUARD JUST YET.
IF THIS MISSION WEREN'T SO VITAL TO HUMANS AND FAIRIES, I WOULDN'T LET YOU GO AT ALL.
I KNOW. I WILL BE CAREFUL. I PROMISE.
WITHOUT YOU BY MY SIDE, OLD FRIEND, I'LL FEEL AS THOUGH ONE OF MY LIMBS IS MISSING.
JULIET WILL KEEP YOU SAFE. I KNOW SHE WILL.
I'LL BE FINE. TRUST ME. I'M A GENIUS.
EC14M1965

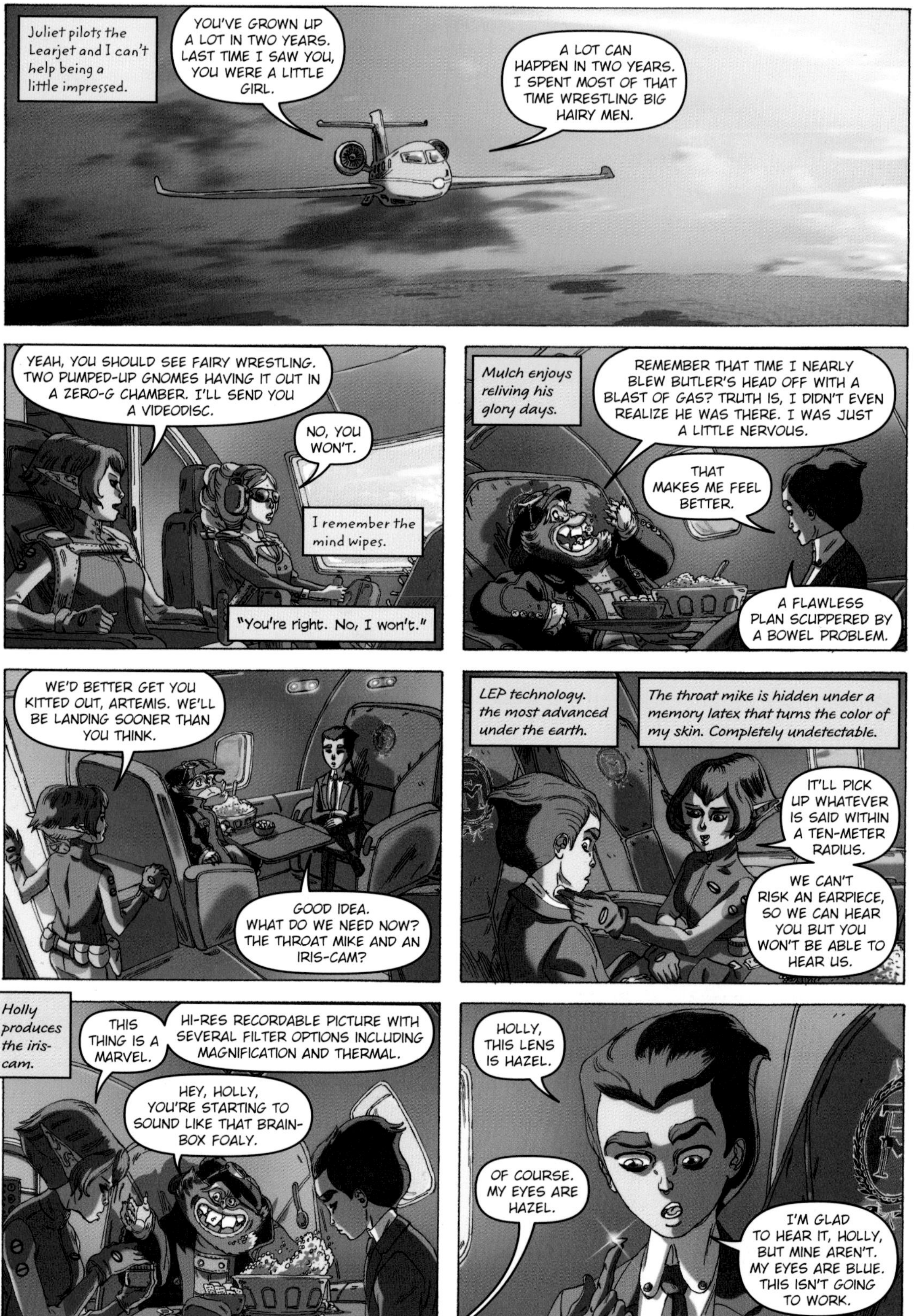

Juliet pilots the Learjet and I can't help being a little impressed.
YOU'VE GROWN UP A LOT IN TWO YEARS. LAST TIME I SAW YOU, YOU WERE A LITTLE GIRL.
A LOT CAN HAPPEN IN TWO YEARS. I SPENT MOST OF THAT TIME WRESTLING BIG HAIRY MEN.
YEAH, YOU SHOULD SEE FAIRY WRESTLING. TWO PUMPED-UP GNOMES HAVING IT OUT IN A ZERO-G CHAMBER. I'LL SEND YOU A VIDEODISC.
NO, YOU WON'T.
I remember the mind wipes.
"You're right. No, I won't."
Mulch enjoys reliving his glory days.
REMEMBER THAT TIME I NEARLY BLEW BUTLER'S HEAD OFF WITH A BLAST OF GAS? TRUTH IS, I DIDN'T EVEN REALIZE HE WAS THERE. I WAS JUST A LITTLE NERVOUS.
THAT MAKES ME FEEL BETTER.
A FLAWLESS PLAN SCUPPERED BY A BOWEL PROBLEM.
WE'D BETTER GET YOU KITTED OUT, ARTEMIS. WE'LL BE LANDING SOONER THAN YOU THINK.
GOOD IDEA. WHAT DO WE NEED NOW? THE THROAT MIKE AND AN IRIS-CAM?
LEP technology. the most advanced under the earth.
The throat mike is hidden under a memory latex that turns the color of my skin. Completely undetectable.
IT'LL PICK UP WHATEVER IS SAID WITHIN A TEN-METER RADIUS.
WE CAN'T RISK AN EARPIECE, SO WE CAN HEAR YOU BUT YOU WON'T BE ABLE TO HEAR US.
Holly produces the iris-cam.
THIS THING IS A MARVEL.
HI-RES RECORDABLE PICTURE WITH SEVERAL FILTER OPTIONS INCLUDING MAGNIFICATION AND THERMAL.
HEY, HOLLY, YOU'RE STARTING TO SOUND LIKE THAT BRAIN-BOX FOALY.
HOLLY, THIS LENS IS HAZEL.
OF COURSE. MY EYES ARE HAZEL.
I'M GLAD TO HEAR IT, HOLLY, BUT MINE AREN'T. MY EYES ARE BLUE. THIS ISN'T GOING TO WORK.

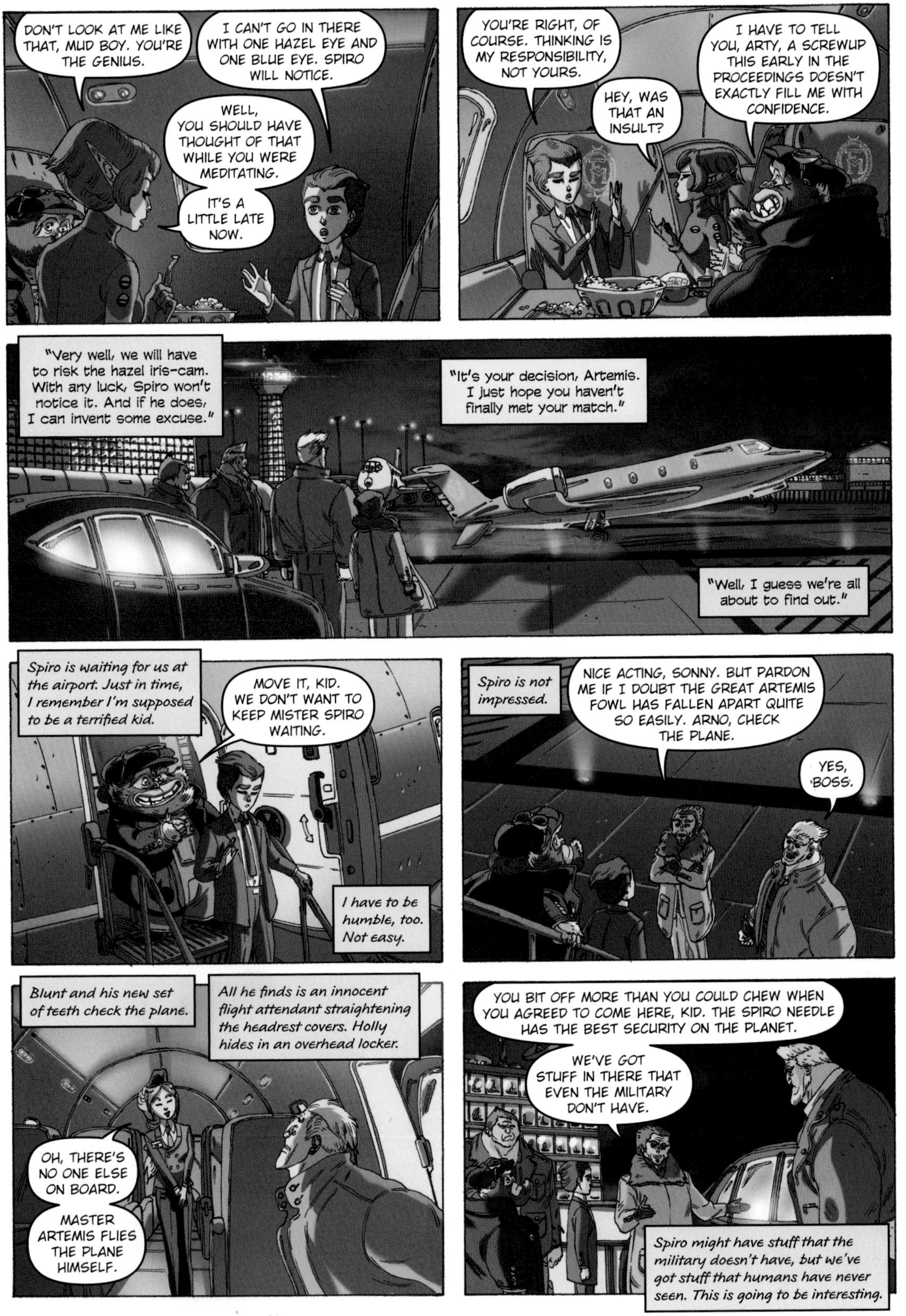
DON'T LOOK AT ME LIKE THAT, MUD BOY. YOU'RE THE GENIUS.
I CAN'T GO IN THERE WITH ONE HAZEL EYE AND ONE BLUE EYE. SPIRO WILL NOTICE.
WELL, YOU SHOULD HAVE THOUGHT OF THAT WHILE YOU WERE MEDITATING.
IT'S A LITTLE LATE NOW.
YOU'RE RIGHT, OF COURSE. THINKING IS MY RESPONSIBILITY, NOT YOURS.
HEY, WAS THAT AN INSULT?
I HAVE TO TELL YOU, ARTY, A SCREWUP THIS EARLY IN THE PROCEEDINGS DOESN'T EXACTLY FILL ME WITH CONFIDENCE.
"Very well, we will have to risk the hazel iris-cam. With any luck, Spiro won't notice it. And if he does, I can invent some excuse."
"It's your decision, Artemis. I just hope you haven't finally met your match."
"Well, I guess we're all about to find out."
Spiro is waiting for us at the airport. Just in time, I remember I'm supposed to be a terrified kid.
MOVE IT, KID. WE DON'T WANT TO KEEP MISTER SPIRO WAITING.
I have to be humble, too. Not easy.
Spiro is not impressed.
NICE ACTING, SONNY. BUT PARDON ME IF I DOUBT THE GREAT ARTEMIS FOWL HAS FALLEN APART QUITE SO EASILY. ARNO, CHECK THE PLANE.
YES, BOSS.
Blunt and his new set of teeth check the plane.
All he finds is an innocent flight attendant straightening the headrest covers. Holly hides in an overhead locker.
OH, THERE'S NO ONE ELSE ON BOARD.
MASTER ARTEMIS FLIES THE PLANE HIMSELF.
YOU BIT OFF MORE THAN YOU COULD CHEW WHEN YOU AGREED TO COME HERE, KID. THE SPIRO NEEDLE HAS THE BEST SECURITY ON THE PLANET.
WE'VE GOT STUFF IN THERE THAT EVEN THE MILITARY DON'T HAVE.
Spiro might have stuff that the military doesn't have, but we've got stuff that humans have never seen. This is going to be interesting.

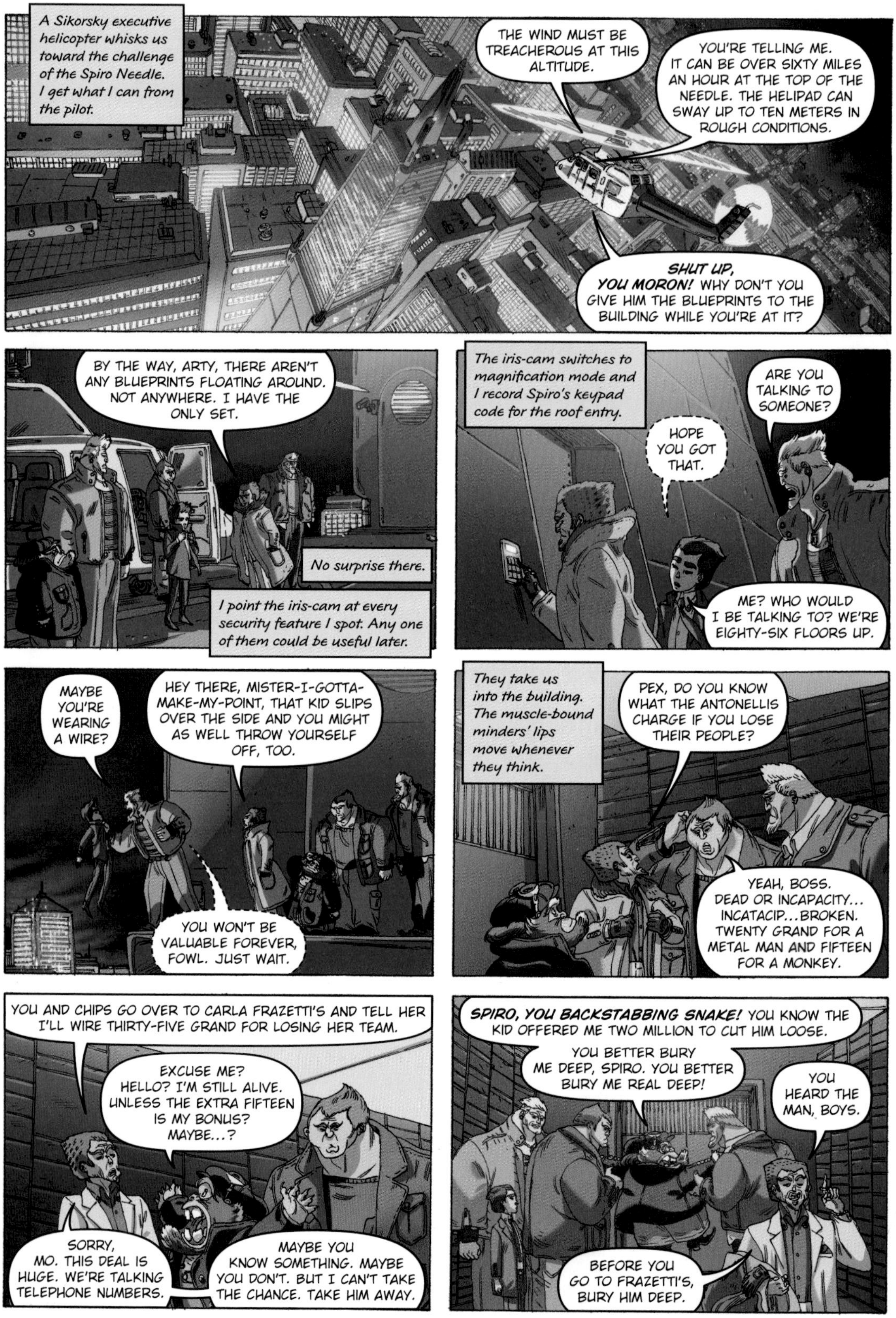
A Sikorsky executive helicopter whisks us toward the challenge of the Spiro Needle. I get what I can from the pilot.
THE WIND MUST BE TREACHEROUS AT THIS ALTITUDE.
YOU'RE TELLING ME. IT CAN BE OVER SIXTY MILES AN HOUR AT THE TOP OF THE NEEDLE. THE HELIPAD CAN SWAY UP TO TEN METERS IN ROUGH CONDITIONS.
SHUT UP, YOU MORON! WHY DON'T YOU GIVE HIM THE BLUEPRINTS TO THE BUILDING WHILE YOU'RE AT IT?
BY THE WAY, ARTY, THERE AREN'T ANY BLUEPRINTS FLOATING AROUND. NOT ANYWHERE. I HAVE THE ONLY SET.
No surprise there.
I point the iris-cam at every security feature I spot. Any one of them could be useful later.
The iris-cam switches to magnification mode and I record Spiro's keypad code for the roof entry.
HOPE YOU GOT THAT.
ARE YOU TALKING TO SOMEONE?
ME? WHO WOULD I BE TALKING TO? WE'RE EIGHTY-SIX FLOORS UP.
MAYBE YOU'RE WEARING A WIRE?
HEY THERE, MISTER-I-GOTTA-MAKE-MY-POINT, THAT KID SLIPS OVER THE SIDE AND YOU MIGHT AS WELL THROW YOURSELF OFF, TOO.
YOU WON'T BE VALUABLE FOREVER, FOWL. JUST WAIT.
They take us into the building. The muscle-bound minders' lips move whenever they think.
PEX, DO YOU KNOW WHAT THE ANTONELLIS CHARGE IF YOU LOSE THEIR PEOPLE?
YEAH, BOSS. DEAD OR INCAPACITY... INCATACIP... BROKEN. TWENTY GRAND FOR A METAL MAN AND FIFTEEN FOR A MONKEY.
YOU AND CHIPS GO OVER TO CARLA FRAZETTI'S AND TELL HER I'LL WIRE THIRTY-FIVE GRAND FOR LOSING HER TEAM.
EXCUSE ME? HELLO? I'M STILL ALIVE. UNLESS THE EXTRA FIFTEEN IS MY BONUS? MAYBE...?
SORRY, MO. THIS DEAL IS HUGE. WE'RE TALKING TELEPHONE NUMBERS.
MAYBE YOU KNOW SOMETHING. MAYBE YOU DON'T. BUT I CAN'T TAKE THE CHANCE. TAKE HIM AWAY.
SPIRO, YOU BACKSTABBING SNAKE! YOU KNOW THE KID OFFERED ME TWO MILLION TO CUT HIM LOOSE.
YOU BETTER BURY ME DEEP, SPIRO. YOU BETTER BURY ME REAL DEEP!
YOU HEARD THE MAN, BOYS.
BEFORE YOU GO TO FRAZETTI'S, BURY HIM DEEP.

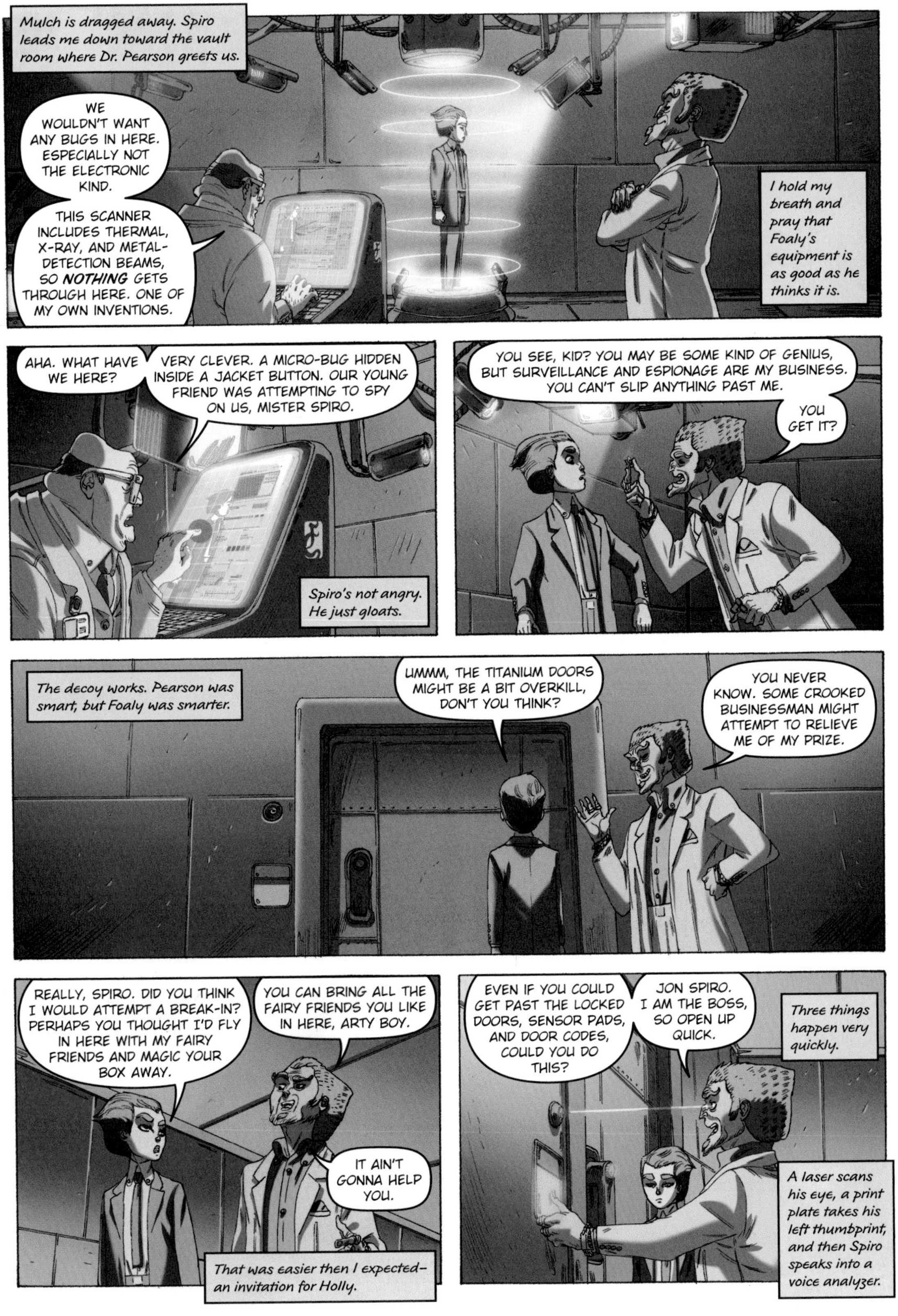
Mulch is dragged away. Spiro leads me down toward the vault room where Dr. Pearson greets us.
WE WOULDN'T WANT ANY BUGS IN HERE. ESPECIALLY NOT THE ELECTRONIC KIND.
THIS SCANNER INCLUDES THERMAL, X-RAY, AND METAL-DETECTION BEAMS, SO NOTHING GETS THROUGH HERE. ONE OF MY OWN INVENTIONS.
I hold my breath and pray that Foaly's equipment is as good as he thinks it is.
AHA. WHAT HAVE WE HERE?
VERY CLEVER. A MICRO-BUG HIDDEN INSIDE A JACKET BUTTON. OUR YOUNG FRIEND WAS ATTEMPTING TO SPY ON US, MISTER SPIRO.
Spiro's not angry. He just gloats.
YOU SEE, KID? YOU MAY BE SOME KIND OF GENIUS, BUT SURVEILLANCE AND ESPIONAGE ARE MY BUSINESS. YOU CAN'T SLIP ANYTHING PAST ME.
YOU GET IT?
The decoy works. Pearson was smart, but Foaly was smarter.
UMMM, THE TITANIUM DOORS MIGHT BE A BIT OVERKILL, DON'T YOU THINK?
YOU NEVER KNOW. SOME CROOKED BUSINESSMAN MIGHT ATTEMPT TO RELIEVE ME OF MY PRIZE.
REALLY, SPIRO. DID YOU THINK I WOULD ATTEMPT A BREAK-IN? PERHAPS YOU THOUGHT I'D FLY IN HERE WITH MY FAIRY FRIENDS AND MAGIC YOUR BOX AWAY.
YOU CAN BRING ALL THE FAIRY FRIENDS YOU LIKE IN HERE, ARTY BOY.
IT AIN'T GONNA HELP YOU.
That was easier then I expected—an invitation for Holly.
EVEN IF YOU COULD GET PAST THE LOCKED DOORS, SENSOR PADS, AND DOOR CODES, COULD YOU DO THIS?
JON SPIRO. I AM THE BOSS, SO OPEN UP QUICK.
Three things happen very quickly.
A laser scans his eye, a print plate takes his left thumbprint, and then Spiro speaks into a voice analyzer.

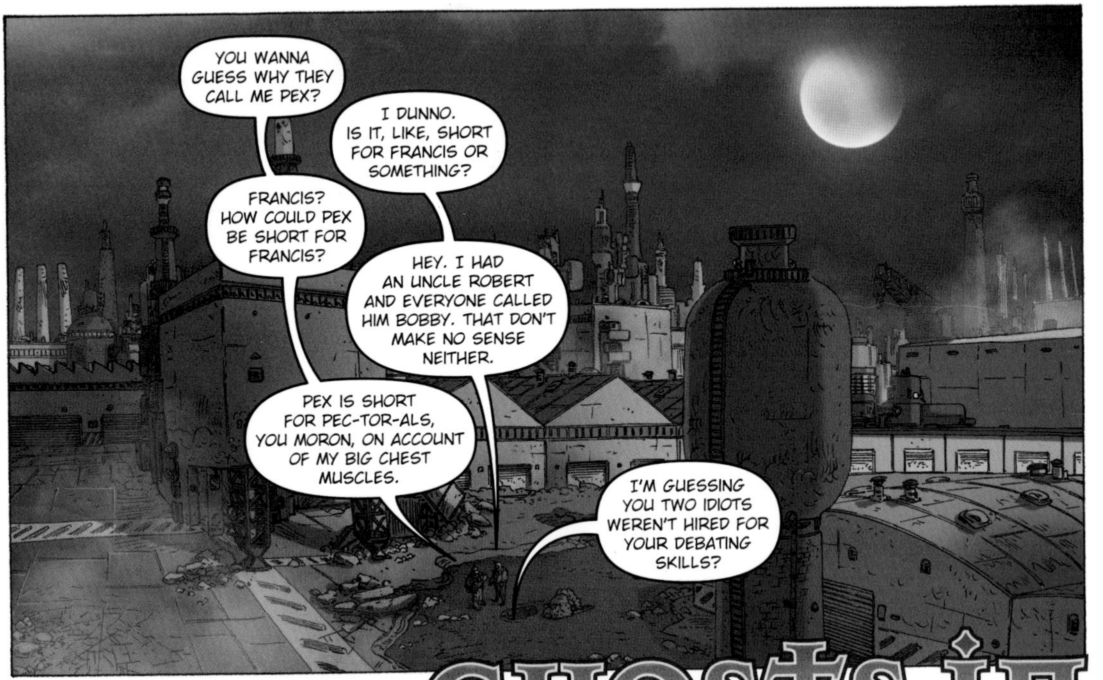
YOU WANNA GUESS WHY THEY CALL ME PEX?
I DUNNO. IS IT, LIKE, SHORT FOR FRANCIS OR SOMETHING?
FRANCIS? HOW COULD PEX BE SHORT FOR FRANCIS?
HEY. I HAD AN UNCLE ROBERT AND EVERYONE CALLED HIM BOBBY. THAT DON'T MAKE NO SENSE NEITHER.
PEX IS SHORT FOR PEC-TOR-ALS, YOU MORON, ON ACCOUNT OF MY BIG CHEST MUSCLES.
I'M GUESSING YOU TWO IDIOTS WEREN'T HIRED FOR YOUR DEBATING SKILLS?

CHAPTER 9: GHOSTS IN THE MACHINE

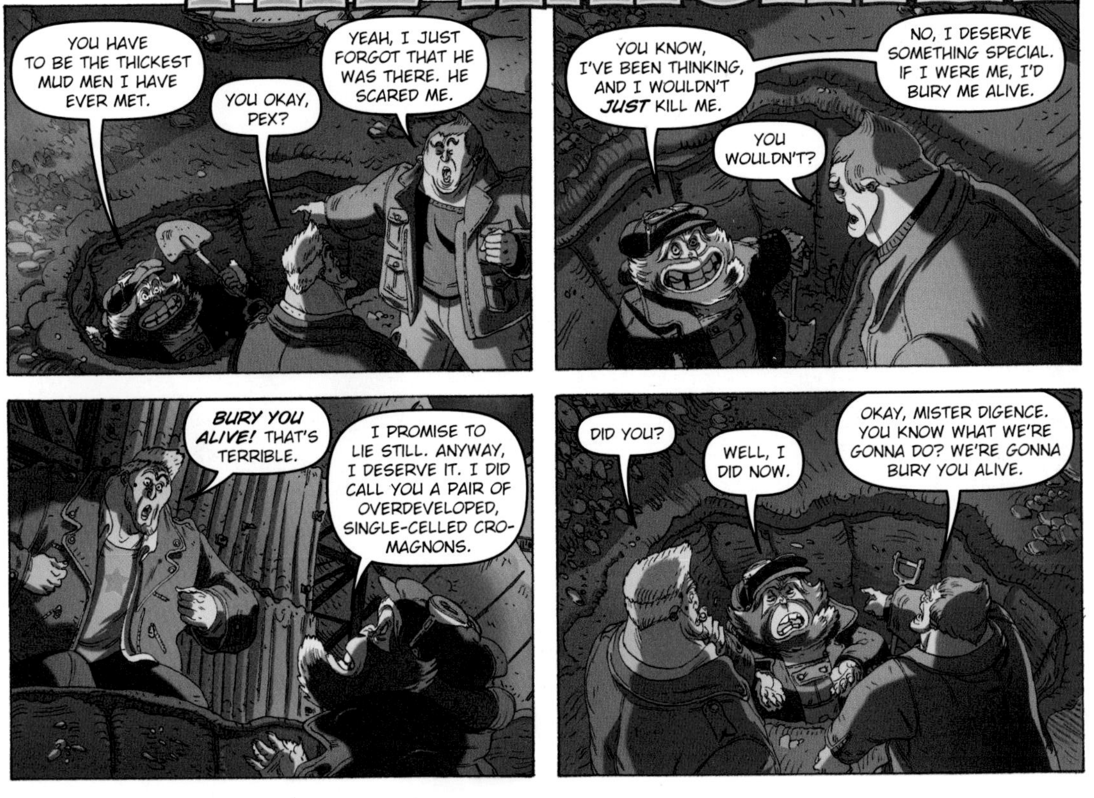
YOU HAVE TO BE THE THICKEST MUD MEN I HAVE EVER MET.
YOU OKAY, PEX?
YEAH, I JUST FORGOT THAT HE WAS THERE. HE SCARED ME.
YOU KNOW, I'VE BEEN THINKING, AND I WOULDN'T *JUST* KILL ME.
NO, I DESERVE SOMETHING SPECIAL. IF I WERE ME, I'D BURY ME ALIVE.
YOU WOULDN'T?
BURY YOU ALIVE! THAT'S TERRIBLE.
I PROMISE TO LIE STILL. ANYWAY, I DESERVE IT. I DID CALL YOU A PAIR OF OVERDEVELOPED, SINGLE-CELLED CRO-MAGNONS.
DID YOU?
WELL, I DID NOW.
OKAY, MISTER DIGENCE. YOU KNOW WHAT WE'RE GONNA DO? WE'RE GONNA BURY YOU ALIVE.

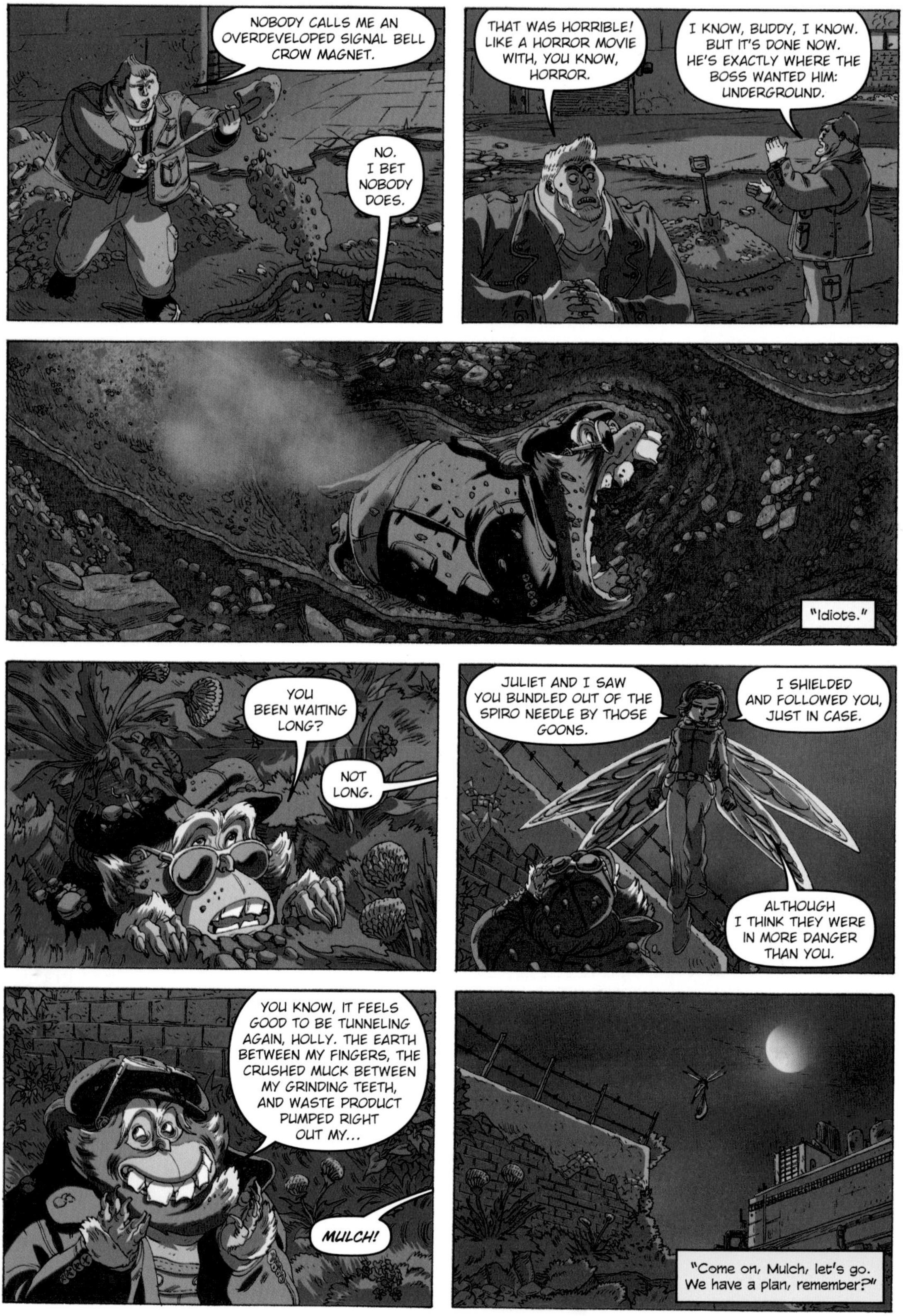
NOBODY CALLS ME AN OVERDEVELOPED SIGNAL BELL CROW MAGNET.
NO. I BET NOBODY DOES.
THAT WAS HORRIBLE! LIKE A HORROR MOVIE WITH, YOU KNOW, HORROR.
I KNOW, BUDDY, I KNOW. BUT IT'S DONE NOW. HE'S EXACTLY WHERE THE BOSS WANTED HIM: UNDERGROUND.
"Idiots."
YOU BEEN WAITING LONG?
NOT LONG.
JULIET AND I SAW YOU BUNDLED OUT OF THE SPIRO NEEDLE BY THOSE GOONS.
I SHIELDED AND FOLLOWED YOU, JUST IN CASE.
ALTHOUGH I THINK THEY WERE IN MORE DANGER THAN YOU.
YOU KNOW, IT FEELS GOOD TO BE TUNNELING AGAIN, HOLLY. THE EARTH BETWEEN MY FINGERS, THE CRUSHED MUCK BETWEEN MY GRINDING TEETH, AND WASTE PRODUCT PUMPED RIGHT OUT MY...
MULCH!
"Come on, Mulch, let's go. We have a plan, remember?"

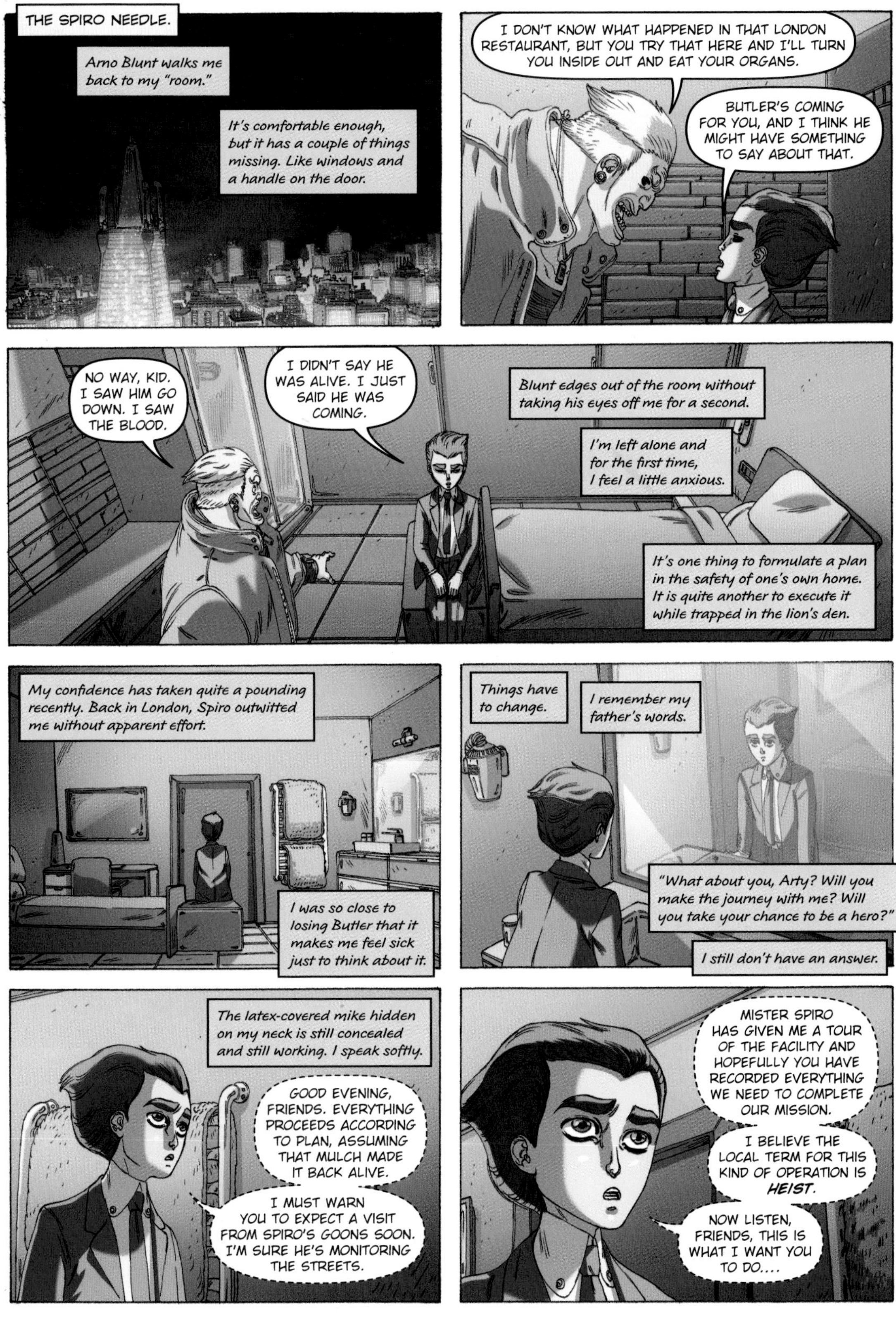
THE SPIRO NEEDLE.
Arno Blunt walks me back to my "room."
It's comfortable enough, but it has a couple of things missing. Like windows and a handle on the door.
I DON'T KNOW WHAT HAPPENED IN THAT LONDON RESTAURANT, BUT YOU TRY THAT HERE AND I'LL TURN YOU INSIDE OUT AND EAT YOUR ORGANS.
BUTLER'S COMING FOR YOU, AND I THINK HE MIGHT HAVE SOMETHING TO SAY ABOUT THAT.
NO WAY, KID. I SAW HIM GO DOWN. I SAW THE BLOOD.
I DIDN'T SAY HE WAS ALIVE. I JUST SAID HE WAS COMING.
Blunt edges out of the room without taking his eyes off me for a second.
I'm left alone and for the first time, I feel a little anxious.
It's one thing to formulate a plan in the safety of one's own home. It is quite another to execute it while trapped in the lion's den.
My confidence has taken quite a pounding recently. Back in London, Spiro outwitted me without apparent effort.
I was so close to losing Butler that it makes me feel sick just to think about it.
Things have to change.
I remember my father's words.
"What about you, Arty? Will you make the journey with me? Will you take your chance to be a hero?"
I still don't have an answer.
The latex-covered mike hidden on my neck is still concealed and still working. I speak softly.
GOOD EVENING, FRIENDS. EVERYTHING PROCEEDS ACCORDING TO PLAN, ASSUMING THAT MULCH MADE IT BACK ALIVE.
I MUST WARN YOU TO EXPECT A VISIT FROM SPIRO'S GOONS SOON. I'M SURE HE'S MONITORING THE STREETS.
MISTER SPIRO HAS GIVEN ME A TOUR OF THE FACILITY AND HOPEFULLY YOU HAVE RECORDED EVERYTHING WE NEED TO COMPLETE OUR MISSION.
I BELIEVE THE LOCAL TERM FOR THIS KIND OF OPERATION IS ***HEIST***.
NOW LISTEN, FRIENDS, THIS IS WHAT I WANT YOU TO DO....

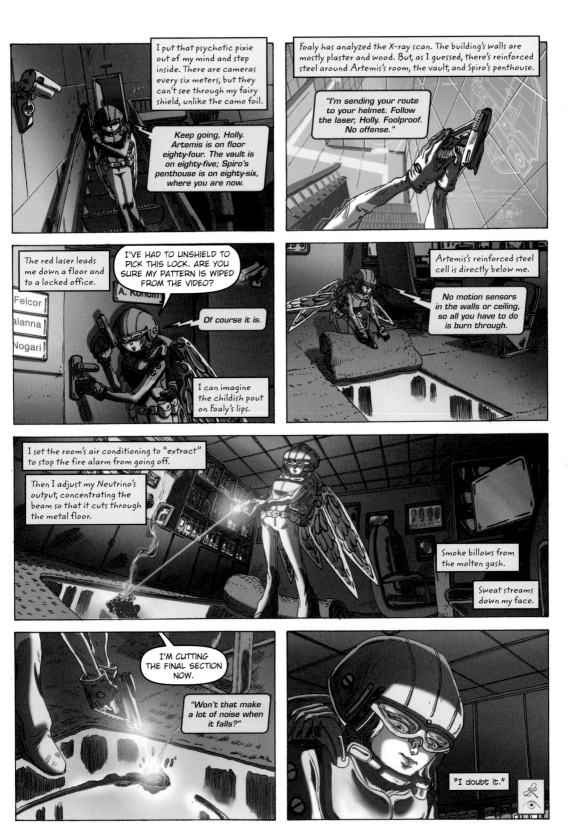

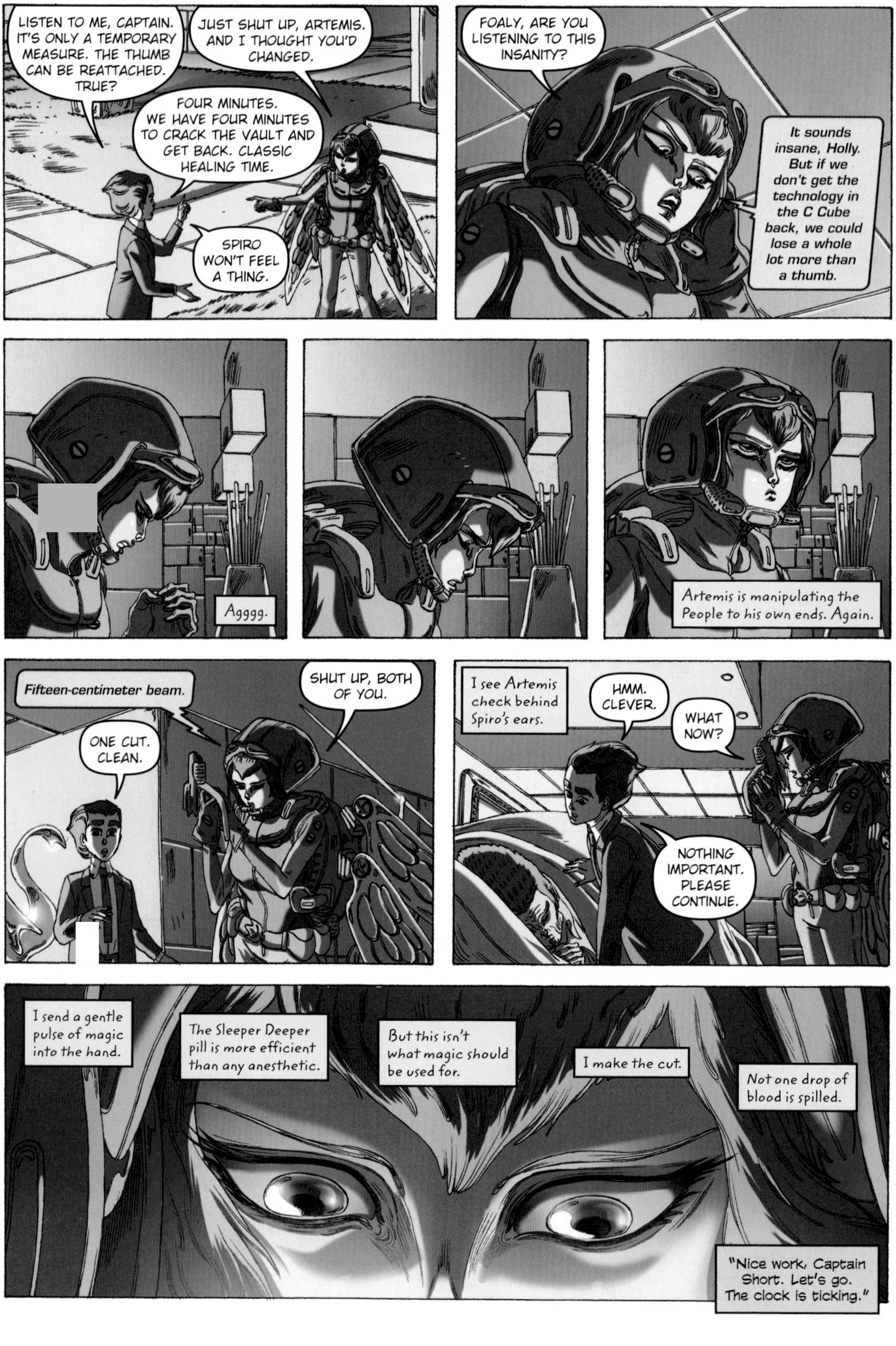
LISTEN TO ME, CAPTAIN. IT'S ONLY A TEMPORARY MEASURE. THE THUMB CAN BE REATTACHED. TRUE?
JUST SHUT UP, ARTEMIS. AND I THOUGHT YOU'D CHANGED.
FOUR MINUTES. WE HAVE FOUR MINUTES TO CRACK THE VAULT AND GET BACK. CLASSIC HEALING TIME.
SPIRO WON'T FEEL A THING.
FOALY, ARE YOU LISTENING TO THIS INSANITY?
It sounds insane, Holly. But if we don't get the technology in the C Cube back, we could lose a whole lot more than a thumb.
Agggg.
Artemis is manipulating the People to his own ends. Again.
Fifteen-centimeter beam.
SHUT UP, BOTH OF YOU.
ONE CUT. CLEAN.
I see Artemis check behind Spiro's ears.
HMM. CLEVER.
WHAT NOW?
NOTHING IMPORTANT. PLEASE CONTINUE.
I send a gentle pulse of magic into the hand.
The Sleeper Deeper pill is more efficient than any anesthetic.
But this isn't what magic should be used for.
I make the cut.
Not one drop of blood is spilled.
"Nice work, Captain Short. Let's go. The clock is ticking."

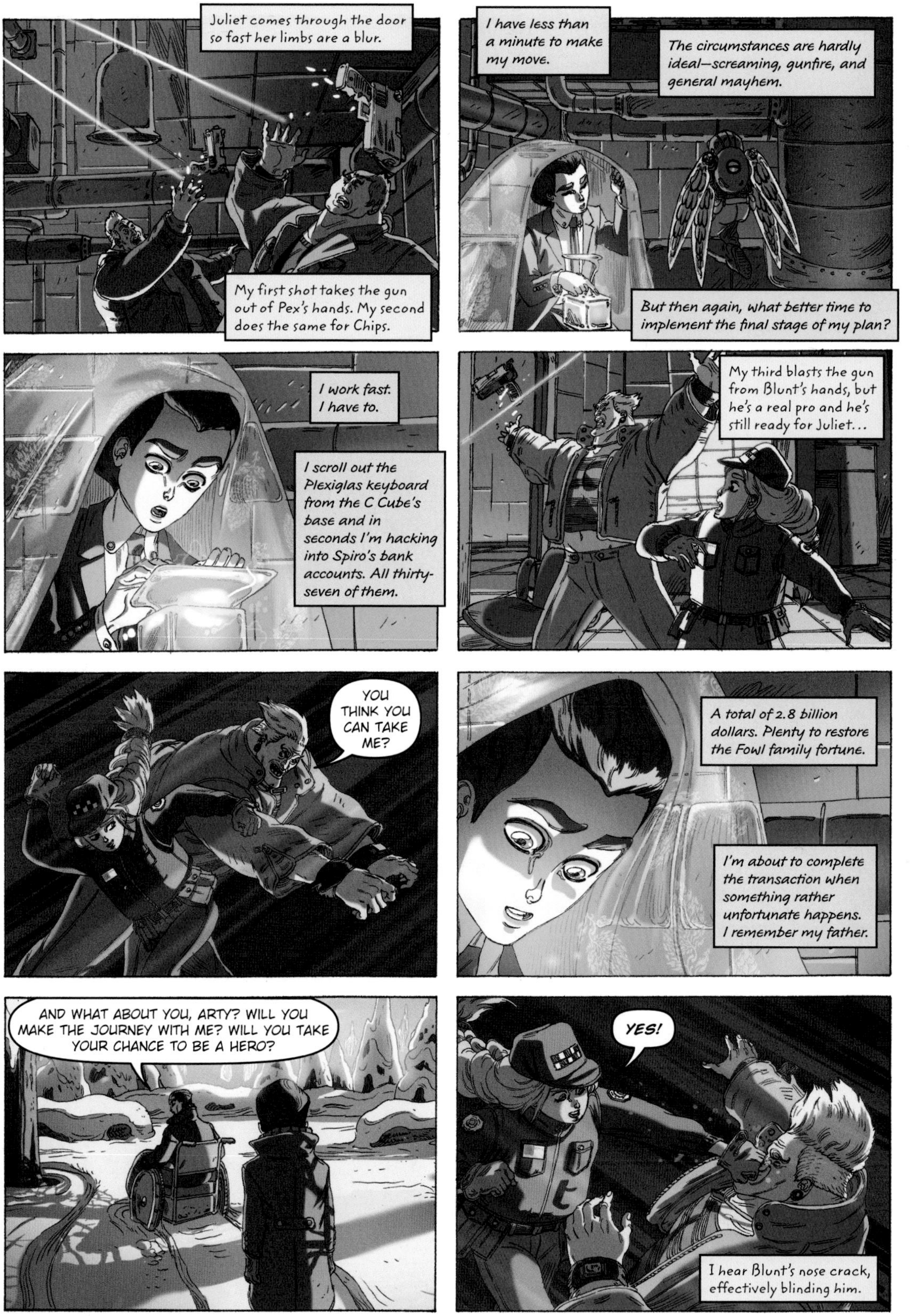
Juliet comes through the door so fast her limbs are a blur.
My first shot takes the gun out of Pex's hands. My second does the same for Chips.
I have less than a minute to make my move.
The circumstances are hardly ideal—screaming, gunfire, and general mayhem.
But then again, what better time to implement the final stage of my plan?
I work fast. I have to.
I scroll out the Plexiglas keyboard from the C Cube's base and in seconds I'm hacking into Spiro's bank accounts. All thirty-seven of them.
My third blasts the gun from Blunt's hands, but he's a real pro and he's still ready for Juliet...
YOU THINK YOU CAN TAKE ME?
A total of 2.8 billion dollars. Plenty to restore the Fowl family fortune.
I'm about to complete the transaction when something rather unfortunate happens. I remember my father.
AND WHAT ABOUT YOU, ARTY? WILL YOU MAKE THE JOURNEY WITH ME? WILL YOU TAKE YOUR CHANCE TO BE A HERO?
YES!
I hear Blunt's nose crack, effectively blinding him.

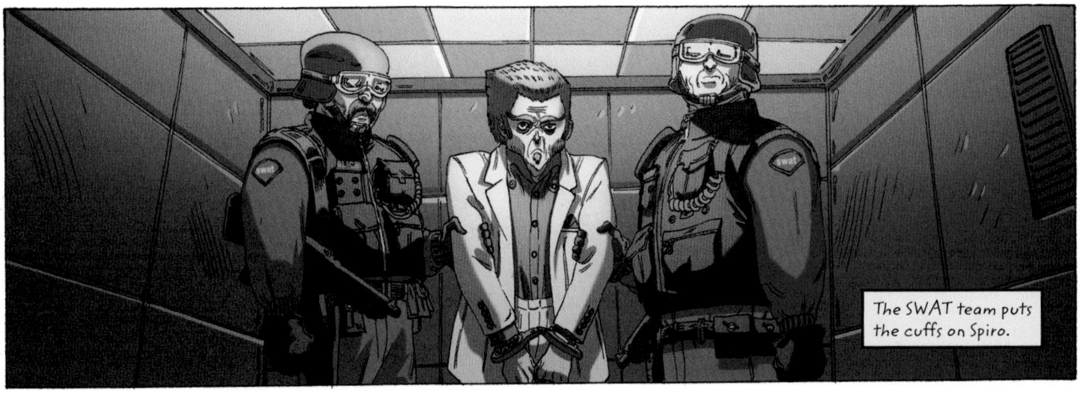
The SWAT team puts the cuffs on Spiro.

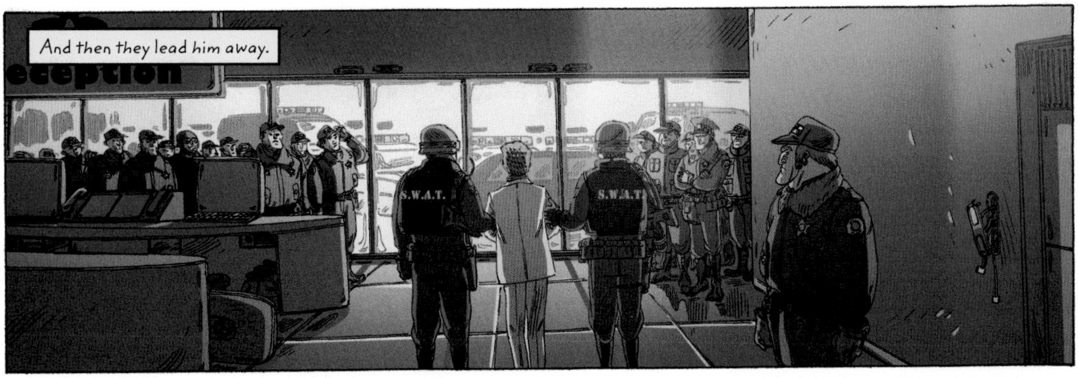
And then they lead him away.
eception
S.W.A.T.
S.W.A.T.

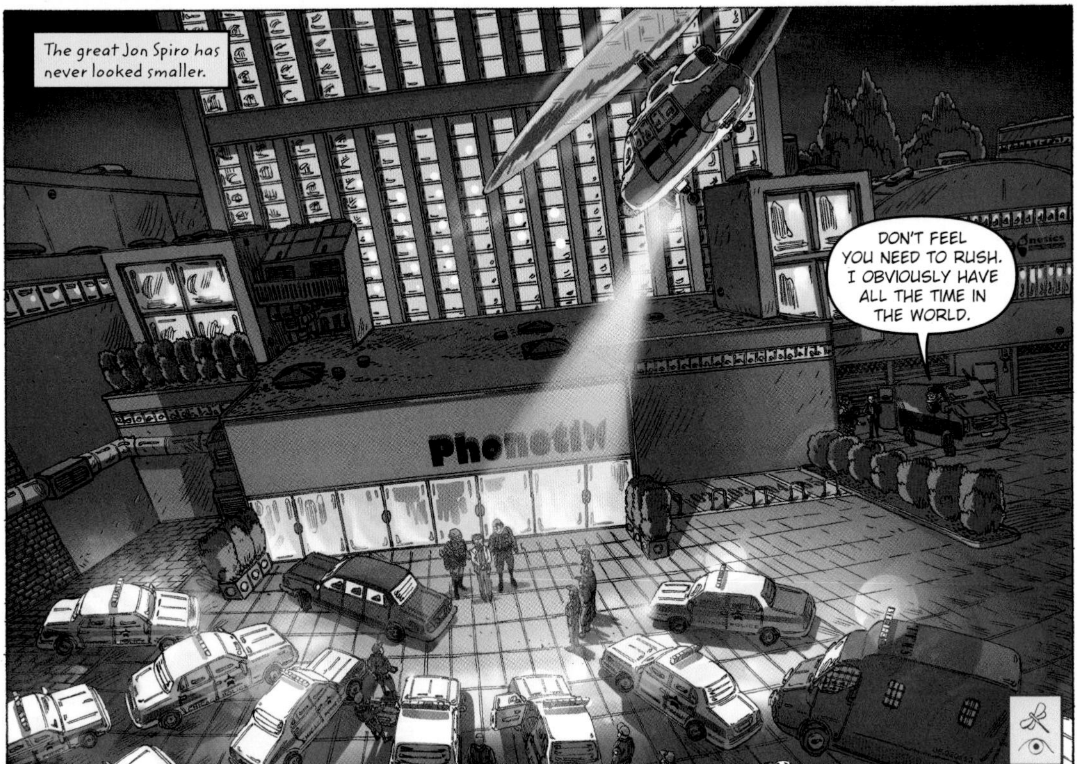
The great Jon Spiro has never looked smaller.
DON'T FEEL YOU NEED TO RUSH. I OBVIOUSLY HAVE ALL THE TIME IN THE WORLD.
Phonetix

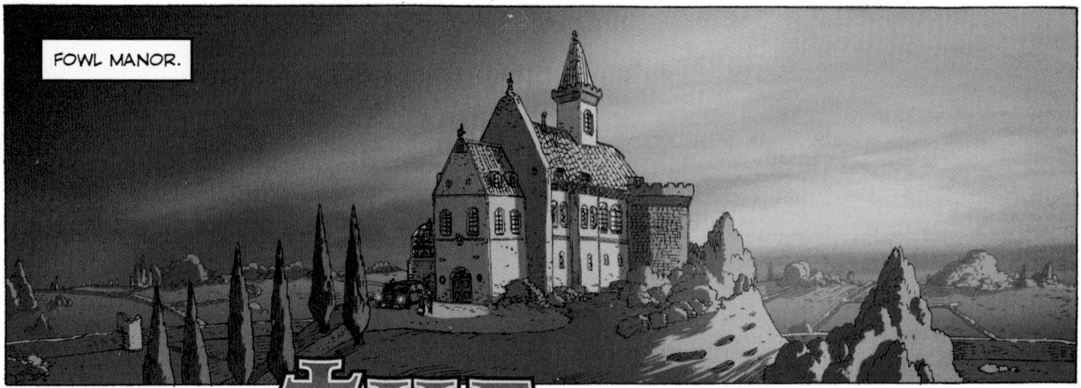
FOWL MANOR.

CHAPTER 11: THE INVISIBLE MAN

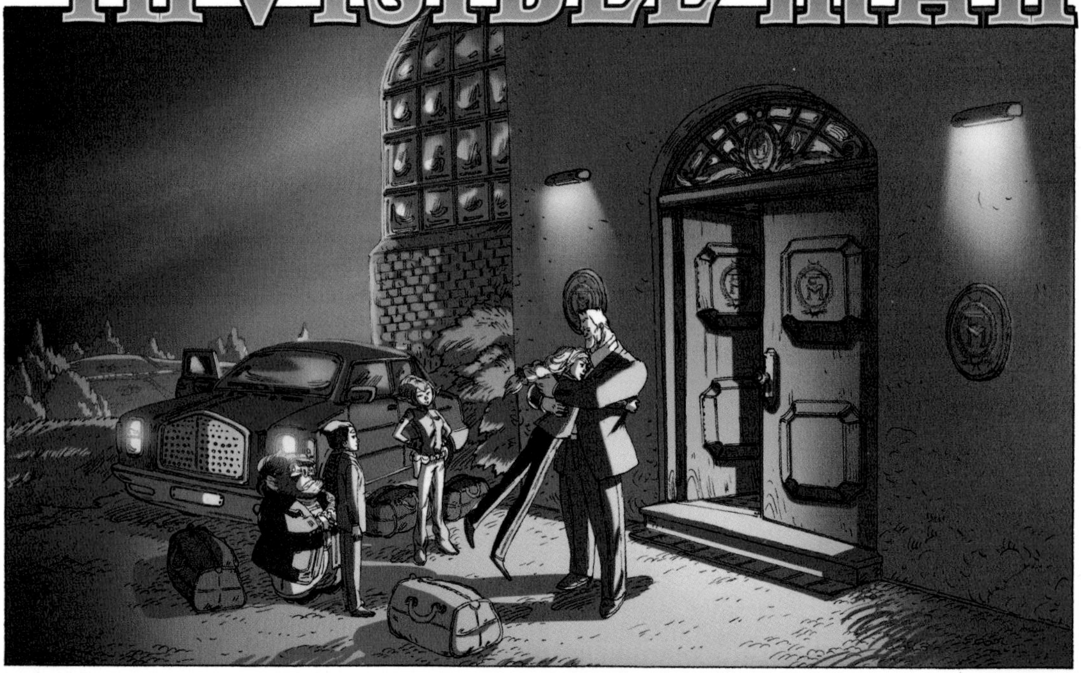

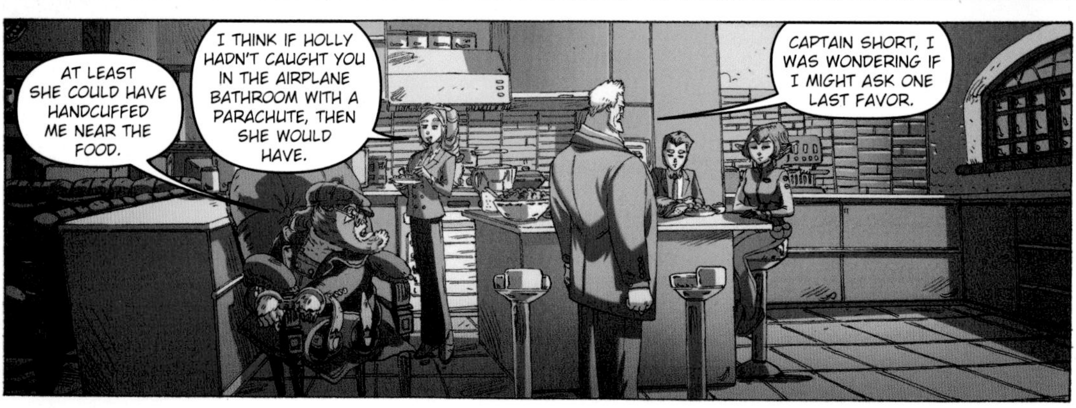
AT LEAST SHE COULD HAVE HANDCUFFED ME NEAR THE FOOD.
I THINK IF HOLLY HADN'T CAUGHT YOU IN THE AIRPLANE BATHROOM WITH A PARACHUTE, THEN SHE WOULD HAVE.
CAPTAIN SHORT, I WAS WONDERING IF I MIGHT ASK ONE LAST FAVOR.

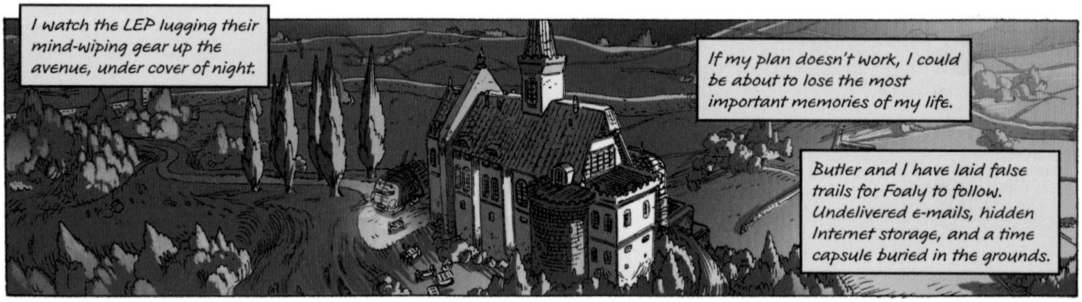
I watch the LEP lugging their mind-wiping gear up the avenue, under cover of night.
If my plan doesn't work, I could be about to lose the most important memories of my life.
Butler and I have laid false trails for Foaly to follow. Undelivered e-mails, hidden Internet storage, and a time capsule buried in the grounds.

CHAPTER 12: MIND WIPE

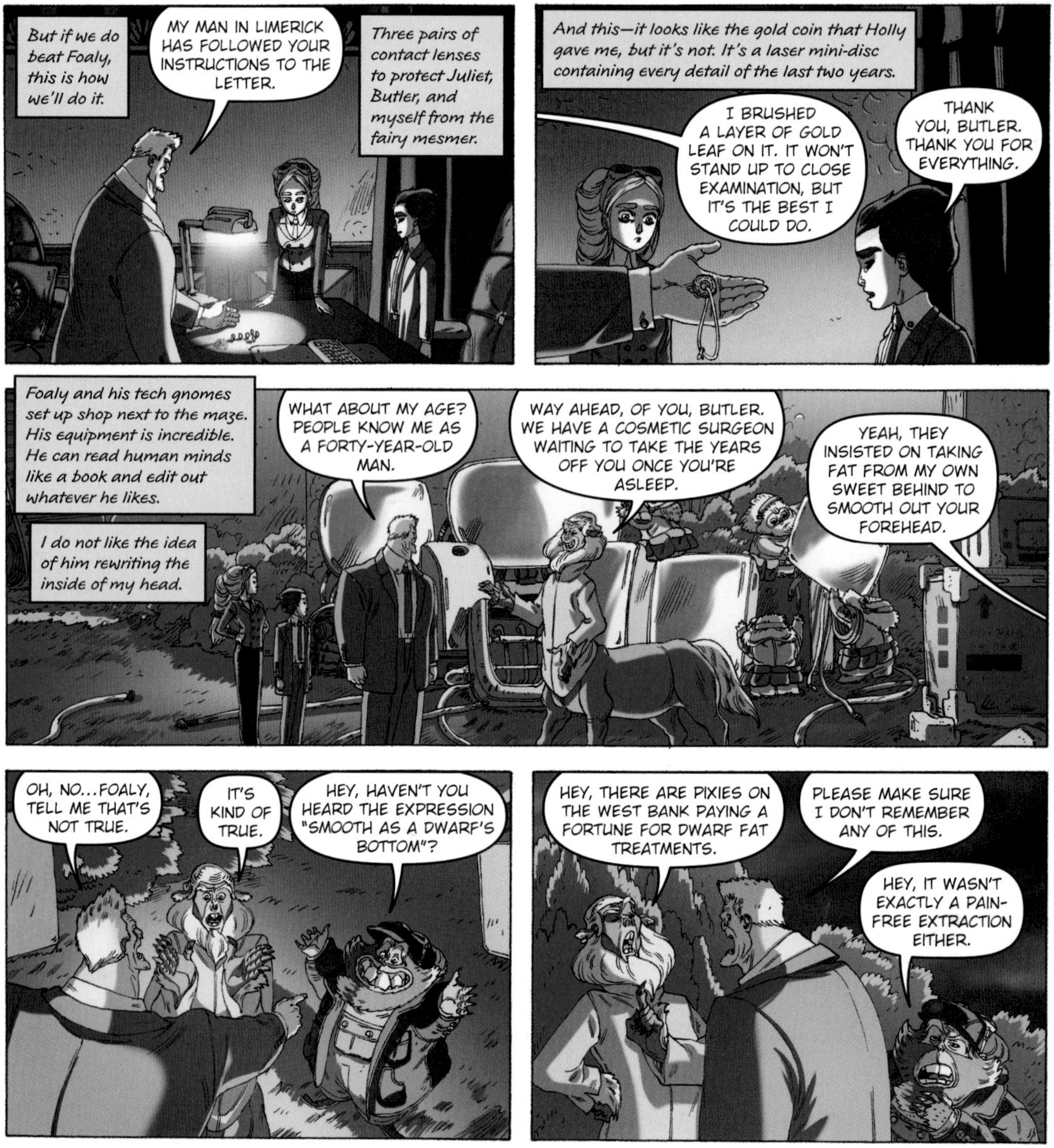
But if we do beat Foaly, this is how we'll do it.
MY MAN IN LIMERICK HAS FOLLOWED YOUR INSTRUCTIONS TO THE LETTER.
Three pairs of contact lenses to protect Juliet, Butler, and myself from the fairy mesmer.
And this—it looks like the gold coin that Holly gave me, but it's not. It's a laser mini-disc containing every detail of the last two years.
I BRUSHED A LAYER OF GOLD LEAF ON IT. IT WON'T STAND UP TO CLOSE EXAMINATION, BUT IT'S THE BEST I COULD DO.
THANK YOU, BUTLER. THANK YOU FOR EVERYTHING.
Foaly and his tech gnomes set up shop next to the maze. His equipment is incredible. He can read human minds like a book and edit out whatever he likes.
I do not like the idea of him rewriting the inside of my head.
WHAT ABOUT MY AGE? PEOPLE KNOW ME AS A FORTY-YEAR-OLD MAN.
WAY AHEAD, OF YOU, BUTLER. WE HAVE A COSMETIC SURGEON WAITING TO TAKE THE YEARS OFF YOU ONCE YOU'RE ASLEEP.
YEAH, THEY INSISTED ON TAKING FAT FROM MY OWN SWEET BEHIND TO SMOOTH OUT YOUR FOREHEAD.
OH, NO...FOALY, TELL ME THAT'S NOT TRUE.
IT'S KIND OF TRUE.
HEY, HAVEN'T YOU HEARD THE EXPRESSION "SMOOTH AS A DWARF'S BOTTOM"?
HEY, THERE ARE PIXIES ON THE WEST BANK PAYING A FORTUNE FOR DWARF FAT TREATMENTS.
PLEASE MAKE SURE I DON'T REMEMBER ANY OF THIS.
HEY, IT WASN'T EXACTLY A PAIN-FREE EXTRACTION EITHER.

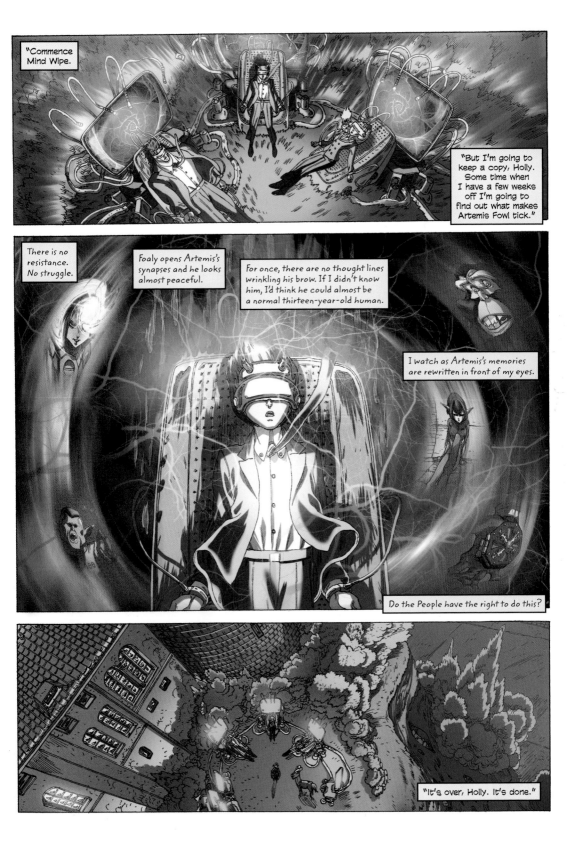

"Commence Mind Wipe."

"But I'm going to keep a copy, Holly. Some time when I have a few weeks off I'm going to find out what makes Artemis Fowl tick."

There is no resistance. No struggle.

Foaly opens Artemis's synapses and he looks almost peaceful.

For once, there are no thought lines wrinkling his brow. If I didn't know him, I'd think he could almost be a normal thirteen-year-old human.

I watch as Artemis's memories are rewritten in front of my eyes.

Do the People have the right to do this?

"It's over, Holly. It's done."

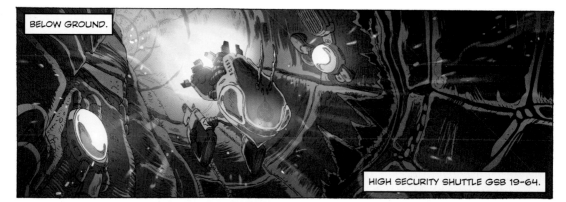

BELOW GROUND.

HIGH SECURITY SHUTTLE GSB 19-64.

OKAY, THEN, MASTER FOWL...

"...let's see what's so important you had to pass it to me secretly."

I have not finished with you yet, Mulch Diggums—

On your return, tell your lawyer to check the date on the original search warrant for your cave. That should get you out. When you are released keep your nose clean for a couple of years. Then bring the gold coin to me. Together we will be unstoppable.

Your friend and benefactor,
Artemis Fowl the Second

WELL, WHAT DO YOU KNOW...

"...maybe there is hope."

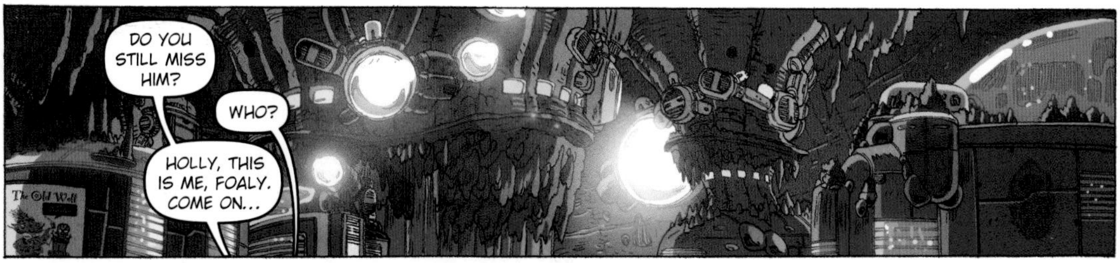
DO YOU STILL MISS HIM?
WHO?
HOLLY, THIS IS ME, FOALY. COME ON...
The Old Well

EPILOGUE II

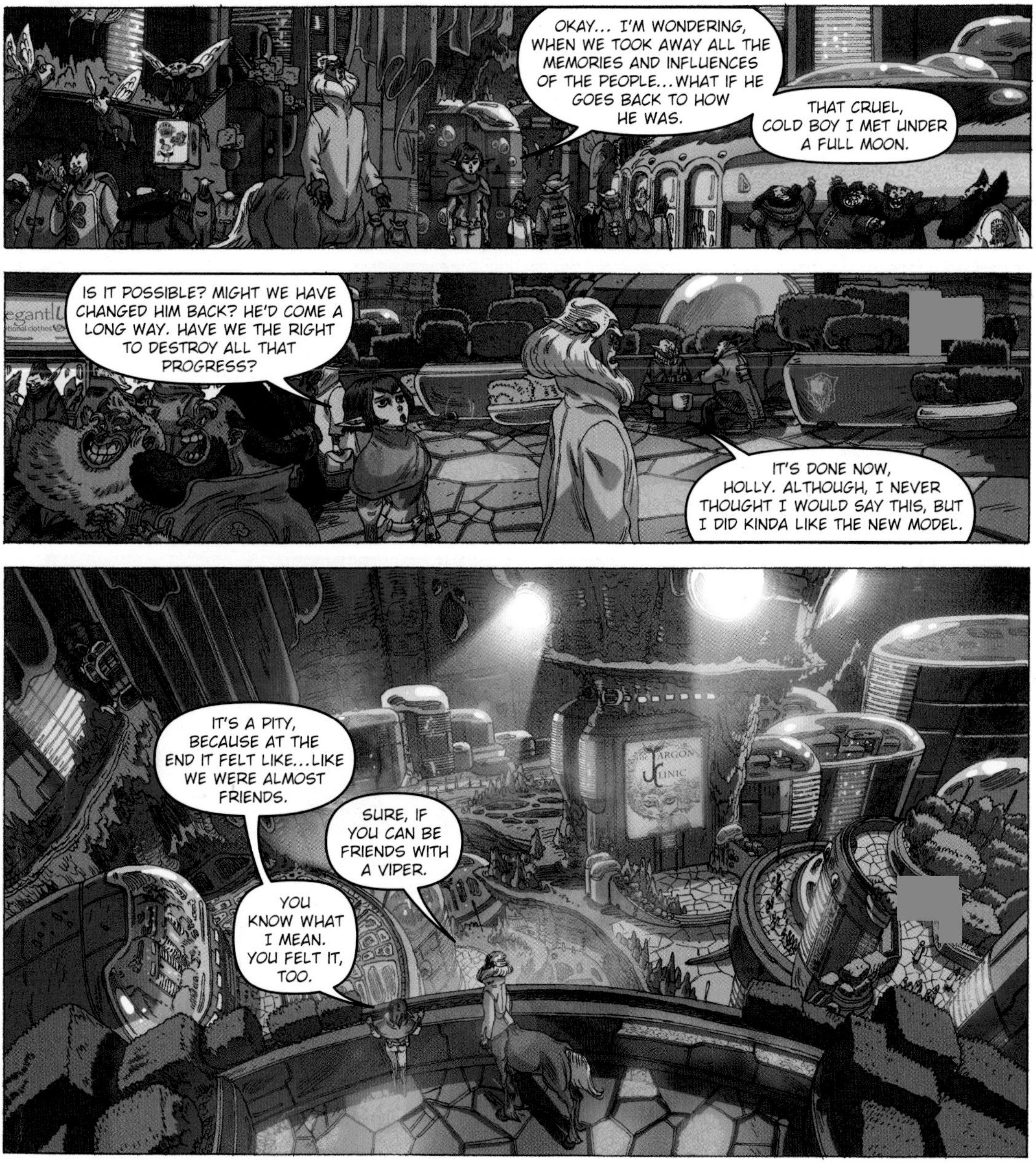
OKAY... I'M WONDERING, WHEN WE TOOK AWAY ALL THE MEMORIES AND INFLUENCES OF THE PEOPLE...WHAT IF HE GOES BACK TO HOW HE WAS.
THAT CRUEL, COLD BOY I MET UNDER A FULL MOON.
IS IT POSSIBLE? MIGHT WE HAVE CHANGED HIM BACK? HE'D COME A LONG WAY. HAVE WE THE RIGHT TO DESTROY ALL THAT PROGRESS?
IT'S DONE NOW, HOLLY. ALTHOUGH, I NEVER THOUGHT I WOULD SAY THIS, BUT I DID KINDA LIKE THE NEW MODEL.
IT'S A PITY, BECAUSE AT THE END IT FELT LIKE...LIKE WE WERE ALMOST FRIENDS.
SURE, IF YOU CAN BE FRIENDS WITH A VIPER.
YOU KNOW WHAT I MEAN. YOU FELT IT, TOO.

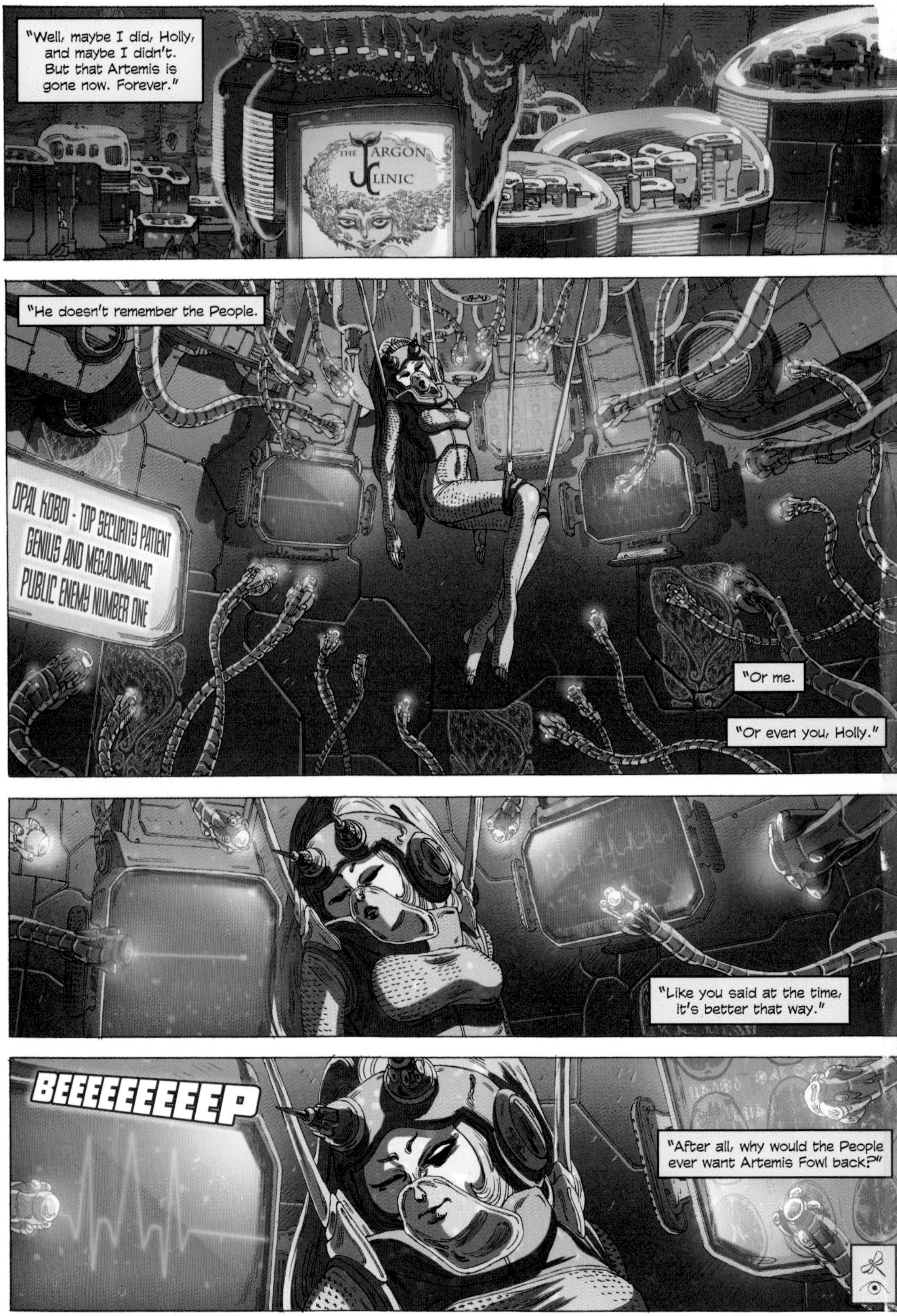
"Well, maybe I did, Holly, and maybe I didn't. But that Artemis is gone now. Forever."
THE ARGON CLINIC
"He doesn't remember the People.
OPAL KOBOI - TOP SECURITY PATIENT
GENIUS AND MEGALOMANIAC
PUBLIC ENEMY NUMBER ONE
"Or me.
"Or even you, Holly."
"Like you said at the time, it's better that way."
BEEEEEEEEEP
"After all, why would the People ever want Artemis Fowl back?"